DIE LAST

TONY PARSONS

arrow books

1 3 5 7 9 10 8 6 4 2

Arrow Books
20 Vauxhall Bridge Road
London SW1V 2SA

Arrow Books is part of the Penguin Random House group of companies
whose addresses can be found at global.penguinrandomhouse.com.

Penguin
Random House
UK

First published in Great Britain by Century in 2017
First published in paperback by Arrow Books in 2018

www.penguin.co.uk

A CIP catalogue record for this book is available from the British Library.

ISBN 9781784755331
ISBN 9781784755324 (export)

Typeset in 12.88/16.65 pt Fournier MT by Jouve (UK), Milton Keynes
Printed and bound in Great Britain by Clays Ltd, St Ives Plc

For Rob Warr of Highbury, Muswell Hill and Hove

'How often have I lain beneath rain on a strange roof, thinking of home.'

William Faulkner, *As I Lay Dying*

DIE
LAST

PROLOGUE
The Girl from Belgrade

The first thing they took was her passport.

The man jumped down from the cab of the lorry and snapped his fingers at her.

Click-click.

She already had her passport in her hands, ready for her first encounter with authority, and as she held it out to the man she saw, in the weak glow of the Belgrade streetlights, that he had a small stack of passports. They were not all burgundy red like her Serbian passport. These passports were green and blue and bright red — passports from everywhere. The man slipped her passport under the rubber band that held the passports together and he slipped them into the pocket of his thick winter coat. She had expected to keep her passport.

She looked at him and caught a breath. Old scars ran down one side of his face making the torn flesh look as though it had once melted. Then the man clicked his fingers a second time.

Click-click.

She stared at her kid brother with confusion. The boy indicated her suitcase. The man wanted the suitcase. Then the man with the melted face spoke in English, although it was not the first language of either of them.

'No room,' he said, gesturing towards the lorry.

But she gripped her suitcase stubbornly and she saw the sudden flare of pure anger in the man's eyes.

Click-click, went his fingers. She let go.

The suitcase was the second thing he took. It was bewildering. In less than a minute she had surrendered her passport and abandoned her possessions. She could smell sweat and cigarettes on the man and she wondered, for the first time, if she was making a terrible mistake.

She looked at her brother.

The boy was shivering. Belgrade is bitterly cold in January with an average temperature of just above freezing.

She hugged him. The boy, a gangly sixteen-year-old in glasses that were held together with tape on one side, bit his lower lip, struggling to control his emotions. He hugged her back and he would not let her go and when she gently pulled away he still held her, a shy smile on his face as he held his phone up at head height. They smiled at the tiny red light shining in the dark as he took their picture.

Then the man with the melted face took her arm just above the elbow and pulled her towards the lorry. He was not gentle.

'No time,' he said.

In the back of the lorry there were two lines of women facing each other. They all turned their heads to look at her. Black faces. Asian faces. Three young women, who might have been sisters, in hijab headscarves. They all looked at her but she was staring at her brother standing on the empty Belgrade street, her suitcase in his hand. She raised her hand in farewell and the boy opened his mouth to say something but the back doors suddenly slammed shut and her brother was gone. She struggled to stay on her feet as the lorry lurched away, heading north for the border.

By the solitary light in the roof of the lorry, she saw there were boxes in the back of the vehicle. Many boxes, all the same.

Birnen – Arnen – Nashi – Peren, it said on the boxes. *Grushi – Pere – Peras – Poires*.

'*Kruske*,' she thought, and then in English, as if in preparation for her new life. 'Pears.'

The women were still staring at her. One of them, nearest to the doors, shuffled along to find her space. She was some kind of African girl, not yet out of her teens, her skin so dark it seemed to shine.

The African gave her a wide, white smile of

encouragement, and graciously held her hand by her side, inviting the girl from Belgrade to sit down.

She nodded her thanks, taking her seat, and thinking of the African as the kind girl.

The kind girl would be the first to die.

Eight hours later the women stood outside a service station, taking turns in the cracked and broken bathroom in a last desperate attempt to keep clean.

The girl from Belgrade looked at the cars on the motorway. The winter sun was rising milky white on what looked like miles of farmland, as barren as the surface of the moon.

'What country is this?' she said.

'Austria?' said one of the young women in the hijabs. 'Germany?'

'A rich country.'

The man came out of the toilet, pulling up the zip of his trousers with one hand and clicking his fingers with the other.

Click-click.

'No more,' he said, and the women must have looked confused. He impatiently snapped his fingers in their faces. 'No stops no more,' he explained, rolling his eyes at their inability to understand his fluent English.

Soon they were back on the motorway.

'No stops,' the kind girl said, her face splitting in that wide white smile. 'No suitcase. No time.'

'No parking!' the girl from Belgrade laughed.

'No smoking!' said an Asian woman.

One of the women in a hijab waggled her dead phone. 'No signal!'

They all laughed together. It was the last time they laughed. For it was cold inside the lorry now, far colder even than midnight in Belgrade in January. At first she thought it was because the ground was steadily rising and they seemed to be passing through mountains.

But then she saw the steam on the breath of the other women.

The cold was not outside the lorry.

The cold was inside the lorry.

And it was getting colder by the moment, far too cold to sleep.

And in the end, far too cold to live.

The girl from Belgrade shivered. Even the air was freezing. It hurt her eyes.

She touched the metal door next to her and it was so cold that it burned her fingertips.

The blood drained from her hands, flooding deeper into her body, trying to protect the organs that kept her alive, and she felt that the icy air had seeped into her blood like poison.

She stamped her feet, flexed her hands, trying to bring some warmth to them, some movement, some life.

The kind girl was looking at her.

'So cold,' the girl from Belgrade said, feeling foolish for stating the painfully obvious.

But the kind girl nodded.

'Yes. Share my gloves.'

'No, no.'

'Please, sister. Put your hands inside with me.'

And so they sat like that for a while, with her numb hands squeezed together inside the kind girl's gloves, palms pressed against palms.

But then her feet began to hurt. And it was so much more than cold. It was the presence of a blinding, aching pain. As she stamped her feet, she felt the muscles in her neck and shoulders tighten. She moved her head in a horizontal figure of eight, the way she had seen her mother do when her neck was tight, and it made not the slightest difference. She saw the kind girl begin to shiver and watched with silent horror as the shivering became a kind of trembling.

She looked around at the other women. One of the women in a hijab was already in something deeper than sleep.

She looked at the kind girl and saw that there were icicles hanging from her thick black eyelashes and the sight of them sent a flood of terror through her.

She stood up, abruptly pulling her hands free from the kind girl's gloves, suddenly aware that the freezing cold that first gripped her hands and feet had now spread everywhere.

Everything was tight. Everywhere hurt. She began to shake with dread.

They were all going to die in here.

She banged on the windowless slab of steel that separated the back of the lorry from the driver's cab. She could smell cigarettes. She could hear voices. A man and a woman.

She banged harder.

The lorry kept going.

But she kept banging on the wall of the driver's cab, the other women silent behind her, although some of them were watching her with half-closed eyes.

And still the lorry kept driving.

Long after she had given up and slumped down next to the kind girl – was it hours or minutes? – the lorry finally stopped. She could hear the sound of big diesel engines, distant voices and – was she dreaming? – what sounded like the horn of a large ship.

She got on to her numb feet and stood alone at the back of the lorry and hammered the door until her hands were bruised and bloody. But the man who drove was as good as his word.

The doors remained closed.

Eventually the lorry pulled off again.

The cold had reached her brain now. She dropped to the floor. Her mind was cloudy. She was going to do something very important – she was certain of that – but now the plan had somehow fled from memory. She stood up and stared at the other women, dumbfounded. What was this glacial fog inside her head? She was very afraid now – a wild, unnameable fear that skittered across her heart and clenched her teeth.

And she had the urge to pee.

And her fingers were covered in small blisters.

And she was very tired.

Above and beyond everything else, there was exhaustion like nothing she had ever known. She sank to the floor again and knew that she would not be getting back up.

Her eyes were closing. She needed to sleep.

As her eyes were closing, she looked around at the unfamiliar faces.

Where was her brother? Why were they apart? They had no one in the world but each other. They should have stuck together. Where was that boy? She would remember if she could only concentrate. Sleep now, she thought. Worry about it all after your long sleep.

It was only the voice of the kind girl that pulled her back.

'Would you please hold me, sister?'

Her eyes jerked open and she stared at the kind girl without recognising her face, although suspecting she had seen it somewhere before.

Now the trembling was more violent and her entire body spasmed with a terrible will of its own. There was a young Asian woman sitting directly opposite and her eyes were wide open and yet she was sleeping. And she knew, somewhere deep inside her foggy mind, that it was the sleep without end.

The faces of the other women seemed to melt in the darkness, dissolving into shapes that had nothing to do with human faces. Then one of the women stood up and began removing her clothes. Ripping at them, not bothering with buttons, desperate to be free of them.

'I am burning,' the woman said in English, and then abruptly sat down, curled into a foetal ball and closed her eyes.

The girl from Belgrade stared dumbly at the boxes that seemed to crowd in on them. *Birnen – Arnen – Nashi – Peren*, said the boxes.

Grushi – Pere – Peras – Poires. Pears in what felt like every language except for Serbian, every tongue on the planet except her own.

What was the word for the fruit in Serbian?

'*Kruske*,' she said out loud.

She could hear her mother calling, saying her name

loud and clear, even though her mother was five years in the grave.

How could these things be? How were they possible?

Sleep now, she told herself, and think about it all later.

But the voice pulled her back again.

'Please, sister. Hold me now.'

So she held the kind girl – she had forgotten to do it before – and she kept holding her, long after the kind girl's trembling had stopped. It was all silence in the back of the lorry now and the silence was matched in the world outside, for at some point in the endless night, the lorry had stopped, and remained stopped, even though nobody came to open the door.

She could no longer see the steam of her breath. Indeed, she was no longer aware of the need to breathe.

And as the kind girl died in her arms, she suddenly understood. Dying is easy.

Living is hard.

PART ONE

The Woman Who Fell Through the Ice

1

We thought we had a bomb.

That's why Chinatown was deserted. If the public thinks the police have found a dead body then they get out their phones and settle down for a good gawp, but if they think we have found a bomb then they will get on their bikes.

The lorry was outside the Gerrard Place dim sum restaurant that marks the start of London's Chinatown, parked at an angle with its nearside wheels up on the pavement.

The lorry itself looked no different to the convoy of lorries that were lined up bumper to bumper all down one side of Gerrard Street, making their early morning deliveries to the shops and restaurants of Chinatown. But half up on the pavement and parked at a random angle, this lorry looked dumped, as if the driver couldn't get away fast enough, and that makes our people think only one thing.

Bomb.

Under the bobbing red lanterns that hailed the lunar new year, Chinatown was abandoned apart from armed response officers in their paramilitary gear, paramedics from half a dozen hospitals, firemen from the station on Shaftesbury Avenue, uniformed officers from New Scotland Yard, detectives from Counter Terrorism Command, dogs and their handlers from the Canine Support Unit, and our murder team from West End Central, 27 Savile Row, a short walk from Chinatown.

It was actually a lot of people, all wound up tight, and our breath made billowing clouds of steam in the bitterly cold air. But there was nobody who was not meant to be there.

The public – the deliverymen to Chinatown, the early workers cutting across Soho to their offices in Mayfair or Marylebone or Oxford Street – had scarpered as soon as the police tape went up and the word went out. Only one local was still here – the elderly Chinese man who had seen the lorry and dialled 999. He was a short, sturdily built man who had probably spent a career carting crates of Tsingtao beer into the stores and restaurants of Chinatown, and there was a hard-earned toughness about him despite the modest frame.

The weak winter sun was still struggling to rise above the rooftops. January's feeble attempt at a sunrise. Without looking at my watch, I knew it must be around eight by now. I sipped a triple espresso from the Bar Italia, my eyes on the abandoned lorry, as DC Edie Wren interviewed the Chinese man.

'So you didn't see the driver?' Edie asked him.

The man shook his head. 'As I believe told you, Detective, I saw no sign of the driver.'

His accent was a surprise. He spoke with the buttoned-up formality of a BBC radio announcer from long ago, as if he had learned his English listening to the World Service.

'Tell me again,' Edie said. 'Sir.'

'Just the lorry.' He gestured towards it. 'Parked on the pavement. The driver was already gone.'

'Was the driver Chinese?'

'I didn't see the driver.'

Edie paused.

'You're not protecting anyone, are you, sir?'

'No.'

Edie stared hard at the old man.

'Do you have permission to be in this country, sir?'

The man, never tall, straightened himself up to his full height, his back stiffened with wounded pride.

'I have had a British passport for many years. But what's that got to do—'

Edie's pale face did not look up from her notebook.

'Just answer my questions, sir. Did you touch the lorry? Is there any reason why we might find your fingerprints on the vehicle?'

'No,' he said. 'I called 999 and the police came immediately. And they said it could be a bomb.'

I lifted the POLICE DO NOT CROSS tape and held it up as a handler ducked under with her sniffer dog. The handler was a young uniformed officer, shockingly relaxed, and her dog was a brown-and-white Springer Spaniel that pulled on its lead, anxious to get cracking.

'Good girl, Molly,' the handler said, and we all watched the pair of them approach the lorry.

The Canine Support Unit uses the kinds of dogs who struggle to get adopted at rescue centres – high energy, endlessly curious dogs that don't know how to stop moving. The same qualities that are all wrong in a household pet are a huge plus in a sniffer dog looking for explosive devices.

Molly sniffed the chassis of that abandoned lorry as if it was a long-stemmed rose.

I held up the tape for them when they came back.

'What does Molly think?' I said.

'Molly thinks it's not a bomb,' the handler told me.

I scratched the dog behind the ears.

'That's good enough for me,' I said.

I looked over at a slight, bespectacled woman who was standing with an armed officer whose face was entirely covered by a ballistic helmet and a balaclava.

She was holding a skinny latte from the Bar

Italia – cops favour the Bar Italia because the coffee is so good and because it stays open for twenty-two hours a day – while he was holding a SIG Sauer SG 516 semi-automatic carbine assault rifle. The woman was my immediate boss, DCI Pat Whitestone, and the man must have been the commanding officer of CTU. I nodded and DCI Whitestone acknowledged the gesture with a salute of her coffee.

This was our case now.

'Let's open it up,' I shouted, ducking under the perimeter tape.

A fireman from the station on Shaftesbury Avenue fell into step beside me. He grinned at me, bleary with exhaustion, and I guessed he must have been kept on after pulling the graveyard shift. Over one shoulder he carried bright red bolt cutters, four feet long, and as we reached the lorry, he swung them down and set the steel jaws against the rust-dappled lock that secured the back door.

He looked at me, nodded briefly, and put his back into it.

The cheap lock crumbled at first bite.

We both grabbed one door and pulled it open.

I stared into the darkness and the cold hit me first. The temperature in the street was in the low single digits. But in the back of that lorry, it was somewhere below freezing.

I climbed inside just as my eyes cleared.

And that is when I saw the women.

Two lines of them, facing each other, their backs pressed against the sides of the lorry.

All young, all silent, none of them moving, as though they had died where they sat. There was a thin coating of frost on their faces.

Some of them had their eyes open. Some of them had ice hanging from their mouth, their nose and their eye-lashes. The ice had stuck and clung and froze wherever there was moisture.

I felt my breath catch in my throat.

Some of them had their clothes ripped, as though they had been assaulted. There was no smell of death in the back of that freezing lorry, and yet death was everywhere.

I felt myself sink forward, as if I had been punched in the stomach.

And then I straightened up and turned back at the street.

'We need help in here now!'

Paramedics were already running towards the lorry.

I stepped back to let them inside.

I looked down at Edie Wren, her notebook still in her hand as she bent at the waist, her hand pressed up against the shuttered window of the dim sum place, waiting to retch. Nothing happened. She straightened up and stared at me, her freckled face even paler than usual.

We nodded at each other.

I turned back to the paramedics. They were at the far end of the lorry, working back to back, each crouching over the woman closest to the cab.

DCI Whitestone stood at the open doors of the lorry, staring into the darkness. She shook her head as her eyes took in the unmoving women, her gaze settling on their torn clothes.

'What the hell happened in here?'

Then Edie was by her side.

She had something in her hands.

'I've found passports,' she said. 'From the cab. Under the dashboard. How many bodies you got in there, Max?'

I did a quick count. There were six of them on either side.

'Twelve,' I said.

Edie was flipping through the passports.

'Are you sure there's only twelve?'

'I'm sure.'

Edie shook her head.

'But I've got thirteen passports.'

'Count again,' Whitestone said. 'Both of them. The bodies and the passports.'

I counted the women in the lorry. Edie counted the

passports in her hand. The passports were of blue and red and green. These women were from everywhere.

'Turkish, Serbian, Nigerian,' Edie said. 'Syrian, Syrian, Syrian. Afghan, Iraqi, Iranian. Pakistani, Chinese, Somalian.' She held them up to me. 'And another Turkish,' she said. 'There are definitely thirteen passports.'

'And there are twelve women in here,' I said.

'So who's missing?' Whitestone said.

I shook my head, and turned towards the medics as they moved down the lorry.

'Dead,' one said, not looking round.

'Dead,' the other replied.

They moved on.

The two women closest to the back door were locked in an eternal embrace, like figures from the last hours of Pompeii. The way they clung to each made them look like sleeping siblings, although one of them was ebony black and the other had skin as white as milk.

I touched the wrist of the young black woman. Then I touched the wrist of the young white woman. And I could feel nothing but the cold.

'No pulse rate,' I told the paramedics.

One of them shook her head and cursed.

'Leave it to us, will you?' she said. 'It's different when they freeze, OK? Different to anything you've ever seen before. Their heart rate and breathing slow to next to nothing. Just because you can't find a pulse doesn't mean they're dead.'

'Can you wait on the street, Detective?' the other one said.

I looked at the women with the clothes torn from their body.

'It looks like they were attacked before they died,' I said.

The paramedic who had told me to wait on the street did not look at me.

'Chances are they did that to themselves,' she said, more patiently now. 'There's an old saying about hypothermia – *you're not dead until you're warm and dead*. That's what happens right at the end. They believe they're burning up.'

I turned back to the two women curled up beside me.

The black woman's eyes were open. But the white woman's eyes were closed. I felt for her pulse again but I could feel nothing. Her skin was colder than the grave.

How old was she? Nineteen? Twenty?

I hung my head, feeling a wave of grief pass over me.

And her fingers reached out and took my wrist.

Then I had her in my arms and I was screaming for an ambulance and hands were reaching out to help me get her out of the back of that death truck and on to a stretcher that we loaded into an ambulance parked in the middle of Shaftesbury Avenue, the swirling blue lights piercing the frozen winter morning. We tore through the city, the sirens howling at the world, telling it to get out of our way.

'You're safe now,' I said, trying to stay on my feet in the back of the rocking ambulance, squeezing her hands, trying to get some warmth back into them. 'We're getting you help. Don't give up. Stay with me.'

She did not reply.

'Don't give up, OK?' I said.

And she did not reply.

I had never felt anything colder than that young woman's hands.

'Will you tell me your name?' I asked.

'My name is Hana,' she whispered.

2

If you have a cardiac arrest in London – or if your heart rate has fallen off a cliff because you are freezing to death – then paramedics and ambulance technicians have the authority to bypass the nearest Accident and Emergency department and take you directly to one of eight specialist heart attack centres, immediately doubling your chances of survival.

And that's what they did with Hana.

The ambulance sped north and I stayed by her side until she was rushed into the Intensive Care Unit at the Royal Free in Hampstead. And then I waited. After I had downed two cups of scalding black coffee, a doctor came out to see me, a young man of around thirty who looked as though he hadn't slept since leaving medical school. Dr Patel, it said on his name tag.

He glanced at my warrant card and nodded.

'Do we have a name for the victim, DC Wolfe?' he said.

'I only know her first name,' I said. 'Hana.'

'Hana has severe hypothermia. Which is easy to diagnose and hard to treat. She's suffering from what we call afterdrop – her core temperature is continuing to fall after removal from cold stress. And her core temperature is likely to drop for the next few hours. We are going to give her a heart-lung bypass where we withdraw blood from the body, warm it up and return it to the body. She's on a CPB pump to maintain blood circulation and keep her oxygenated.' He paused. 'Do you know how long she was exposed to sub-zero temperatures? Anything at all about her medical history?'

I shook my head.

'When can I talk to her?'

He looked at me as if I still didn't quite get it.

'Hypothermia is next door to death, Detective – it suppresses heart and brain function and the internal organs all stop working. Do you understand? Everything that keeps you alive suddenly stops.' He ran a hand through his already thinning hair. 'We're not even allowed to declare someone dead until their body is warmed to a near normal body temperature.'

And finally I understood.

Hana was dying.

When I arrived at West End Central, a stocky Chinese man in his sixties was standing under the big blue lamp that marks the entrance to 27 Savile Row.

I recognised him as the man that Edie had been interviewing before we opened up the lorry, the man who
had called it in. They must have taken him to the station
for a longer interview and now they were done with
him. He looked at me warily as I came up the steps.

'Thank you for your help, sir,' I said.

He shook his head.

'I'm not sure I was very much help.' He glanced back
at the entrance to West End Central. 'I told your
colleagues everything I saw but I don't think they
believe me.'

I was struck once again by his formal, old-fashioned
English and I could feel the gap between the courtly,
well-mannered country he imagined when he first heard
the language coming out of a radio in Hong Kong and
the harsher reality he had found in London.

And I believed him – he had not seen the driver and
he didn't have much more to tell us. I could see he felt
ill used.

I held out my hand and told him my name.

He shook my hand although his grip was so soft I
regretted the gesture.

'Keith Li,' he told me, one of the generation of Chinese who had automatically adopted an Anglo name,
usually the kind of name that the British had stopped
using two or three generations ago.

'You speak very good English, sir.'

'In China, I was a teacher.' He laughed bitterly. 'In England – nothing.'

I went up to Major Incident Room One.

Whitestone and Edie were wearing blue nitrile gloves and poring over the passports of assorted nationalities in red and blue and green they had spread out before them like a deck of cards.

Trainee Detective Constable Billy Greene was at a workstation, his long, gangly body hunched up as he scrolled through still black-and-white images of vehicles, their number plates showing in yellow and black at the foot of the screen.

And there was a tiny middle-aged man with milk-bottle glasses sitting between Whitestone and Edie who was also wearing gloves, and sliding what looked like a Syrian passport into some kind of clunky silver box. The machine resembled a computer printer from when the world was young. He looked a bit like a mole.

'Did you talk to her, Max?' Whitestone said.

I shook my head.

'The Royal Free are going to call me when she comes out of the ICU. How many more made it?'

'None,' Whitestone said. 'The rest of them were pronounced dead at the scene. It took the Divisional Surgeon quite a while. Apparently it's hard to tell when they freeze to death. Something to do with the heart rate

26

slowing to next to nothing. So we have eleven dead.' She tapped a burgundy passport with a golden coat of arms. 'And *Hana Novak* fighting for her life at the Royal Free.'

'So we still have that thirteenth passport,' Edie said. She nodded at the man with the silver machine. 'Ken here is from Visas and Immigration at Heathrow.'

'I'm the Questioned Documents guy,' Ken told me. 'Running your passports through my VSC40 here to see how many of them are kosher.'

'What does the machine do?'

'It reads microchips, assesses paper quality and scans surface features such as visa stamps,' he said. 'It sniffs out fake watermarks, bogus metallic strips and home-made ink.' He grinned shyly at me, warming to his theme. 'Basically it's a lie detector for travel documents.'

His gloved hands danced lightly above the passports. The dark red of Iran. The deep blue of Syria. The green of Pakistan. The burgundy and gold of Serbia. And two Turkish passports – one in maroon and one in green.

'There are a thousand ways for a passport to be forged,' he said. 'Passports that are genuine but have had the photograph changed on the ID page. Passports that are real but have had bogus stamps inserted. The VSC40 sees through them all.'

Ken's profession explained his mole-like appearance. I imagined that most of his working day would have been spent in a darkened room at Arrivals at Heathrow Airport. And I had no doubt that he would not have been brought to West End Central unless he was the best in the business.

'How we doing so far?' I said.

'These passports are all as fake as a nine-euro note,' Ken said, allowing himself a smile of professional pride. 'We see the best forged passports in the world at Heathrow. But this bunch is not the best in the world. This is amateur hour. Apart from *this* one. This one is real.'

It was the passport that Whitestone had tapped. Ken held up a burgundy-coloured passport with two inscriptions in gold Cyrillic script either side of a gold coat of arms. I pulled on a pair of blue nitrile gloves and took the Serbian passport. Hana Novak's solemn young face stared out at me from the identity page.

She had long, straight brown hair that looked as though it had been curled up at the end by some kind of heating tongs. It was a curiously moving attempt to look attractive from a young woman who was already beautiful, even if she did not know it yet.

Ken ran his fingers over the stack of fakes.

'I wouldn't expect these passports to be decent forgeries,' Ken said. 'The back of a lorry is the budget option for sneaking into the UK. At Heathrow we see people – professionals from Damascus and Baghdad – who have paid fifteen grand and more for bogus travel docs that have been made by a master.'

'These people smugglers,' I said. 'Are they more likely to fly someone in than put them in the back of a lorry?'

'Depends how much money you've got,' Ken said. 'If you're a big spender, you can get a speedboat from Dunkirk to Dover for twelve grand. But if money's tight, you can buy a passage to England for as little as a hundred quid in Calais. They sell it as a guaranteed entry on social media – and these traffickers have hundreds of accounts online – but really that hundred quid just buys you one attempt to squat in the back of a lorry heading for Dover. Not that they confine themselves to the south coast these days. As security tightens up around Dover the smugglers' speedboats are heading for Portsmouth, Whitstable, Tilbury, Hull – you name it. And if they make it, most of them can stay forever. Nobody gets shipped back to a war zone.' He indicated the passports. 'I'll tell you something about these girls.'

I stared at the solemn beauty of Hana Novak's passport photo.

'What's that?' I said.

He sighed. 'They were unlucky,' he said.

'I've found the lorry,' Billy Greene said, excitedly swivelling in his chair. 'Got it on ANPR.'

Automatic Number Plate Recognition is the system

we use for storing registration numbers, even for vehicles that we are not looking for at the time. Around eight thousand ANPR cameras photograph over thirty million numbers every day, and the details are stored for two years.

'The lorry is a five-ton refrigerated Sinotruk that was bought for cash at an auction in Kent last summer,' Billy said. 'It's a Chinese make, although the plates were Turkish. That's what they do – the people smugglers – they pick the rides up for cash at auction. Makes it as hard to trace as a pay-as-you-go phone.' He turned in his chair to peer at his screen. 'It entered the UK yesterday on the last ferry from Dunkirk. Landed at Dover.'

'Any CCTV of the driver?' Whitestone asked.

'I'm still looking, ma'am,' Billy said.

'So we're assuming the owner of the thirteenth passport wasn't driving?' I said.

'It's unlikely,' Whitestone said. 'Because the owner of the thirteenth passport is a woman and the drivers who smuggle in illegals are all men. At least, that's how it has been until now. It's not an equal opportunities profession. Find the thirteenth woman and then you find the driver. Find the driver and you find the scumbags who run the whole stinking operation.'

'Why did the driver do a runner?' Edie said.

'Perhaps he looked in the back, realised the women were dying or already dead, and panicked,' I said.

'Perhaps he didn't get paid. Perhaps there was nobody there to meet him.'

'But why was it below freezing in the back?' Edie said. 'He smuggled a lorryload of girls into the country and then froze them to death. It makes no sense.'

'The big ports see these refrigerated lorries all the time,' Ken said. 'Before I was in Heathrow I worked in Dover. Their refrigeration works just like your central heating – on either a timer or a thermostat. The cold air kicks in when the temperature gets above a certain level or at a specific time. My guess would be that it never crossed the driver's tiny mind that those women could freeze to death back there. There's no market for dead women. He didn't turn the refrigeration on deliberately, and he didn't know enough to turn it off until it was too late. He's unlikely to be any kind of criminal mastermind.'

'So he saw what had happened and he legged it,' Edie said.

Whitestone nodded grimly. 'The driver's fear seems to be a major component in every possible scenario.' I saw she was trembling with anger. 'This is not a trafficking offence, Max. This is not smuggling illegals. We have eleven dead bodies at the morgue. I want these bastards for murder.'

'Any leads inside the lorry?' I said.

'The women each had one small bag,' Edie said. 'That's

clearly all they were allowed. The contents are remark-
ably similar. They each had a little bit of make-up and
they each had a phone, and the batteries were all dead
by the time we found them. We're charging the phones
and calling in the relevant translators to examine text
messages.' She indicated the United Nations of passports
before her. 'It's going to be a lot of translating. And the
embassies are not going to be any help because it looks
like only one of the passports is kosher. We can't ID the
dead if they're travelling on a fake passport.'

Whitestone pulled off her gloves and went to stand
before the giant map of London that covers one wall of
MIR-1.

'Are we working on the theory that Chinatown was
the final destination?' I said.

Whitestone nodded.

'It's unlikely those twelve young women were coming
here to pick potatoes in East Anglia or collect cockles
in Morecambe Bay. They were coming to London, Max.
And they were coming to do one thing.' She exhaled
hard. 'I want to put the squeeze on every pimp between
Chinatown and the Watford Gap. You've got a CI in
Chinatown, right?'

I must have looked surprised.

'A CI?'

'The Filipina,' Whitestone said with a touch of irritation. 'Ginger Gonzalez.'

'Ginger's not really a Criminal Informant,' I said. 'She's more of a friend.'

Ginger Gonzalez ran one of the most successful prostitution rings in the city, although she preferred to call her business – Sampaguita, named after the national flower of the Philippines – a social introduction agency.

She had once helped me bust a paedophile ring wide open. She had arranged company for my colleague DC Curtis Gane when he had been paralysed in the course of duty and needed someone to hold in the last days before his death. I believed the end of his life had been made easier by Ginger.

So I had plenty of reasons to feel grateful to Ginger Gonzalez.

'Your friend puts wealthy men in contact with beautiful young women, right?' Whitestone said.

Ginger found Sampaguita's clients in the swankier bars of London hotels – the Coburg at the Connaught, the American Bar at the Savoy, the Rivoli at the Ritz, and the Fumoir at Claridges – and then put them in contact with the ever-changing stable of young women who were on her books.

'But she doesn't think of herself as a pimp,' I said.

Whitestone bit her bottom lip, as if I was testing her patience to the absolute limit.

'She can call herself what she likes, Max, but I call it pimping. Do you really want to give her a pass?'

I was certain that the lorry in Chinatown was nothing to do with Ginger. There was no coercion involved in what she did. She was a businesswoman.

'She's a good kid,' I said simply.

Whitestone's face flushed with anger.

'Those women in the back of that lorry? I bet they were all good kids, too. Your first job is interviewing Hana Novak in the hospital. But then you're coming back here and we are going to see your friend, Max. That's your second job.'

It wasn't a suggestion.

'Yes, ma'am,' I said.

'Ma'am, why are you so certain they were coming here to go on the game?' Edie asked Whitestone. 'We don't know that for sure, do we? They might have thought – I don't know – they were coming here to be models, or dancers, or waitresses.'

'But the men who brought them in knew,' Whitestone said, looking at me. 'Didn't they?'

'Yes,' I said. 'The men knew.'

My phone began to vibrate.

DR PATEL CALLING, it said.

'Hana's not going to make it,' he told me.

By the time I got up to the Royal Free they had moved Hana Novak from the ICU to a small private room where the lights were low and the temperature was warm and you could hear the buzz of traffic drifting up from Pond Street as they slowly climbed one of the steepest hills in London.

The nurses had tucked her up to keep her comfortable and, with only her face showing above the bedding, she looked very young.

'I suppose there's no point in asking about next of kin?' Dr Patel said.

'We're trying,' I said. 'Her passport's real. Probably the only one of the bunch that is real. We're in touch with the Serbian embassy about next of kin.' I looked from the young woman in the bed to the doctor who had done his best to save her. 'We should hear soon. But I don't know if it is going to be soon enough. How long has she got?'

'She'll slip away soon,' he said. 'She's not in any pain.' He wiped his eyes with the back of his hand. I don't think I had ever seen a man more tired. 'But there was too much internal damage before we reached her.'

'May I stay with her?' I said.

'Of course.'

As soon as Dr Patel was gone, I took the only chair in the tiny room and pulled it close to the bed. When I spoke, my voice was as soft as a prayer.

'Who did this to you, Hana?' I said.

But if she heard me, she did not speak, and if she knew I was there, then she gave no sign, and so I sat by the bedside of Hana Novak and I stayed there until she had gone.

3

Night was falling on Chinatown.

There was no sign of what we had found outside the dim sum restaurant in the freezing sunrise. It all seemed a lifetime away. The white lorry had been impounded by forensics. The police tape had all come down and been neatly disposed of. And the only clue that the dead bodies of twelve young women had been discovered on this spot was the tide of flowers that was piling up by the entrance to Gerrard Street.

DCI Whitestone glanced at the flowers as we walked through the archway to Chinatown, and I knew she was in no mood to go easy on Ginger Gonzalez, whatever favours my friend had done for us in the past.

'Is this difficult for you?' Whitestone said.

'We have to talk to her,' I said. 'I don't see that we have a choice.'

Halfway down Gerrard Street there was an open doorway by a duck restaurant where a long queue of stylish young Cantonese queued for a table. We went up a short flight of stairs to a white door with a simple sign.

SAMPAGUITA

Social Introduction Agency

Whitestone laughed. 'She even advertises,' she said bitterly.

Without knocking we went inside a small white room. It was almost nothing – just a spartan little cube of a room above a Chinese restaurant. Ginger Gonzalez was sitting behind her desk.

She was a thirty-year-old Filipina and everything about her proclaimed that she was a high-flying London businesswoman – the giant iMac, the well-thumbed copy of that morning's *Financial Times* on her desk and her black-rimmed glasses. The only thing that made her look as though her career possibly was not in the financial sector were the tattoos that I knew ran down her lower inner arms.

Ginger's studious face broke into a smile when she saw me and then faded immediately she saw Whitestone.

'Max,' she said. 'How can I help?'

There was a scented candle in a small glass holder on Ginger's desk and it disguised the smell of Peking duck that drifted up from the restaurant below. Whitestone stared thoughtfully at the flame, leaving it to me.

'It's about the lorry we found this morning, Ginger,' I said.

'One hundred metres away from where we are now,' Whitestone said, picking up the scented candle.

'It's terrible,' Ginger said in an accent that hovered somewhere between Manila and Manhattan. 'I left flowers.'

'Big of you,' Whitestone said. She put down the candle. 'Remind me again how it works.' She gestured towards the door. 'You know. Your Social Introduction Agency. What would I find if I Googled Sampaguita?'

Ginger glanced at me and then back at Whitestone.

'You will not find Sampaguita online. We leave no digital footprint.'

'We? That's the royal "we", is it? Or do you mean you and your whores?'

Ginger folded her hands. 'What I mean is that I prefer to make personal contact with clients,' she said pleasantly.

Whitestone almost smiled. 'In other words, you pick up men in bars and then you put them in touch with one of your girls?'

'I introduce men to women. That's what I do. And I pay my taxes——'

Whitestone lifted a hand to silence her.

'Spare me the waffle about how respectable you are.' She nodded at me. 'I know that you and Max are friends. And I know that you have helped him – and our people – in the past. But here's the problem. You run a prostitution ring.' She again raised a hand. 'You can call it what you like, but we both know that is what it comes down to.' She pushed her spectacles up the bridge of her nose and nodded to the window. 'And first thing this morning a dozen young women who were being brought into the country to make a living on their backs – whether they knew it or not – were found at the end of this very street. And now they're all dead.'

Ginger took a breath.

'It's a tragedy. But it's nothing to do with me.'

Whitestone continued as if Ginger had not spoken. 'Max here might believe whatever rubbish you tell him, but not me. See, you make it sound far too much like *Pretty Woman*. You make it sound almost romantic. Lonely, rich men and willing, beautiful women.' She laughed. 'You make it sound as though the men are all Richard Gere and the women are all Julia Roberts. And it's not quite like that, is it?'

Ginger looked at me for help.

'Ginger. We have no leads,' I said. 'We're on a cold trail. So anything you can—'

Whitestone hurled the small glass candle against the wall. It shattered with a crack like gunshot. Without the scent of the candle, the room began to fill with the smell of roasting meat.

'Answer my question,' she said.

Ginger stared back at her.

'No, it's not always like a remake of *Pretty Woman*. That's true. Sometimes the men are less than gentlemen – especially as they are all rich, privileged men who are accustomed to being obeyed and getting what they want. And – although I have a rigorous recruitment programme – my staff are constantly changing and on occasion they are not as honest or reliable as I would wish.'

Whitestone shook her head and looked at me.

'Her staff, Max,' she said. 'She calls them her staff!'

I saw the first flash of anger in Ginger's eyes. 'None of my girls are forced into doing anything they do not want to do. There is no violence. There is no coercion. I have been out on my own since I was sixteen years old—'

'Am I meant to feel sorry for you?' Whitestone said.

'I don't care what you feel about me,' Ginger said. 'But I know the law, Detective. It's illegal to buy sex from anyone who has been subjected to force – and none of the staff at Sampaguita is ever subjected to force. It is illegal to buy sex from someone under the age of eighteen – two years older than the age of consent – and none of my staff gets a job without verified photo ID. And prostitution itself is not illegal – only soliciting in a public place, running a brothel and kerb-crawling.'

'And pimping,' Whitestone said quietly. 'Don't forget pimping. That's illegal, isn't it?'

Ginger stared at her for a moment. Then she nodded.

Whitestone got off the desk and went to stand by the window. It was dark now and Chinatown blazed with its nighttime colours of red and gold.

'I could shut down your little business tonight,' Whitestone said. 'If the judge is sufficiently senile, then he might buy your line about Sampaguita being a – what is it? – Social Introduction Society. My guess is that would be laughed out of court. My guess is that you would get done for causing or inciting prostitution for gain. And – again, this is just my opinion – I think you would serve a custodial sentence.' She looked back at Ginger. 'You tell me – could you do jail time?'

Ginger stared at her defiantly.

'You would not believe what I've had to do to survive,' she said quietly.

'I doubt that,' Whitestone said. 'Because you see, Ginger, I've been clearing up the mess of commercial sex since I was in uniform. I've seen poor little cows who should have still been in school sold to twenty men in one night. I've seen girls with their front teeth knocked out because they disobeyed some evil stinking pimp. I've kicked down doors and found women who thought they were coming here for a better life. I've seen the lot.'

'That's not me,' Ginger said. 'That was *never* me. If that was me, Max would have busted me the first time we met.'

Whitestone nodded. 'I know.'

Ginger looked genuinely confused.

'Then what do you want from me?'

Whitestone suddenly seemed very tired.

'We had to look at eleven dead women before breakfast.' She nodded at me. 'Max watched another one die – Hana, her name was Hana – at the Royal Free. So before I can sleep tonight, I just need to feel like I'm fighting back.'

'Busting me is not fighting back,' Ginger said. 'It's lashing out.'

'Ginger,' I said. 'Where do they come from? The women who work for you?'

'They come from everywhere, Max. Europe. Asia. South America. They come from everywhere except here.'

'How do they get in?'

'Student visas. Tourist visas. But of course if they're from one of the countries in the European Union, they come in through the same immigration line as you.'

'And what about the ones who don't have student or tourist visas?' I said. 'What about the ones who don't come from Europe?'

'What are you asking?'

'I'm asking if there's one of your girls who came into

this country in the back of a lorry,' I said. 'If there was anyone who was smuggled in. If there's someone who works for you who came in the hard way.'

She hesitated.

'There was one,' she said at last. 'Turkish. Years ago. When I was starting out. I know she came here in the back of a lorry. Her name was Asuman. She said it meant daughter of the sky. Asuman Ata. Sweet kid. Very shy. She certainly came here the hard way.'

'And how did you meet Asuman?' Whitestone said.

'She had been working at some kind of lap-dancing club just off the M25. Some scuzzy joint selling blow jobs with the beer. That's where she was taken after being smuggled into the country. She didn't elaborate on how she got in. She talked more about this place she worked. The Champagne Room. And how all the girls there were the same as her.'

'You mean they were all illegals?' Whitestone said. 'They only used illegals at this place – the Champagne Room?'

Ginger nodded. 'Nothing but,' she said.

'You're not going to tell me you've lost contact with her, are you?' Whitestone said.

Ginger's right hand flew across her keyboard.

'Asuman Ata,' she said. 'I've got an address for her. She's Asuman Jenkins now. She's married. To an Anglo.'

'And why would that matter to me?' Whitestone said.

Whitestone and Ginger stared at each other but I sensed that something had been resolved between them. Ginger had given us enough. She wasn't going to be busted tonight.

'This club,' I said. 'Why did they only like using illegals?'

Whitestone looked at me as if she should not have to explain these things.

Then she glanced at Ginger and let her answer my question.

'Because illegals are easier to control,' Ginger said.

4

It was close to midnight when I parked the old BMW X5 on Charterhouse Street. The city was closing down for the night but my neighbourhood was just coming awake.

At 77A Charterhouse Street, a former meatpacking warehouse, the clubbers were filing in to dance the night away at Fabric. Directly across the street a convoy of meat trucks was lined up outside Smithfield meat market. A roar of activity was coming from inside the majestic old building and it would not stop until dawn. On Charterhouse Street late diners lingered over coffee and dessert at Smiths of Smithfield, four floors of beautiful blasted brickwork, reluctant for the evening to be over.

But I was bushed and climbed the stairs to our top-floor loft with a bone-deep exhaustion. Mrs Murphy, who took care of us, had been asleep in an armchair but woke at the sound of my key in the lock and was getting to her feet, patting her immaculate white hair. Stan, our ruby-coloured Cavalier King Charles Spaniel, did not bother to get up but watched me with his perfectly round black eyes. Mrs Murphy waved away my apologies for the lateness of the hour.

'Those girls in Chinatown,' she said, and the shake of her head became a shudder. 'A terrible thing.' I followed her to the kitchen. 'Everybody's been washed, walked and fed,' she said, looking at Stan. By everybody she meant Stan and Scout, my six-year-old daughter. Mrs Murphy collected the airmail envelope that contained her money for the day. For some reason, both of us preferred me to not actually hand over money directly. Perhaps because Mrs Murphy felt like the closest thing that Scout and I had to family.

'Scout thought you might be here to tuck her in.'

'That was the plan.'

I knew I had let all the good things of the day slip away. Meeting Scout from school. Eating dinner with my daughter. Walking Stan in the streets and squares of Smithfield. I would have to try harder to make them happen tomorrow. We walked to the door. Mrs Murphy pulled on her coat and patted my arm.

'You'll make up for it, I'm sure. Scout mentioned pancakes at Smiths of Smithfield.'

I smiled. 'OK.'

'We should be nice to our children,' Mrs Murphy advised. 'They choose our care home.' At the door she jabbed a finger at the laptop. 'And don't turn *that* thing on or you will never get your sleep.'

When Mrs Murphy had gone I crossed the loft, Stan padding behind me, the lavish plume of his tail wagging, and I slipped quietly into Scout's room. It felt that until quite recently she had slept like a baby, on her back with her raised fists in the air, like a victorious boxer. But tonight she was curled up on her side, her hair falling across her perfect face. Now she slept like a little girl.

I gently pulled up her duvet and let myself out, ushering Stan before me. The pair of us sat by the giant floor-to-ceiling windows, watching the lights burning at the meat market.

Despite my weariness, I knew that sleep would not come soon or easily tonight.

So I slipped Stan a dental chew and, as he crunched it contentedly in the middle of that massive open space we called home, I powered up the iMac and found the home page for Europol, the European police intelligence agency responsible for the war on people smuggling.

And I learned it was a war they were losing.

The figures were staggering: 90 per cent of migrants into Europe used smuggling and trafficking networks. The smugglers came from more than a hundred countries. Hana Novak and the eleven other young women who died in the back of that refrigerated truck were part of a criminal industry that was worth almost £5 billion a year.

This was far more than big business.

This was the fastest-growing industry on the planet.

Europol charted the varied routes of the smuggling, a tide of trafficked humanity heading west and north.

Across the Mediterranean from Morocco and Algeria into Portugal and Spain. From Tunisia and Libya into Sicily and the islands of southern Italy. And from all points east – Turkey, Syria, Iraq, Afghanistan, Pakistan – into Turkey and Greece then across the Balkans and the dream of life in northern Europe.

I checked my notes on the thirteen passports we had found in the cab. Three Syrian. Two Turkish. And one each from Nigeria, Afghanistan, Iraq, Iran, Pakistan, China, Somalia and Serbia – Hana Novak.

There was no doubt in my mind that the lorry had taken the Balkans route.

We knew that the truck had entered the country at Dover on a ferry from Dunkirk. I worked my way backwards through what Europol called the major smuggling hubs.

Dover. Dunkirk. Paris. Stuttgart. Munich. Zagreb. And Belgrade.

Had Hana been the last passenger to join the lorry? It seemed likely. My finger traced the likely route before they picked up Hana. Skopje in Macedonia. Athens in Greece. And then one of the Greek islands in the Aegean Sea – Kos or Lesbos or Symi, a short hop from the Swiss cheese coastline of Turkey. And before that, all they were fleeing from – a world of war, suffering and poverty.

And I read about the casualties.

The unknown thousands who drowned unnoticed, uncounted and unmourned in the seas of Europe. The fifty-eight Chinese who were found dead in a Dutch lorry at Dover in 2000, the largest mass killing in British criminal history. And the twelve young women who had died in London this morning.

I remembered Hana Novak, and the few hours of her life that she had spent at the end of the rainbow, and how she had looked in her hospital bed at the Royal Free.

And I thought about the thirteenth passport.

And as my eyes fell shut and my head nodded forward, and I folded my hands to rest just for a moment, I tried to imagine where the woman who got away was sleeping tonight.

I jolted awake in the crystal light of another freezing dawn. My daughter and my dog were by my side, both watching me with disapproval. Scout was still in her pyjamas and holding a purple toothbrush, clearly realising that I had not made it to bed when she was cleaning her teeth.

'Scout,' I said, still blurry. 'Can I get you some breakfast?'

She nodded briskly.

'Don't stay up all night,' she said. 'It's bad for you. OK?'

'OK.'

She turned away. Stan trotting beside her, gazing up with adoration.

'And I'm having pancakes,' she called over her shoulder, as if our breakfast menu had been decided a long time ago.

5

Scout and I sat at a window seat at Smiths of Smithfield, eating our breakfast – a stack of pancakes for her and porridge with honey and berries for me. We were watching the cars go by.

'Mazda MX5,' she said through a mouthful of pancakes. 'Porsche 911.' Her brown eyes widened. 'BMW X5 – like us!'

I looked out at the morning traffic on Charterhouse Street.

'That's a BMW X6.'

Scout craned her neck, looking doubtful. 'Is it?'

'You're slipping, kiddo. The X6 has a smaller back window than the X5.'

Scout was not convinced.

'What – you don't believe me?' I said. 'You used to think I was infallible.'

I thought she might ask me what *infallible* means – she couldn't possibly know at six years old, could she? – but instead her face split into a happy smile, revealing a gap

51

where she had lost a couple of her lower centre milk teeth.

'Edie,' she said.

Through the steamed-up windows, we watched Edie Wren coming our way. It was another freezing day, the sky steely grey and too cold for snow. Edie was dressed to climb mountains. Puffa jacket, boots, her red hair tucked up inside a beanie. She pushed through the big glass doors of SOS, grinning when she saw Scout. Stan stirred between our feet.

'You should get the pancakes, Edie,' Scout said. 'They're very good in here.'

'Pancakes are good everywhere,' Edie said, scratching Stan behind the ears. 'I bet even the worst pancake you ever had was still pretty good, right?'

They smiled at each other. But Edie's face was lined with exhaustion. I could see she was still shaken up from what we had discovered in Chinatown yesterday morning. I pulled out a chair for her, wondering what she wanted, but she lifted her chin, indicating that it could wait until we were alone.

'You two enjoy your breakfast,' she told me.

When the pancakes and porridge were gone, we all walked to school, Edie holding hands with Scout, Stan trotting by my daughter's side, the dog expertly slipping between the meat porters and their empty trolleys as they wound up business for the night. As we got closer to the school, the sound of the children rose like bird-song in the bitterly cold air. Someone called Scout's name and she was immediately off, never looking back. She was with her friends now. Edie and I were forgotten.

We stood in silence at the school gates, listening to the sound of the children. Then a bell rang from some-where inside the school and we turned away.

'Anything in Chinatown?' Edie said.

'Ginger Gonzalez gave us a name,' I said. 'Asuman Jenkins. Formerly Asuman Ata. Turkish. Asuman is of interest because she was trafficked into the country and worked at some kind of lap-dancing joint where they only used illegals.'

'So they can keep the girls on a tight leash, right?' Edie shook her head. 'Bastards.'

'The place this Asuman worked was out on the M25. Then she did a bunk and found Ginger in London. She's still here. You and I will pay her a visit. But it's huge now, Edie. Human trafficking. It's bigger than drugs. It's the biggest criminal racket in the world.'

Edie nodded, pausing to take a deep breath. A wave of nausea seemed to pass. I touched her lightly on the sleeve.

'You all right?'

'Bad night.' She exhaled hard, in control again. 'Do you know what we do with the bodies that nobody knows and nobody wants?'

'The official policy with the unclaimed dead? I didn't know there was one.'

'There's not,' Edie said. 'There's no policy with the unclaimed. In this country we get around one hundred and fifty unidentified bodies every year, everything from dead newborn babies to bodies with their heads chopped off. Once the law has had a think, and scratched our heads, and come up blank, then it's the coroner's call if the unclaimed are stored at the morgue or buried in unmarked graves.'

'And you think those dead women in Chinatown are going to remain unclaimed? We only found them yesterday morning, Edie.'

'But how can anyone claim them if we don't know who they were? We're investigating multiple unlawful deaths where eleven of the twelve victims are unidentified – and likely to stay that way because they had fake travel documents. I've been talking to the embassies, Max. They don't want to know. None of them. They don't want to hear about a bunch of fake passports. It's not their problem because they don't even know if it's really one of their nationals. The only luck I've had is with the genuine passport.'

'Hana Novak,' I said.

'The Serbs have found a next of kin in Belgrade. They're flying him in from Belgrade tomorrow to formally identify Hana.'

'Parent?'

'No, both the mother and father are long gone,' she said. 'But Hana Novak had a kid brother.'

'This is how you freeze to death,' said Elsa Olsen, forensic pathologist, deep inside the Iain West Forensic Suite at the Westminster Public Mortuary. 'Breathing slows then stops. Blood slows then stops. The heart rate slows then stops. The metabolism shuts down. And that's what happened here.'

The twelve bodies of the young women lay on stainless steel tables, two rows of six, pushed close together. I shivered in the near-freezing temperature, those carefully maintained single digits of centigrade that make it possible to examine and inspect the dead.

My eyes drifted to Hana Novak, at the far end of one of the lines.

She did not look at peace.

I could not believe the comforting clichés we tell ourselves about death. She looked like someone else, someone other than the young woman who had spoken to me to tell me her name in the ambulance, someone other than the young woman who I saw fight for her life in the Royal Free. Whatever spark had made Hana Novak the person who climbed into the back of that lorry in search of some better life, it had gone forever. This was not Hana Novak any more, although perhaps it was the shadow of who she had once been. I thought for a moment about her brother, wondering how old he could be, knowing that whatever age he was, he was far too young to come to this place to look upon the shell of his sister.

'It's a hell of a thing,' Elsa said to herself in the clipped English of a Norwegian who had spent most of her adult life in London.

She walked between steel tables, a tall dark woman in a white coat and latex gloves, as each of our team stood at the end of one of the lines, wearing blue scrubs and hairnets. Whitestone and Edie and Billy and me. DCI Whitestone, our Senior Investigating Officer, wanted all our team to witness what had been done to the women we found in Chinatown.

So we stared at the bodies on the steel tables, and it seemed as if the victims came from every race on earth and from every corner of the planet.

'Despite some abrasions, there are no defensive wounds or signs of violence on the victims,' Elsa said. 'Therefore I looked at three possible causes of death.' She counted them off with a nod of her head. 'Asphyxiation due to lack of oxygen. Carbon monoxide poisoning due to inhaling toxic fumes. And multiple organ failure due to fall of body temperature.' She looked at Whitestone. 'And I am satisfied that the cause of death was multiple organ failure due to stage four hypothermia – profound hypothermia.'

'So it's as we thought – they froze to death,' Whitestone said.

Elsa nodded.

'We call it freezing to death although there's no precise core temperature at which the human body can no longer survive. It's what the exposure to sub-zero conditions does to the internal organs that causes death. And it was cold enough in the back of that lorry to kill anyone.' She glanced at Hana Novak with something like fondness. 'It is a miracle that they didn't all die before you found them.'

'Some of them had their clothes torn off,' Edie said. 'Indicating some kind of assault before death.'

'The clothes torn and removed are attributable to what is known as paradoxical undressing,' Elsa said. 'When someone has profound hypothermia they remove their clothes as a response to what feels like extreme heat. When I was growing up in Norway, mountain climbers who died of cold would often be found in a state of undress.'

I remembered what the paramedics had told me in Chinatown.

'You're not dead until you're warm and dead,' I said.

Elsa nodded.

'The cold makes the brain enzymes less efficient,' she said. 'Their cerebral metabolic rate drops rapidly with every degree of core temperature. At first you can't think straight. And then you can't think at all. You would struggle to recognise your mother's face. Time would have no meaning. Blood thickens. Blood pressure drops. It's a cruel delusion. At the moment the cold is about to kill you, you're not hot – but you think you are. And then perhaps – right at the end – there would be a moment of terrible clarity.'

I took a step closer to Hana Novak. The skin on her hands seemed torn away. I noticed that a few of the victims had the same injury, as if they had been fighting off an attacker.

'You say there are no defensive wounds, Elsa,' I said.

'That's right.'

'And you're certain nobody attacked them? Nobody assaulted them? They didn't fight anyone off?'

'Correct, Max.'

'Then what are those marks on their hands?'

Elsa picked up Hana Novak's right hand and stared at the torn skin on her fingertips. I saw that there was also skin missing from the palms of her hand.

'The abrasions on their hands are where they beat the door,' Elsa Olsen said. 'Those marks are from where they tried to get help.' She struggled to control her breathing and I saw that the tall Norwegian pathologist had tears in her eyes.

'Those marks are where they tried to stay alive,' she said.

6

The locals were gone.

The pub at one end of the street was now a mosque. The church at the other end of the street was boarded up and used as a car park. The working-class families who had built their lives here had long ago moved out of this far-flung corner of east London to Essex and Kent and East Anglia. The only sign that they had ever been here were the net curtains that still hung in every single window.

'My nan still has net curtains like that,' Edie said as we sat in the BMW X5 outside the address we had been given for Asuman Jenkins, formerly Asuman Ata.

The newcomers had not removed the net curtains. Not the Bangladeshis who had first moved in, and not the East Europeans who came later, and not the most recent arrivals, who had brought their food and their faith to the street but left the net curtains in place, even as they turned yellow and frayed with age.

'My nan's net curtains are cleaner, of course,' Edie said.

I remembered a book from school, and the fifty-year-old wedding dress of a woman who had been left alone at the altar on her wedding day. That's what all those rotting net curtains looked like. Miss Havisham's wedding dress in *Great Expectations*.

It was a street of modest terraced houses built after the war, the places that went up when the slums were bombed out or torn down, with probably two bedrooms and what they used to call a box room and not one place in the house where you could not hear everybody else going about their business.

There would be a garden out back and there had once been smaller patches of grass out front but these token gardens had long been concreted over, converted into parking spaces for the cars and vans that crowded the road as if they were the true owners.

It was late afternoon and the hazy winter sun was already calling it quits for the day. My stomach rumbled and I was suddenly aware that I had not eaten since I had breakfast with Scout that morning.

Towards the former pub end of the street there was a sad-looking strip of shops, some of them with graffiti-stained shutters down for the day or possibly forever, some with TO LET in the dusty windows and hills of junk mail piled under the letter box. But some were still open for business. Halal butchers. Polish supermarket. A chicken joint where a little crew of apprentice bad boys idled on their bikes, giving us the evil eye. There was a betting shop and I couldn't tell if it was open or closed. And there was a Chinese take-away, Double Fortune.

'We could get some noodles from the Chinese,' I said. 'Double Fortune. Sounds good.'

Edie took a breath and shook her head. She placed the palm of her hand on her midriff and slowly exhaled.

And suddenly I got it.

I stared out at the street, letting it sink in.

'Edie,' I said. 'How far gone are you?'

Silence.

I looked at her. The pale face, the untidy red hair tucked inside a beanie, the bluest eyes I had ever seen. How old was she now? Her mid-twenties? Still young.

I kept looking at her. I was waiting.

'Ten weeks or so,' she said.

I nodded, winded and wordless.

For as long as I had known Edie Wren, she had been involved with a married man. I had seen him once, a good-looking man in a suit and tie, like a politician who wants your vote, no spring chicken – the far side of forty – but a handsome man who knew it and who had always known it. I had only glimpsed him in a doorway for a moment. But I saw his wedding ring. Or perhaps I imagined that I saw it. But it was there.

Edie Wren's married man. Mr Big.

I could not, off the top of my head, even remember his real name. But I knew with total certainty that he was too old for her, and that he was too married for her and that he was nowhere near good enough for her. He did not deserve her and he did not deserve to be the father of her child. I felt an anger and grief that I could not explain. And I felt totally absurd at the depth of my feelings.

Why can't you just wish the girl well, Max?

I looked at her, and she was fingering the small crucifix around her neck. Edie Wren was London-Irish Catholic. And nothing in the world would stop her having this baby.

'Congratulations,' I said, looking away. 'I guess.'

'What's wrong with you?'

'Nothing,' I said. 'Here she comes now.'

Asuman Jenkins was perhaps thirty, but her dark face was lined with exhaustion and made her look years older. Under her black unbuttoned North Face jacket you could see the light blue uniform of an NHS staff nurse. She was fiddling with her key in the front door when we came up the concrete garden path.

'Asuman Ata?' Edie said.

She turned to stare at us, a look of horror on her tired face.

'Jenkins,' she insisted. 'My name is Asuman *Jenkins*.'

Our warrant cards were in our hands.

'Please,' I said. 'There's no need to be alarmed, Mrs Jenkins.'

'But we need to talk about when you were Asuman Ata,' Edie said.

We followed her through the front door. I thought I knew these houses but inside it was more compact than I had imagined. I had been spoiled by my years in a Smithfield loft, living in more space than me or my little family would ever fill. But in the tiny box-shaped living room where the widescreen TV was exactly the same size as the sofa, three was a crowd.

Edie and I sat on the sofa and Asuman Jenkins perched uneasily on the footstool of a La-Z-Boy. It is not her chair, I thought, as her knees almost pressed against mine. As she sat there in her light blue uniform, I tried to imagine her as the young woman who had been smuggled into the country.

'We understand that you entered this country illegally, Mrs Jenkins,' Edie said.

She immediately stood up.

'I have a British passport now. I'll show you. My husband—'

I held up my hand. 'We're not questioning your right to residency. We wanted to ask you about how you found work after you arrived here.'

'The travel agent arranged it,' she said, slowly sinking on to the edge of the big black easy chair.

'The *travel* agent?' I said.

'You mean the trafficker,' Edie said. 'The smuggler.' Edie looked at me and grinned. 'Travel agent!'

For the first time, I saw a flash of defiance in the woman's face.

'To you – he was a trafficker,' Asuman said. 'To me – he was a travel agent. I wanted to come to this country. In my home . . .' She shook her head. 'There was nothing for me. My father was very strict.' She bit her lower lip, then shook off the memory. 'So I went to the travel agent. And I paid him money. And he arranged my trip.' She glanced at her watch. 'But all this is a long time ago. You must leave before my husband comes home.'

'It doesn't work like that,' I said.

'We leave when our questions have been answered,' Edie said. 'If you want us to be gone by the time your husband gets home, then we should get cracking.'

'Where did you meet this travel agent?' I said.

'There's an area in Istanbul called Aksaray. They call it Little Syria. That's where the travel agents are. If you want a travel agent – you go there. Ten years ago or today. *I paid £1,240.*'

She looked at us with suppressed rage, as if the steep price made the journey legitimate. The sudden sound of a car outside turned her head towards the window.

'Mrs Jenkins,' I said quietly. 'We're investigating the death of the twelve young women who were found in a lorry in Chinatown. If you've seen the news over the last twenty-four hours, I know you will have heard about it.'

'Terrible,' she nodded, getting to her feet. Edie and I looked at each other. Why was she so afraid of her husband?

'We are talking to you now because we know a little of your history,' I said. 'We spoke to Ginger Gonzalez.'

Her face flushed. She would not meet my eyes.

'That was a long time ago,' she said. 'Another life.'

'How did your travel agent get you here?' Edie said. 'Boat to a Greek island?'

'No,' she said. 'I caught a taxi. It was all overland. No boats to Greece in those days. Nobody drowning in the sea at that time.' She took a breath. 'A car from Turkey to Sofia in Bulgaria. Then a car to Niš in Serbia, then on to Belgrade in the same car. Then a different car to Zagreb and then a lorry to Stuttgart. And the same lorry all the way to England. And then on the ferry. Across the sea.'

'The journey ended in London?' I asked.

She shook her head.

'There's a big road from London to the north of England. The M1.'

'Rings a bell,' Edie said.

'There is a place for petrol and food where the M1 meets the M25. That is where the travel agent dropped us.'

'London Gateway service station,' I said.

'But all this is ten years ago!' she protested.

'And who found you work?' I said.

She bit her lower lip and looked towards the window again. But there were no cars out there now.

'There were men waiting to meet us at this place on the M1,' she said, reluctantly sitting on the La-Z-Boy. 'They knew we were coming. One of them gave me work. Me and another girl from – I don't know. I think her country was Thailand.'

'You worked at the Champagne Room,' I said.

She drew an audible intake of breath.

'But you ran away from the Champagne Room,' I said. 'You went to London. And you met Ginger Gonzalez.'

A car pulled on to the tiny driveway.

'Please,' she said. 'I don't know anything about those women.'

'How did those men know you were coming?' I said. 'How did it work? Did the travel agent arrange this job for you?'

A key turned in the front door.

'I don't want to get into trouble,' she said. '*Please.*'

Her husband walked into the room. He was a large and burly red-faced man, who looked as though he had played rugby twenty years ago, or at least watched a lot of it.

And he was a sergeant in the Metropolitan Police.

He came into the little living room with a smile on his ruddy face and it fell away when he saw Edie and me, standing to meet him with our warrant cards in our hand.

'Sergeant Jenkins, I'm DC Wolfe and this is DC Wren of West End Central,' I said. 'We're here—'

'I can guess why you're here,' he said. 'Ash doesn't know anything.'

Ash was his nickname for her.

As if she was someone else now.

And perhaps she was.

'Now get out of my house before I throw you out.'

Most people think that detectives outrank uniformed officers but it is not true. Plain clothes mean nothing to a police officer. As a sergeant, Jenkins outranked us.

Edie and I glanced at each other. I could see it in those blue eyes. We were not going to get much more out of Asuman Jenkins unless we played rougher and brought her in for a formal interview. And I suspected that leading us to the Champagne Room was about as far as she could take us.

We made our way to the door. Asuman Jenkins stayed in the living room but Sergeant Jenkins dogged our steps. Edie slipped out the front door and I turned to look at the big sergeant.

'One more thing,' I said.

'No,' he said. 'Nothing else. Sling your hook.'

'Where did you meet your wife?'

His face flooded with a tearful fury.

'Why should she have to beg to be inside this country?' he said. 'And in case you are fucking wondering, she wasn't a whore. She was never a whore. She came to this country to be a nurse.'

'But she wasn't working as a nurse for Ginger Gonzalez, was she, Sergeant Jenkins? And she wasn't working as a nurse in the Champagne Room.'

'Do you want me to take you outside and punch your lights out?' he said.

'You could try. You might even succeed.' I sized him up. 'You're bigger than me. Stronger than me. But I'm in much better shape than you and I've probably had a lot more training than you.'

He sneered at me.

'What are you meant to be then? Some kind of Mixed Martial Arts bad ass?'

'Nothing so modern.'

He looked at the bend in my nose.

'You're a boxer,' he said. 'Nobody's born with a snout like that.'

He didn't seem impressed. I didn't expect him to be.

I was here to talk to his wife about her former life in prostitution and the thing that he wanted most in the world right now was to rip my throat out.

'But you know that rolling about on the pavement with me would not make anything easier for your wife,' I said.

'She's a nurse. Ash is *a nurse.*'

'I know.' I took half a step closer to him. 'But we have twelve young women who died following pretty much the same route that your wife took into this country. That's why we're here today. That's the only reason we're digging up the past. Because we have twelve bodies and no leads. You following me, Sergeant Jenkins?'

He nodded. But he still did not answer me.

'So I'll ask you one last time,' I said. 'Where was Mrs Jenkins working when you met her? At the Champagne Room?'

No reaction.

'Then was she working for Ginger Gonzalez?' I said.

He looked away, and he shook his head, but somehow it was the exact opposite of a denial.

'I would have thought that Ginger's staff were out of your pay grade,' I said, and I took half a step back as I watched his fists clench by his sides. But he did not raise his hands. He raised his head and I saw that finally he wanted to get it over with.

'Janice,' he said. 'My first wife – her name was Janice. She died of breast cancer. I went off the rails. Alcohol mostly. But I had these fits of rage.' He shook his head. 'I was angry. I thought – why her? Why anybody? It made me a violent man. On the job, I mean. On our job, Detective. There was a crew of little hoodies on Lewisham High Street, mugging the old white ladies for their cat-food money. I got hold of one of these little hoodies.' His voice became very quiet at the memory. 'And I nearly killed him,' he said.

Edie was waiting for me on the street. I nodded at her, afraid to move or speak in case it stopped Sergeant Jenkins from speaking.

'One of my colleagues knew about Ginger Gonzalez. This is years back, when Ginger was fresh off the banana boat. I met her in a pub. I think her business – Sampaguita is the name of her business, right? – was not quite so upmarket back in the day. She wasn't operating out of the big five-star hotels in those days. This is long before the Savoy and the Ritz and Claridges. She met men in pubs. Same deal – Ginger made the introductions. But she took what she could get. Even serving police officers. So a date was set up for me and one of Ginger's girls.'

'And that was Asuman,' I said. 'That was Ash.'

'She wanted to be a nurse. She wanted a decent life. She wanted to take a different road from the one she was on.' He looked at me and for the first time I felt that there was no possibility of us ending up punching each other. 'I made it happen,' he said. 'That new life.'

'One date and then you rescued her.'

He looked at me.

'I'm not sneering at you,' I said. 'Thank you.'

As I turned away I felt a powerful hand on my arm.

'Look in the Champagne Room,' he said. 'I know those bastards are still out there. And look at those service stations where the motorways meet. Where London ends and the country begins. It hasn't changed in ten years, you know. The whole rotten business just gets bigger and bigger. The whole world wants to come here. And they'll do anything to get in.'

I thanked him and I watched him go inside his house.

Then Edie and I drove away from the street of filthy net curtains.

'So are you and me going to check out this club?' Edie said. 'The Champagne Room, toast of the M25, the hottest spot north of London Gateway service station?'

She was grinning. I didn't smile back.

'No,' I said. 'It's better if I go with Billy.'

Silence.

'Why are you angry with me?' she said. 'Because I'm pregnant? What's it got to do with you, Max?'

'Nothing,' I said. 'Two men just works better. In fact, two men is the only thing that works. Look – the Champagne Room is somewhere between a lap-dancing club and a knocking shop. We're not going to be kicking down doors, Edie. We'll go in undercover as a couple of punters. And see if they're still working from the same business model.'

Her phone was ringing. After a moment she took the call, listened, murmured assent and hung up.

'That was DCI Whitestone,' she said. 'The boy has landed. Hana's brother. Nenad Novak is sixteen years old. And later today he is going to ID his sister's body at the Iain West.'

My stomach knotted at the thought of a sixteen-year-old boy staring at his next of kin in the mortuary.

'Whitestone wants you to be there,' Edie said.

'Why me?'

Edie smiled a little sadly.

'You're good with children,' she said.

7

There was a flurry of snow in the evening air as I walked
from 27 Savile Row to the Westminster Public Mortuary
on Horseferry Road. A man and a boy were waiting
outside. They were an odd couple. The man was a
tall lean figure with a briefcase, a sleek and affluent
professional ready for the last of the day's business. The
boy – a young-looking sixteen – was in an unbuttoned
coat that was frayed by previous owners and two sizes
too big for him. His spectacles had been broken and
mended more than once.

'DC Wolfe?' the man said, shaking my hand. 'I'm
Dejan Jovanović from the Embassy of the Republic of
Serbia.' He turned to the boy with a show of formality.
'And this young man is Mr Nenad Novak.'

I could see his sister in his face.

I shook the boy's hand.

'I'm sorry to meet you under these circumstances,' I
said, as his eyes behind his broken spectacles slid away
from me. His second-hand coat was unbuttoned despite

the temperature hovering just above zero. I felt that he had a lot of things to learn. 'Shall we go inside?'

They followed me into the Westminster Public Mortuary. I addressed both of them. 'Identification is necessary to establish that the person reported as having died is truly that person in order to complete the certificate of death,' I said.

'Of course,' nodded Jovanović of the embassy. The boy said nothing, his face a glum mask, as if he had been brought to this country, this city and this place against his will.

I looked at him until he finally met my eye.

'Nenad,' I said. 'I am afraid we believe that body is your sister, Hana.'

His mouth twitched with emotions that I could not read. Grief. Shock. Adolescent embarrassment. I wished there was a way around this bleak ritual.

I met her, I wanted to tell him. *I found her alive. I held her hand in the hospital. I was with her when she died. And I promise you that I am going to nail the bastards who did this to your sister and all those other women.*

But I said nothing. I put my arm around him, guiding him to a chair, but never quite touching him. We all remained standing.

He was very young for what he had to do today. Seeing his sister's body would bring home the full reality of loss. I realised that it was best to ask him anything I needed to know now, before he saw her.

'Nenad? Why was Hana coming to this country?'

'She was a nurse,' he said in near-perfect English.

'Do you know what she was going to do in this country? Did she speak about her plans?'

'To work as a nurse.'

'But did she have a job to come to? Or was she planning to look for work?'

He shrugged, shook his head, his eyes once more avoiding my gaze.

'Where did you learn English, Nenad?'

'YouTube. And my sister.'

I turned to Jovanović.

'I recommend that Nenad does not touch the body,' I said. 'Touching can make it all a lot worse.'

Jovanović murmured a sentence in Serbian and Nenad shrugged again, as if none of this had very much to do with him. I felt for the kid. He was a teenage boy in a situation he was not equipped to deal with. In fact, I had never yet seen a fully grown adult who was equipped to deal with this situation.

Elsa Olsen came to meet us in the lobby. I made the introductions and Elsa took us down in the lift to the Iain West Suite. Beyond the glass wall, a lone metal trolley was waiting for us, the body it held covered by a white sheet.

Elsa looked at Nenad Novak and then at me.

The boy stared off into a corner of the room. I nodded and Elsa gently pulled back the sheet to reveal the face of Hana Novak. I was still looking at her when the boy finally spoke.

'That's not her,' he said.

We all looked at him.

'That's not Hana,' he insisted. 'That's not my sister. You're all wrong.'

He turned on his heels and walked out.

'Very irregular,' said Jovanović.

Elsa took a last look at the lifeless face on the trolley and then pulled back the sheet.

'I'm going to have to record her as unclaimed, Max,' she said. 'Like all the others.'

'I'll talk to him,' I said.

I thought I would find him waiting for us in the lobby. But he was already out of the door. I stepped on to the street and saw him walking into the small park on the far side of Horseferry Road. Jovanović was by my side.

'Let me handle it,' I said, and Jovanović nodded and held back.

There is a giant chessboard in Saint John's Gardens and I found Nenad Novak staring at it, as if contemplating his next move.

He looked up at me.

'That's not her,' he said, his eyes shining.

I nodded and put my arm around his shoulder, as if I was ready to believe whatever he chose to tell me. There is a small circular fountain in the middle of the park and we took one of the benches facing it. When the tears came I patted him gently on his second-hand coat and then took my arm away.

It was dark by this time, one of those bleak mid-winter nights that has the world hurrying for home as soon as possible, and the park was totally empty. Just us and the pigeons. But Nenad still covered his face with his hands, ashamed of his tears. He said her name, and it came out as a choke of grief.

'*Hana.*'

'That's your sister in there,' I said. 'Isn't it, Nenad?'

He breathed out, a long slow exhalation that was at once an affirmation and an acceptance of a world that had suddenly changed forever.

'I'm part of the team that wants justice for Hana,' I said. 'We want to find the men responsible for her death. But I need your help, Nenad. I need you to talk to me. And I need you to be totally honest with me.'

'She was a *nurse*,' he said angrily. 'She was not anything else. And it doesn't matter what anybody says about her now. My sister was coming to London to be a nurse.'

'I spoke to her,' I said.

He looked at me.

'I was the one who went into the lorry where we found her,' I told him. 'I went into the lorry where we found Hana and eleven other women. Hana was the only one who was still alive. And she told me her name in the ambulance. And I went with her to the hospital.'

He wiped at his eyes with the back of his hand. He waited as if there was a wealth of details that he knew nothing about. But there was not much more to tell.

'You stayed with my sister?'

I felt a flood of shame. I shook my head.

'I went away,' I said. 'To try to find the men who did this to Hana and the other women. But then I went back to the hospital. I was with her at the end. She died peacefully. In her sleep. She was not alone at the end.'

All the comforting clichés of death, I thought.

But it was true. Even if I had nothing else to give him.

'She looked frightened,' he said. 'She looked so frightened.'

For a moment I was about to mutter some desperate platitude about being at rest now, and beyond all pain, but then I realised with a jolt that he was not talking about the viewing at the mortuary.

He meant the last time he ever saw Hana alive.

'When Hana got into that truck,' he said, wiping his nose with his hand. 'I have never seen her so frightened. She was a brave woman! She was strong! After our parents died, she was the head of our family. It was a shock for me to see the fear on her face. I think it was because they took her passport away.'

I let it settle for a moment.

'You saw her get into the lorry?' I said. 'You were there?'

He nodded.

'I carried her suitcase to the meeting place. But the man – the man from the lorry – the driver – he would not permit luggage. I had to take her suitcase back home with me. And he took her passport. He had all their passports.'

I remembered the stack of passports that Edie had found in the cab. I remembered them spread out on a workstation in West End Central. And for the first time I felt I could feel the presence of the man who put a rubber band around that stack of travel documents and tossed them inside his cab.

'Nenad,' I said. 'Listen to me.'

'Nesha,' he said.

'What?'

'Nesha,' he repeated. 'In Serbian – for Nenad we say *Nesha*.' He looked at me as if for the first time. 'Nesha to our friends.'

'Nesha, this is really important. Anything you can tell me about this man – his nationality, what he looked like, anything at all he said – will help us find justice for Hana and all those other women.'

He took his cheap little phone out of his ragged coat and tapped some buttons. He handed it to me.

There was a photograph on the cracked screen.

Hana and Nesha Novak. Brother and sister. Standing on a frozen street in a blacked-out city that could be anywhere but I knew was Belgrade. A selfie – taken hurriedly – brother and sister holding on to each other, both smiling shyly, a souvenir of that last goodbye.

And in the background of their selfie, I saw a man turning away, his face in profile and out of focus and obscured by the shadows of the sleeping city. But I could see the elaborate scarring that ran down one side of his face, like a parody of tribal markings.

The driver.

'What nationality was this man, Nesha? It's very important.'

'I don't know. Maybe Albanian? Or Turkish?'

'Did he give a name?'

'No name.'

'Any more photographs?'

'No more. He was very quick. He was in a hurry to leave. He rushed us to finish. He wanted to go.'

I stared at the photo on the cheap little phone, desperate for more. But there was no more. Until Nesha Novak spoke. He had stopped crying now.

'One thing I can tell you,' he said, wiping his nose with the back of his hand. 'The driver – he did *this*.'

And the boy clicked his fingers.

8

Click-click.

I placed my right thumb against the pad of my middle finger and pressed twice as I looked up at the wall of MIR-1 where the photograph of Hana and Nenad Novak was blown up to life-size. The driver hovered in the background. Enlarged to life-size it was clear that the scarring on his face was a jagged, asymmetrical mess.

'What did they attack him with?' Edie said. 'A cheese grater?'

She saw me smiling and it encouraged her.

'He's no oil painting,' she grinned. 'Unless it's – what's that one? – *The Scream*!'

Edie placed her hands on her cheeks, opened her eyes and mouth, and we laughed together.

'All right, settle down,' DCI Whitestone murmured, immediately restoring order.

'The Serbian embassy is flying Hana Novak's brother back to Belgrade tomorrow,' I said. 'I'll talk to him again, but I don't think there's a lot more he can give us.'

I held Nesha's cheap little plastic phone in my fist. I had promised to give it back to him before he left.

'And the boy has no idea of the route they were taking?' Whitestone asked. 'No idea what the plan was at this end?'

'Hana was coming here to work as a nurse,' I said. 'That's what his sister told him. And that's what he still believes.'

Whitestone stared at the blown-up selfie, looking beyond the smiling brother and sister at the scarred man in the shadows.

'The good thing about villains,' she said, 'is that they're too stupid to stop before they get caught. This guy – Mr Click-Click – he is out there right now. And he's taking the same chances with lives. I know it. I can feel it. We just have to find the bastard.'

TDC Billy Greene was placing hard copies of the photograph in front of us and I saw the old burns scarring the palms of his hands where he had rescued a woman from a basement fire when he was still in uniform. There was a little stiffness in both his hands from the injury that had not been severe enough to stop him becoming a detective. But it meant that most of Billy's duties were behind a computer in West End Central and not out in the field. Which always struck me as ironic, as Billy Greene was probably the bravest cop in 27 Savile Row.

'This image is already with the border force agencies across the south coast,' he said. 'If the unsub comes in or out of a major port, Customs and Immigration will be watching.'

Whitestone nodded.

'But watching and seeing are not the same thing. These border forces have got their hands full meeting and greeting returning jihadists. So smugglers are getting bumped way down the list of priorities. I have a feeling we are going to have to do our own heavy lifting. What have you got on the Champagne Room, Edie?'

'The Champagne Room is an alleged lap-dancing club near the junction of the M25 and M11 motorways,' Edie said. 'It has been open for ten years and currently has an entertainment licence of only six months – a year's licence is the norm for this kind of place – because of concerns about what goes on in the club. Over the years our colleagues in Essex police have investigated numerous allegations of prostitution. Nothing has stuck although, around the time that Asuman Ata was shaking her sweet little thong there, the owner was arrested for kicking a customer all the way to hospital. A charge of common assault was later dropped when the victim declined to press charges. And this is the best part of all. The owner of the Champagne Room is one Steve Warboys.'

Warboys was one of those family names that always rang bells.

Back when Reggie and Ronnie Kray ran the East End, and Eddie and Charlie Richardson ruled south of the river, Paul and Danny Warboys were the kings in west London. But that was fifty years ago. Paul Warboys had crossed my path – his brother Danny had died inside when they both went away for murder – but he was an old man now.

'Is he any relation to Paul?' I said.

'Steve Warboys is the grandson of Paul Warboys,' Edie said. 'Steve's father is Barry Warboys – Paul's son who went straight. There had to be one in the family, right? Privately educated, MBA, runs his own company – Barry Warboys owns that big chain of retirement communities, Golden Years.'

'That's Paul's son? Golden Years?' I said. 'They're everywhere these days.'

'*Elderly care for every pocket*,' Whitestone said, quoting the company slogan. 'We're all going to get shipped off to a branch of Golden Years one day.'

Edie said, 'But Steve Warboys was determined to enter the family business. The problem is – Steve is strictly small-time. Unlike his dear old granddad, Steve Warboys never made it out of the minor leagues. Steve has a criminal record but it's amateur-hour stuff – a bit of dealing in his youth, receiving stolen goods in young manhood, the assault charge that got binned, and all those allegations about what really goes on at the Champagne Room.' She leaned closer to her screen. 'And there was one charge of criminal damage that was dropped. Eleven years back. Second-degree arson.'

Second-degree arson is the torching of an unoccupied building.

'What did Steve Warboys burn?' Whitestone said.

'He was acquitted, ma'am.'

'Sorry, Edie — what *didn't* Steve Warboys burn?'

'Steve had a bar in Brentwood called Studs that went up in flames. The insurance company howled but in the end it was put down to an electrical fault. So he walked and started the Champagne Room with the insurance money. This is Steve.'

Edie hit her keyboard.

On the big HDTV a man appeared, looking furtive and hostile as he emerged from a courthouse into blazing sunlight. He was an overweight thirty-something with fair hair, cropped close and thinning. I stared hard at Steve Warboys and tried to see his grandfather in him. Paul Warboys was a proud, lean, fit man even in his old age. Apart from the almost-albino pallor that all the Warboys clan seemed to share — although for decades old Paul had toasted his milky complexion with a Costa del Sol tan — there was little family resemblance. Steve Warboys had none of the swaggering charisma of his legendary grandfather. Steve looked like exactly what he was – a small-time thug trading on the family name.

'The Warboys dynasty is scraping the bottom of the gene pool with young Steve here,' Whitestone said. 'But that doesn't mean he's not a people smuggler. In fact, I'd say it makes it quite possible. This herbert ever come up on your radar, Max?'

'No, ma'am.'

'How long since Asuman Ata worked in the Champagne Room?' Whitestone said.

'Ten years,' Edie said.

'Who runs girls in this town?' she said.

'The Turks in the north,' I said. 'The Somalians in the south. The Yardies in the west. The Bangladeshis in the east. The idea of one of the old family firms being involved in prostitution sounds unlikely. But maybe I'm wrong. We don't expect the Krays and the Richardsons and the Warboys to be anywhere these days, apart from our local cinema. And perhaps that's a mistake. Asuman Ata – Mrs Jenkins – tells us that the girls in the Champagne Room were all illegals in her day.'

Whitestone nodded. 'And it's worth checking if that is still the case. Since Mrs Jenkins jumped off the back of a lorry, this country has had the greatest wave of migration in its history. There's certainly no shortage of new recruits and only one possible reason to stick with the illegals.'

'Why would they risk prosecution by employing illegals?' Billy said.

'Because in the end a lap-dancing club is no different from a major corporation,' Whitestone said. 'Every boss on the planet loves a docile workforce.'

I arrived home to find Scout already in her pyjamas, Stan out for the count and Mrs Murphy clutching a well-thumbed copy of *Diary of a Worm* by Doreen Cronin.

She handed it to me.

'*This is the diary of a worm,*' I read to Scout. '*Surprisingly, a worm not that different from you and me. Except he eats his homework. Oh, and his head looks a lot like his rear end.*'

We grinned at each other.

After I had kissed her forehead, tucked her in and turned out the lights, I left Mrs Murphy and Stan on the sofa and I went to pick up Billy Greene from the small house where he still lived with his mother in Tottenham.

And then we drove out to the Champagne Room.

9

'Members only.'

He was a big man in a black coat and he stood with his legs far apart and his hands behind his back in front of the dinky red rope that guarded the entrance to the Champagne Room. Mixed race, hair in tight man braids, south London drawl in every vowel. I felt like I had seen him somewhere, perhaps fighting halfway down the undercard at York Hall.

He had certainly been a boxer.

He looked like a light heavyweight who had turned out to be too slow to go far in the pro game, but was vain enough to stay in shape. He wore no hat, despite the bitter temperature of the Essex midnight. Behind us there was the buzz of the boy racers on the motorway, and beyond the doorman I could see the pulsing twilight of the club. The bassline of some golden oldie from the Nineties was so loud I could feel it in my back teeth.

The Champagne Room looked like the lap-dancing

club at the end of the universe – a squat, ugly concrete building surrounded by a car park the size of a football pitch and, beyond that, the endless blackness of all those flat Essex fields. The front of the building was illuminated by a pair of red neon female lips wetly wrapping around the harsh yellow neon of a champagne flute.

'We'll join,' I said.

The big man flinched as if I had insulted his mother.

'Two-fifty,' he said.

'Fine.'

He looked over my shoulder at the lanky figure of young Billy Greene. We had both put on suits and wore shirts with no ties, anxious not to look too formal, but buttoned up to the neck, because it was below freezing.

We looked like junior members of the Iranian Government.

'Each,' the doorman said.

'No problem,' I said, reaching for the thick wad of petty cash that I had inside my jacket. The bouncer took a step closer to me and I could see the spiteful streak in him. He looked in my eyes and not at my money.

'Membership's closed,' he said, waiting for me to contradict him.

A Range Rover swung into the crowded car park that separated the Champagne Room from the howling motorway. It parked next to my BMW X5, casually, couldn't-give-a-monkey's sideways, as if the driver owned the place.

Which he did.

Steve Warboys got out of the Range Rover, a good couple of years older and five kilos heavier than the image that Edie had pulled up, and quickly made his way to the club.

The bouncer respectfully lifted the red rope and Steve Warboys gave me a blank stare as he brushed past. He gave an almost imperceptible nod to the doorman.

'All right, Steve,' said the doorman.

And he turned to me, thawing a little.

'That's five hundred then, brother,' he said. 'Enjoy your evening.'

It took a long moment for my eyes to adjust to the dark inside the Champagne Room. When my sight came back I saw elevated stages, each one featuring a young woman in minimal pants and maximum heels winding herself around a silver fireman's pole.

Tattoos stained naked flesh like the symptoms of some contagious disease. There were more women lurking in the shadows, wearing diaphanous see-through clothes that were possibly nightwear, roaming the perimeter of the club, judging their next move. The place was huge – a perk of building it by the side of a motorway in the middle of all those fields rather than the middle of London.

The men were divided into two groups. There were the loud, drunken City boys in suits and ties who had been moving money in the financial centre of the world a few hours earlier, and there were the older, solitary figures who sat alone at the bar or with a girl astride them at one of the numerous tables that lurked in every nook and cranny of that cavernous space. The groups of City boys acted as if they were having the time of their life and the men who were alone acted as if they were having root canal treatment. The only reveller who didn't fit into either clan was a neatly bearded Middle Eastern man in a Yankees baseball cap at the bar, with a woman on each knee.

A soft hand touched my arm.

She was a pretty blonde, only in her mid-twenties but with many miles on the clock. She was small, but her heels added five inches, and she wore a black sleeveless cocktail dress that seemed to stop before it had even begun. She tugged modestly at its top, a gesture that seemed to emphasise her semi-nakedness rather than disguise it.

'You want party?' she asked.

'How about a drink?' I said.

I looked around for Billy and saw him being led into the darkness by two women in baby dolls. There goes the budget of the Metropolitan Police for another year, I thought, as I was gently steered in the opposite direction.

She found us a table.

A waiter – a young woman dressed in black tie – was immediately by our side, taking the order. My new friend crossed her legs and again pulled up the top of her dress, her manner veering between brazen and modest.

It was even darker at the table, but not so dark that I could not see the bruises on her arms, as mottled as camouflage.

'What happened to you?' I said.

'Oh,' she said, rubbing at the bruises as if that might make them disappear. 'Sometimes I am so clumsy.' She suddenly paid attention as the waiter returned with a bottle of Prosecco.

I looked at the label.

'Champagne, sir,' the waitress said, with just the right note of defiance. I signed the chit she offered and a red velvet curtain was pulled in front of us, hiding us from the rest of club.

My new friend was still massaging her bruises.

'What's your name?' I said.

'Bianca.'

'Is Bianca your real name or your bar name?'

She smiled. 'We're in a bar, aren't we?'

She poured us two drinks, the fizz spilling over the top of first one flute and then the other.

'Whoops,' said Bianca. 'I did not think you would

want me.' She sighed elaborately. 'There are so many beautiful girls in the Champagne Room. I thought you would want . . .' She seemed to search for a phrase that she remembered from her English lessons of long ago and far away. 'Fresh meat,' she said.

She self-consciously pulled up her pants. When we sat down on the low velvet chairs, I saw that there were dark bruises on her knees, a deeper, darker hue than the ones on her arms.

'Where are you from, Bianca?'

'Bucharest. But I have been out for – oh, ten years.'

'Where are the other girls from?' I asked.

She leaned close to me and whispered her great secret. 'Everywhere but here,' she said.

Then the waitress was back.

'Steve wants you in the VIP room now, Bianca,' she said. And then to me. 'We'll get you another girl, sir – what flavour do you like?'

I waved her away.

'You have to go?' I said to Bianca, who was already on her feet, a tiny woman tottering on heels as long as hypodermic needles.

She tugged at the top and bottom of her little black dress.

'Steve is the boss,' she said, placing a chaste kiss on my cheek. 'But you come back,' she said, looking at me for the first time. 'I like you, you're nice.'

'Bianca?'

'Yes?'

'What happens in the VIP room?'

Another secret to be purred into my ear.

I could smell the vodka and the cigarettes and her total despair.

'Everything,' she said.

I watched her walk away and the sound of her heels cut through the music.

Click-click, they went. *Click-click*.

Then the doorman was standing before me. When he turned sideways to glance back into the Champagne Room I saw that his nose had been punched so flat that it was as vertical as a sheer cliff face, just one long straight line of flattened cartilage, bone and scar tissue.

'The boss wants a word.'

'Bit busy right now,' I said, grinning foolishly and acting drunker than I felt after a mouthful of sparkling wine.

'Now, Detective,' he said.

I looked at him.

And now I knew where I had seen him before.

I never saw him fight. I never saw him at York Hall. It was at Smithfield ABC. Banging the bags at Fred's gym. A few years back now, it must have been. He had turned pro and then almost immediately been put away for running around town with a gun, waving it in the face of known drug dealers.

I could even remember his name. Peter Chivers.

'Working the doors now, Peter?'

'It's not Peter any more. It's Mahmud X.'

'Converted inside, did you?'

'Saw the light.'

And then Steve Warboys was there, tired of waiting for me to show up in the VIP room. His eyes flitted and moved, frowning at the puddle of alcohol that Bianca had left on the table. There was a natural intelligence about his grandfather Paul that had nothing to do with academic education and his father Barry must have been no slouch to build up his business.

But Steve Warboys looked as though his lift stopped a few floors from the top.

'So your theory is that we're bussing in illegals from bongo bongo land?' he said. 'Getting our girls under the counter?' He laughed. 'You've seen too many Liam Neeson films, Detective. Why would we? Look around. The whole *world* wants to live in this country. And they will do anything – *anything* – to stay here.'

'Well – Steve – if I may call you Steve – the word is you favour using illegal migrants because they are easier to control,' I said. 'Not quite so fussy about pension plans and health care as the locals and the legals.'

He laughed.

'*None* of them are easy to control!' Steve Warboys said. 'They've all got their *issues*. Issues with their daddy, issues with their boyfriend, issues with their body, issues with substance abuse.' He looked hurt, misunderstood. 'In this job, people see only the glamour. They see only the glitz. But it's hard keeping a stable of girls.'

He must have seen some doubt in me because he grinned.

'People smuggling is an industry,' he said, as if I needed to understand. 'But it's not my line of work. Now I'm not denying that we might have had a few employees who fell off the back of a lorry in our time. Like dear old – what was her name again, Mahmud?'

'Asuman,' the bouncer said, and it sounded like a threat. 'I can't remember her bar name.'

They both smiled at my surprise.

'What – you think you can talk to a former employee and we don't get to hear about it immediately?' Steve Warboys said. 'We like to maintain close contact with our former employees.' His face clouded. 'Especially when they run off halfway through a contract. Asuman gave us a head's up that you'd been round.' He touched his heart and I saw the thick gold rings on his right hand. 'For which I am grateful,' he said. 'And, yes, it's possible that her visa papers were not completely in order when she worked here. But that was some years ago, Detective. And in those days, their visa was not the first thing I looked at. Know what I mean? But that was then. And it's a different world now.' A cloud drifted across his sly, slow features. 'I think you might be looking to fit us up, copper.' He held back the red velvet curtain. 'So get out and don't come back.'

I was naturally curious.

'And what happens if I come back?'

'Your new friend – Bianca – will say she gave you a Southend shoeshine,' he said. 'Know what one of those is?'

'I can make an educated guess.'

'Believe me, the allegation will be enough to bring in the IPCC,' he said, referring to the Independent Police Complaints Commission, the body that investigates charges of misconduct against the police. 'Enough to embarrass your family,' he said. 'Enough to get you and your colleague suspended.'

He held out his phone to reveal half a dozen strippers draped all over PC Billy Greene. One of them was grinning at the camera as she fiddled with his belt. I had to admit it didn't look good. And it would look even worse sat in an interview room with the IPCC. Perhaps Steve Warboys was not quite as thick as he looked.

I stood up and smiled at him. I have seen a lot of young hoods that tried walking like the Richardsons, the Warboys and the Krays – *the twins* – as if Reggie and Ronnie were the only twins ever born.

It's a natural aspiration for the criminally inclined, like a singer wanting to be bigger than Elvis. Steve Warboys did it better than most, but in the end he was not the king of anywhere apart from a pole-dancing joint by the side of the motorway.

And I wasn't scared of him.

'I've met your grandfather,' I said. 'And you've got that same colouring. But as far as I can see, that's all you got from Paul Warboys. You've got the name but not the game. Sorry.'

'Get the bats, Mahmud.'

It is stupid to hurt a cop. However big your gang is, our gang is bigger. However much firepower you have, we have far more. And we have the full weight of the state behind us. Yes, it is stupid to hurt a cop. But stupidity is the distinguishing feature of criminals.

Even the smart ones are stupid.

Mahmud X came back with a couple of cricket bats. He gave one to Steve, who hefted it in his hand, grinned at me and strolled back to the bar. The Middle Eastern man with the neat beard still had a woman on each knee. They both shrieked and fled when they saw Steve Warboys and Mahmud X advancing with the cricket bats. And I suddenly saw what they were planning to do.

Mahmud hit the man across the side of the face.

Warboys knocked him off his bar stool.

Phone lights suddenly appeared in the darkness. But

there was a sign on the wall. NO FILMING, it said — standard protocol in any lap-dancing joint. Warboys slapped the sign with his open palm and all the smart phones were quickly put away.

I went to help the man on the ground and found my path blocked by two gorillas in evening wear. They were not quite as big as Mahmud X but they were enough to keep me back.

'You can't stop it,' one of them said, sounding almost wistful.

And he was right. I couldn't stop it.

Warboys and Mahmud laid into the bearded man as he sprawled on the ground and women in high heels and bikinis and baby dolls covered their mouths and screamed at the horror and the drunken City boys kept a respectful distance. Now nobody was even thinking about filming the fun on their iPhones and Samsung Galaxies. They contented themselves with just watching. It was a new experience for them.

The doorman and the club owner both gave the man on the ground a good hiding but the way they worked was very different. It was the difference between a professional hard nut and a raving nut case. Mahmud the doorman beat the man with a calm but vicious professionalism.

But Steve Warboys enjoyed it.

He beat the man with the neat beard until his bat was broken in half. When it was over he stood before me, sweating and panting, gesturing at Mahmud X with his shattered cricket bat.

'Get the girls together,' he said. 'All of them.' He gestured at the man at his feet. 'And get this one to the hospital. He's only half-dead. You can leave him on the pavement outside A&E. And turn on the lights. Now!'

The girls were corralled.

The house lights came on.

The man on the floor was not moving.

'Tell him where you're from,' Warboys told the women. The girls hesitated, anxious not to do anything wrong, unsure of the rules to this parlour game, not understanding that he was trying to prove to me that they were all here legally.

He shouted in the face of a tall, doe-eyed woman in some kind of cheap satin shift.

'*Tell him where you're from!*'

'Italy!'

'That's the idea. You!'

'France.'

'Latvia.'

The women were forming an orderly queue now. They nervously told me their country and then stepped aside, tugging self-consciously at their hair or their pants or the hem of their nightdress.

'Russia. Student visa.'

'China. Student visa.'

'See?' Steve Warboys said, and he laughed at last. 'Do you understand? It's a new century, Detective! And a different business model.'

And then Bianca was standing there, and Warboys roughly shoved her towards me.

'Romania,' she said shyly.

And as she turned away, self-consciously adjusting her pants, I saw Steve Warboys' blood-smeared handprint on her bare back, the bones beneath her skin as fragile as a wishbone.

10

The motorway unfurled into the night, the flat fields of Essex stretching off out into the blackness, TDC Billy Greene silent and sheepish by my side, the lipstick traces on his face looking like a tropical disease.

'Your fly's undone,' I said.

He quickly adjusted himself, and started to stutter out an apology.

'Don't be sorry – be more careful,' I said. 'They're all nice girls but they all follow orders. They don't have the luxury of doing anything else.'

I was thinking about Bianca.

'Nothing happened,' he said.

'I know you're not that dumb,' I said.

Just young, I thought. *And green behind the lugholes.*

I had called in the assault to Essex police but it wouldn't mean a thing if the bearded man had no desire to press charges when he woke up in that hospital bed.

There was a knot of shame in my gut that I had been unable to stop a pair of career thugs handing out a beating but I could not worry about that now. And I wasn't worried about Warboys' hamfisted threats to smear us with snaps of Billy buried under a scrum of lap dancers. The law is not so easily blackmailed. What worried me – what scared me to death – was that TDC Billy Greene was clearly as raw as sushi.

And that was dangerous.

For him. For me. And for anyone he worked with.

'I wanted to do well tonight,' he said. 'In the field, I mean.' His scarred hands rubbed together, as if he were washing them. 'I never planned to be a canteen cowboy.'

Just as the Eskimos have fifty different words for snow, so policemen have many names for cops who never leave their desk. Station cat. Clothes hanger. Shiny arse. Olympic torch (never goes out). Bongo (Books On, Never Goes Out). Flub (Fat, Lazy, Useless Bastard).

But I flashed on the night that Billy Greene ruined his hands. I remembered the basement in a suburban house where we cornered a man called Ian Peck, far better known as Bob the Butcher, currently serving a life sentence for murder. I remembered that basement as a place of damp and dust and death, the black hole where my boss DCI Victor Mallory received a fatal knife wound to the neck.

It was very dark down there, one weak bare light bulb illuminating the horror, and even now I could feel the ache in my ribs beyond the dent in my Kevlar Stealth where Bob had tried to stab me. Bob was small but possessed with the simian power of the insane, and he took me out of the game almost immediately. But through the stars in my vision brought on by a blow to the back of the skull I watched PC Billy Greene throw himself into the flames of a barbecue pit for roasting human flesh.

It was a ragged hole that had been doused with petrol and a naked woman was screaming inside it, a journalist called Scarlet Bush who Bob had abducted, and I remembered the smell of burning flesh and what Billy had looked like in his hospital bed, his hands wrapped in oozing bandages, months of care ahead of him, his future uncertain. But what I remembered most of all was that he had never hesitated to throw himself into the flames.

'I never think of you as a canteen cowboy, Billy,' I said. 'OK?'

'OK. Thanks.'

'Where were your new friends from?'

'Vilnius and Budapest,' he said, confirming what Steve Warboys had insisted. The women of the Champagne Room were all in the country legally. Give or take a dodgy student visa or two, they were even working more or less legally. The Champagne Room did not import its dancers in the back of a lorry. They didn't need to. I heard Billy's stomach rumble.

'You want to stop for something to eat?' I asked him. 'My mum will have something waiting for me,' he said. 'Let's just get back home, shall we?'

Going home was always fine by me. And it should have been an easy run. It should have been an hour cruising on the empty late-night motorways that snake through all that Essex countryside and then back home to London, dropping off Billy to his mum, who would be waiting up for him, and then to Smithfield, where Mrs Murphy and Stan would be dozing on the sofa.

But it didn't work out like that.

The motorway miles drifted by and Billy and I had lapsed into silence until we saw the blue and red lights of trouble piercing the darkness somewhere ahead of us.

'Looks like an accident,' Billy said.

We had turned off the great looping motorway that encircles the city and come down the long straight stretch that runs all the way to the lights of north London. Round midnight on most nights of the year, it is a strip of road much favoured by the boy racers of Essex. They speed here. They preen here. And too often they die here.

On the other side of the road, I could see the lights of the emergency services winking far ahead where the blackness of the country began to be lit by the orange sodium lights of the city. Blue for the law, red for the ambulances, and plenty of both. The traffic on that side of the road had begun to slow and thicken and as we got closer I saw the sickening sight of two cars crushed like cigarette packets by the side of the road.

I slowed the BMW X5 as we passed, close enough to see the expressions of the fire crews and paramedics and the police, their faces taut with shock, and as I pulled away, I saw jagged scraps of metal, careering skidmarks and, glinting like tossed diamonds, the crushed glass of the windscreens. A body bag was being zipped.

I put my foot down. Our side of the road was almost empty but on the other side, where the accident had happened, the traffic was slowing down. As we went faster, it was coming to a total stop. Motorists were getting out of their vehicles.

And then I saw the lorry.

It was stopped in the fast lane, the traffic stagnant both ahead and behind, perhaps five hundred metres from the accident.

The driver had not joined the other motorists who were stretching their legs and checking their phones. He stayed in the cab, but as we passed the lorry the back door of his vehicle came open.

And two men jumped out.

'Max!' said Billy Greene, looking back.

'I see them,' I said.

And I watched in my rear-view mirror as the men did

the one thing that the guilty can always be guaranteed to do.

They ran like hell.

I pulled down hard on the steering wheel and did a U-turn up on to the central reservation, and suddenly we were heading in the other direction. The stalled traffic was too thick to allow us on the road and so I bumped along the frost-hardened grass at a teeth-jolting twenty miles an hour.

Half a mile ahead of me was the stopped lorry, getting closer every second. The back door was wide open now.

A head stuck out.

A young man emerged, sniffed the air and jumped to the ground. He stood for a moment in the fast lane of the motorway with nothing moving, looking warily at all the blue lights of all the authorities waiting ahead.

Then he made a dash for the hard shoulder and beyond.

And then another man emerged, older this time. He too looked at the blue lights of the law, didn't fancy them much, and took off exactly in the opposite direction. They were all heading for the blackness that surrounded this final stretch of road.

And then the doors of the lorry were flung wide open and more were pouring out, perhaps a dozen of them, mostly men but also a couple of women in headscarves.

They all looked at the blue lights and legged it.

I approached the lorry just as the traffic began to move. The emergency services must have opened up a lane. Vehicles began to crawl away, then quickly picked up speed. Including the lorry. I bounced along the central reservation, level with the rear doors of the lorry, flapping wildly as it picked up speed. Men continued leaping out of the back and taking off into the black fields. One of them narrowly avoided a Nissan Micra doing thirty.

'I've got them,' Billy said, the passenger door already open, and I touched the brakes as he jumped out, furious horns of accelerating cars blaring all around him as he fell into the oncoming traffic.

I could see the stowaways legging it into the fields. Billy body-swerved a couple of accelerating cars and went after them. I saw him launch a rugby tackle at the nearest man and bring him down.

Then I put my foot down, swerving back on to the motorway, the lorry directly ahead.

It was pulling away from me. The emergency services had all three lanes open now and as I sped past their blue and red lights for the second time, this time in the opposite direction, I again caught a glimpse of the two heaps of smashed metal, glass and rubber, and the strained faces of the emergency service teams.

The lorry was getting further away from me.

So I put on my blues and twos. The lights pulsated

under the BMW grille and the two-tone siren split the night.

The lorry immediately began to slow. It takes a lot of nerve to make a dash from the blues and twos. And the driver of the lorry didn't have that kind of nerve.

He indicated, slowed down and pulled over to the hard shoulder. I parked just ahead of him, the X5's rear bumper right up against his grille just in case he had a change of mind.

I walked back to the lorry, the motorway traffic hurtling past. I could not see Billy but figures were loping desperately across the fields, lit by moonlight.

By the time I reached the driver's cab he had the window down and an ingratiating smile plastered on his round, rosy face. He looked like a man who had spent a lifetime sitting down.

'Good evening, brother,' he said in a West Country accent that was a perfect fit with his stout, yeoman's mug. 'Nasty accident back there. These boy racers, eh? How can I help you?'

'Get out of the cab before I drag you out.'

I waited for him to lower his considerable bulk on to the ground. He walked round the cab and faced me, still smiling. He had his driving licence and insurance documents all ready for me. I glanced at his licence. His enormous cropped head stared out at me. Lee Hill.

'Where have you come from?'

'I come from Augsburg, bruv. Over there in Germany.'

'I know where Augsburg is. Where did you enter the UK?'

'Dover, bruv, off the ferry from Dunkirk. Nice journey, if a bit choppy near the white cliffs.' He was the picture of benign innocence. 'What's all this about then?' he said.

'What's your load?'

He pursed his lips like the class dunce trying to remember an answer he really ought to know.

'I'm carrying car batteries, bruv, bound for a warehouse in Birmingham.'

'What else?'

'Bruv?'

'Let's have a look in the back.'

The lorry doors had swung shut.

I indicated to Lee Hill and he pulled them open.

Beyond the crates of car batteries, a young woman in a hijab held her newborn baby to her breast. She looked at me without fear or expectation, as if I was just the latest in a long line of unfortunate events.

'You and your baby are safe now,' I told her. 'Do not attempt to leave this vehicle.'

I looked at Lee Hill and I waited.

'They must have sneaked on board at Calais,' he said. 'You have got no idea what it's like, bruv! Every run!

Every time! They light fires now to slow us down. Every Paki, blackie and Iraqi on the planet wants to hide in the back of your lorry!'

I stared at him and wondered if there was any possibility that he was telling the truth.

I knew it happened.

I knew that there were plenty of innocent lorry drivers who entered the country every day with human cargo they knew nothing about, and had absolutely no desire to be transporting.

'Let's have a look in your cab,' I said.

A used condom sat in the footwell like a burst party balloon. There was a coat on the passenger seat, a worn coat that looked as though it had done service in far too many winters.

I looked at the driver, snug in his leather jacket.

'Who does this belong to?'

'Me, bruv.'

One of the worst things about my job are the lies that you hear every single day of your working life. It would not be so bad if they were good lies – credible lies, half-believable lies. But usually they are rubbish lies.

'Then put it on,' I said.

He looked appalled.

'The . . . condom?'

'The *coat*. Let me see you put this coat on. Come on. Do it.'

He slipped out of his XL leather jacket and struggled to fit into the size-8 winter coat. He managed the arms, sort of, just about, but the worn-out material groaned and split with the strain as it tried to stretch across his broad back.

I looked down the hard shoulder. Billy was emerging from the darkness with a bedraggled gang of dark-skinned men. The two women in their hijabs followed behind at a demure distance. He had rounded up perhaps half of them. I nodded to the back of the lorry and Billy started loading them back in.

I turned to Lee Hill.

'Do you know what the sentence is for trafficking people for labour and other exploitation under the Asylum and Immigration Act?'

'Bruv, I had no idea they were in the back of the lorry!'

'Twelve months to fourteen years. You could do twelve months, no sweat, but I don't fancy your chances with fourteen years. The good news is, that's only if you are found guilty. Only if the jury thinks you are lying through your back teeth about knowing nothing about what was in the back of your lorry.'

'I want a lawyer.'

'Get a good one. Who paid you to bring those people in?'

'Anarchists,' he said. 'You know – they don't believe in borders. They think all men are brothers. They don't believe in the nation state, as such. They think that if we invite the Third World to come and live here, then mankind will all live happily ever after in a fairer world.' Billy and I stared at each other. It might even be true.

'What's the name of the anarchist group?' I said.

'Imagine.'

'Imagine?'

'Like the John Lennon song.'

He began singing the chorus.

'Stop singing or I swear to God I will arrest you now,' I said.

I took out my phone and called up the photograph of Hana and Nesha Novak. Their smiling faces huddled together in the Belgrade night, the unsmiling profile hovering behind them like a bad moon.

I showed it to the lorry driver.

'Not a bad-looking woman,' he said.

'I want you to look at the man in the background.'

'OK, bruv.'

'He's a lorry driver. Like you. Exactly your kind of lorry driver. The scumbag kind.'

'Bit harsh, bruv, bit harsh.'

'Ever seen him on your travels? Dunkirk? Calais? Dover?'

'He's an ugly bastard, I'll give him that.'

'And who are you? George Clooney?'

He gave me back my phone.

'Don't recognise him.'

I slipped my phone into my pocket.

'So is that who you work for?' I said. 'This anarchist group? Imagine?'

He snorted at the very thought.

'Those mad hippies? I'm self-employed, bruv. A small businessman.'

I nodded.

'You work for me now,' I said.

We stared at each other.

The traffic zoomed by. It was very cold and I was very tired. I wanted to be under the same roof as my daughter and my dog. I wanted to be away from the liars and the desperate. I wanted to be home.

'OK, bruv,' the driver said.

'And one more thing,' I said.

His fat face waited patiently for my instructions.

'Stop calling me your brother,' I said.

11

When I got to West End Central the next morning, Dejan Jovanović of the Serbian embassy was waiting for me alone.

'Where's the boy?'

He looked at me apologetically.

'What's the expression? Our young Mr Novak has *done a runner*.'

I could not believe it. It's a ten-minute walk from the Embassy of the Republic of Serbia at 28 Belgrave Square to 27 Savile Row. It should have been simple.

'How can he have done a runner, Dejan? Your embassy is only a mile away.'

'We were having breakfast in a coffee shop on Piccadilly. He went to the bathroom. Or at least I *thought* he went to the bathroom.'

I looked at the cheap telephone in my hand. Nenad Novak's phone. And I was angry. I didn't have any great expectation that the boy would be able to tell me anything more about the night his sister climbed into the back of that lorry in Belgrade. But it felt like the kid had condemned himself to a life on the streets of London. The dumb little bastard.

'Did he say anything else about his sister? Anything about the driver of the lorry?'

'He again made the point that his sister was coming to London to be a nurse. And then he went to the bathroom. And then he was gone.'

I shook my head.

'What does he think is going to happen to him here?' I said. 'In London – in the middle of winter – no money, no friends, no family. Nowhere to go. What exactly does he think is going to happen to him here?'

Jovanović sighed as though he had seen all this before.

'Something better than if he stayed home,' he said.

'I find that hard to believe,' I said.

'But it's why they all come. You have had peace and prosperity here for so long that you think it is the normal state of affairs. And it's not. You know, I was a soldier once,' he said, smiling gently at how unlikely that seemed, his dark eyes twinkling behind his spectacles. 'No – I was a soldier *twice*. In two of the wars that were fought after the old Yugoslavia came apart. In Bosnia and later in Kosovo. I didn't have to shoot anyone. I was supposed to save them.'

'You were a medic?'

He nodded.

'And we picked up everyone. There was no difference between them when they were lying broken on the ground. Whatever their god, whatever their flag, whatever their uniform, they all looked the same when they were broken. And then one day in Kosovo we picked up a solider of the Serb Volunteer Guard. They were also known as Arkan's Tigers. Did you ever hear of Arkan?'

'A paramilitary leader.'

'His real name was Željko Ražnatović. And we took this wounded Tiger to a house where there were wounded men from every flag, from every god. And of course we did our best to save him. And then Arkan came and we hid the Muslims in the basement because we did not know what might happen to them. And Arkan thanked us and said, "Do your best to save my Tiger." And Arkan said, "Do you need anything?" And we said, "We need everything. We need *everything*." And Arkan came back with three lorries of medical supplies. And that helped us to save many lives.'

'And did the Tiger die?'

He seemed surprised by the question.

'I don't remember,' he said. 'But this boy reminds me of that time. What does he need? He needs *everything*. Because he is a boy who has nothing.'

* * *

There is a corner of the Black Museum in New Scotland Yard that is dedicated to the family firms that ran London half a century ago.

Reggie and Ronnie Kray.

Charlie and Eddie Richardson.

Paul and Danny Warboys.

The exhibit features the electrical generator that the Richardsons relied on for extracting confessions, the bolt cutter the Warboys enlisted for removing a talkative lawyer's tongue and a crossbow that the Krays were planning to use in an assassination. But your eyes drift past these dusty items to the black-and-white photographs behind them.

Reggie and Ronnie sharing a cup of tea in an East End parlour with flowered wallpaper. Charlie and Eddie posing outside the main gates of their South London scrapyard. And Paul and Danny grinning and raising flutes of champagne in one of their Soho nightspots.

It feels like a lost world, that criminal aristocracy of Sixties London – all smart suits and skinny ties and noses that had been broken in the boxing ring, tight bands of brothers with their hair cut short and neat, a leftover from the last generation to do National Service. And the last of the celebrity criminals, pictured in all their swaggering pomp shortly before getting sent down for some of the longest sentences ever handed out at the Old Bailey.

'You'll not find him up there,' said a voice behind me. 'Steve Warboys never made it to this place.'

I turned and gratefully took a mug of steaming tea from Sergeant John Caine, the keeper of the Black Museum – or, to give it the official title, the Crime Museum of the Metropolitan Police.

'Hit a brick wall, have you, Max?'

I smiled at him.

When my colleagues found an investigation leading down a dead end, they turned to the full resources of the Metropolitan Police – Police National Computer, CCTV, recognition systems for everything from faces to fingerprints to number plates. But not me. When I was at a loss for my next move, I went up to Room 101 of New Scotland Yard and had a cup of tea with John Caine in the Black Museum.

I watched him carefully straighten a framed photograph of the teenage Krays posing in their boxing kit.

'You never crossed paths with Steve Warboys?' I asked.

John shook his head.

'I heard a few rumours when I was still in uniform,' he said. 'You always keep your ears open for up-and-coming villains. Especially when they have a name you know. I heard he was some kind of fire starter.'

'His first club burned down,' I said. 'The law liked him for it but he walked.'

'Studs,' he said. 'I had a lager there once. Rough old gaff. No, I understood it was more than just his own bar that burned down. I heard it's how he started out — torching places for the insurance money. It's what he was and what he still is, as far as I can make out — a small-time hood trading on his granddaddy's name.'

I looked at a portrait of Paul Warboys fifty years ago. He grinned back at me.

'Why is Steve Warboys of interest?' John said.

'Chinatown,' I said. 'We had a lead that he was employing illegals in the place he has now, the Champagne Room. We thought they might be coming in by the same route as those twelve dead women.'

'But these days they all fly into Luton airport.'

'Looks like it. You had any dealings with people smugglers, John?'

'After my time. But it's going to be bigger than drugs. I know the smugglers all think of themselves as travel agents and that the service offered varies wildly. Some of them get you where you paid to go, some of them go out of business and leave you stranded. Just like travel agents. The experts will tell you that people get trafficked for all different reasons. Sexual exploitation. Forced marriage. Forced labour. Organ harvesting. And sometimes they just want a better life. It's always difficult to fight human nature. What's your instinct tell you about Steve Warboys?'

I looked at the hard, shrewd faces of all those pairs of brothers from long ago.

'I don't think he's smart enough for people smuggling,' I said.

John shrugged.

'You stick a bunch of desperate people in the back of a lorry – or in some rubber boat – or in the boot of a motor – and then you let them take their chances. And sometimes they make it across the border and sometimes they get turned back, and sometimes they drown and sometimes freeze to death in a lorry dumped in Chinatown.' John sipped his tea. 'How smart would you have to be?' he said.

I looked closer at the display of Paul Warboys.

In one black-and-white photograph the legendary villain, not yet thirty years old, was posing in a boxing ring with a spindly little boy, perhaps five years old, who was wearing shorts, vest and a pair of Lonsdale boxing gloves that were larger than his head. The man and the boy both had their fists raised as if they were about to start fighting.

Paul Warboys' face was split in a broad smile.

But the small boy looked terrified and on the verge of tears.

Paul's laughing henchmen, all busted noses and Ben Sherman shirts, chortled in the background, their heavy arms leaning on the ropes of the boxing ring.

'Who's the child?' I asked.

John studied the photograph.

'Now that is Paul's son – Barry Warboys. Steve's old man. Barry is the one and only Warboys who went straight. The one who made a packet in business. He started this chain of care homes – Golden Years. And apparently he's nothing like his father. Or his son.'

We stared at the photograph together in silence.

Half a century gone, and the boy's face still radiated terror.

'A boxing ring's not a good place to be small or scared,' I said.

Sergeant John Caine nodded.

'It's tough enough if you're an adult,' he said.

The police can hold you for up to twenty-four hours before we either have to charge you with a crime or release you.

So after letting the lorry driver stew for a night and a day, DCI Pat Whitestone and I took the lift down to the custody suite of West End Central. The lift doors opened and a female uniformed officer was waiting for us.

'Ma'am,' she said, slipping a set of keys from her belt and opening up holding cell D.

Lee Hill was lying half-awake on a blue, easy-to-clean mattress that was not quite as large as a camp bed and built close to the floor to avoid drunks falling off and cracking their drunken skulls wide open. The holding cell itself was a beige-tiled cube, clean but airless, with a toilet in one corner and a frosted-glass window high on one wall to let in natural light. In terms of holding cells, this was one of the nicer ones.

'Lee Hill? I'm DCI Whitestone and I am arresting you for facilitating the entry of illegal immigrants.'

The lorry driver jumped up from his easy-to-clean mattress, his jaw open with shock.

'But I thought we had a deal,' he said to me.

I shrugged.

'My SIO here doesn't want a deal,' I said.

Whitestone looked at Hill like he was something she had almost stepped in.

'You do not have to say anything but it may harm your defence if you do not mention when questioned something you later rely on in court,' she said.

'Wait, wait,' he said, desperately looking at me.

'Anything you do say may be given in evidence,' Whitestone continued. 'Do you understand?'

He shook his head.

'No,' he said. 'I don't understand anything. What is this? Some kind of good-cop-bad-cop routine?'

He took a shaky step towards Whitestone.

'Nice and calm now,' murmured the uniformed officer, narrowing her eyes, and he came no closer.

'I was going to be your grass,' he said to me.

'Criminal Informant,' I said. 'You were going to be my CI. That was the initial plan. "Grass" sounds derogatory. And when you are smuggling people into the country, you don't get to look down on anyone. But I spoke to my Senior Investigating Officer, DCI Whitestone here, and she's not interested.'

'Because you told DC Wolfe that you never saw the individual we're looking for,' Whitestone told Hill. 'And – as I understand it – you don't sound remotely optimistic about ever seeing him again.' She showed him her empty hands. 'So what good are you to me, Mr Hill?'

'But I was going to work for you!' he protested.

'What do they hand out for trafficking these days, Max?' Whitestone asked. 'Fourteen years?'

'I wasn't *trafficking* anyone,' Hill protested. 'You think those people were coming to this country against their will? You think anyone had to hold a gun to their hijabs? It's their wildest dream to get here!'

'Spare us the subtle distinction between trafficking and smuggling,' Whitestone said. 'If your passengers hadn't been spooked by all those blue lights on the motorway, you would have collected money for importing people who have no right to be here.'

Lee Hill looked from me to Whitestone and back again.

'Sorry,' I said. 'DCI Whitestone doesn't think you'll deliver the goods.'

'If we don't lock you up, all you're ever going to deliver is another lorryload of illegal migrants,' Whitestone said. She nodded to the uniformed officer and took a step towards the holding cell door.

'Show me the photo again!' Hill said. '*Please.*'

I laughed.

'Why? So you can tell me – oh, yeah, *now* I remember – I saw him munching a croque-monsieur in Dunkirk last week?'

'No lies,' Whitestone said, so quietly that Hill looked at her and could not look away. 'If you are our CI, then you *never* tell us a lie or I will cheerfully watch you buried alive.'

'No lies,' Hill agreed.

I took out my phone and called up the photograph of Hana and Nenad Novak. I put my thumb and index finger on the screen and slid them apart so that their smiling young faces disappeared and all that remained was the enlarged image of the scar-faced man in the background.

'I never saw him,' Hill said. 'But I bet I can find him.'

He sounded far more convinced than when I had first showed him the image.

'Listen – it's not a big world once you get to the French ports,' he said. 'The world – that world – narrows right down by the time you get that close to England. Those refugee camps – they're not cities. They're villages. Reeking, stinking villages. You can't hide in a village.'

'So how does it work?' Whitestone said quietly.

'There's a lorry park in Saint-Omer,' Hill said. 'It's a long way from the migrant camp at Dunkirk – thirty miles or so inland. The clients have already paid the carriers in advance by the time they arrive at the lorry park. They pay by money transfer, Western Union or the like. Once the cash has been collected this side, the clients get the green light to travel. And once everybody's boarded, it's forty minutes to the ferry and on to the UK.'

'Loving these euphemisms,' Whitestone said. 'You never go to the camps for your *clients*?'

'Too dangerous,' he said. 'Too many knives. Too many headcases that have just walked all the way from a war zone. Too many child soldiers. Too many mad blokes with full beards and empty eyes.'

'Tell us about your employers,' I said. 'Tell us about Imagine.'

'Never worked for them before. I told you. Bunch of nutters. Idealists. Anarchists. They want national borders down and the Third World moving into the Home Counties for the good of humanity. Don't hold your breath, far as I'm concerned. But there are all sorts down there. You've got your radicals like Imagine who want

126

people to come in for political reasons. You've got your pimps, your returning Jihadis, your career gangsters. You've got people who just want to bring dear old granny in from Kabul or Damascus or Aleppo so she can enjoy the December of her years in Birmingham or Luton or Leeds. You've got economic migrants and you've even got some poor bastards who just want to avoid having their families blown to bits. Takes all sorts, eh?'

'So the pick-up point is always at this lorry park in Saint-Omer?' I said.

'The pick-up can be anywhere,' he said. 'The pick-up can be when you're lining up to get on the ferry. But that might not be a voluntary pick-up, if you know what I mean. A driver might not even know about it. The lorry park at Saint-Omer is the place where you are least likely to get a knife in your ribs and where you are most likely to get paid for your troubles. You know why I got into this game? Because I once made it to the Watford Gap with a bunch of hairy-armed Afghans who were tucked up behind a load of German washing machines without my knowledge or consent. So I figured – if the great unwashed are going to hitch a ride, then why shouldn't I get paid for it?'

'Fourteen years' hard time,' I said. 'How about that for a good reason?'

He looked wistful.

'If it hadn't been for those Essex boy racers losing control of their Ford Escorts, you would never have nicked me. You think I was the only lorry on that motorway last night with the Third World in the back?'

Whitestone shook her head, her face clouding.

Chinatown, I thought. *She's remembering Chinatown.*

'I don't think we can trust Mr Hill.'

She was not trying to scare him. She truly meant it. This was always the trouble with Criminal Informants. By their very nature, they were duplicitous, two-faced liars. That's exactly who you were relying on for information.

And sometimes it is just not worth the effort.

Whitestone nodded to the uniformed officer and turned away. The key rattled in the lock.

'Wait.'

Hill still had my phone in his hand.

'I'll find him for you,' he said. 'I'll look in the lorry park at Saint-Omer. And if that doesn't work, then I'll even look in the camps and risk a knife in my neck for the trouble. And I'll look for his ugly mug in the bar on the ferry.' He stared at the image on my phone. 'And I'll find him.'

Whitestone thought about it.

Then she nodded.

'You get seven days,' she said.

'And then what happens?' he said.

'Nothing good, Mr Hill.'

I held out my hand for my phone.

'Got a name?' he said. 'Nationality?'

'All we have is that one photo,' I said. 'We know he does the Balkan run. We know he has brought at least one cargo through Dunkirk. And we know he does this.'

I snapped my fingers twice.

Click-click.

'Then you don't know very much, do you?' Hill said, handing me my phone.

'There was a woman who survived,' I said. 'She was in the cab with the driver. We found twelve bodies but thirteen passports.'

'I'm not expected to find her, am I? A woman in the cab with the driver! She's going to be long gone.'

Whitestone stared at him in silence.

'Where was your drop-off last night?' she said.

'A car park,' Hill said. 'If you're doing a planned run, it's always done in car parks. Over there and over here, pick-up and drop-off. It's all car parks. Car parks make the smuggling world go round.'

'And where was last night's car park?' I said.

'Behind some gaff on the motorway,' he said. 'Nice and quiet car park, same as always.' He thought about it for a moment. 'All I had was a postcode tapped into Google Maps.'

'What was the postcode for last night?'

He told us and I tapped it into my phone.

Google Maps honed in on planet Earth, Europe, England, Essex, the roads and streets all as delicate as veins.

I stared at the result for a moment and then showed DCI Whitestone.

'The car park of the Champagne Room,' I said.

12

So Billy and I went back to the Champagne Room and this time we sat in the BMW X5 and looked beyond the red neon lips and the yellow neon champagne flute and the squat ugly building, and we stared into that dark expanse of car park that stretched on forever behind the club.

And now I saw that dark space for what it was — a bazaar.

Figures in the far shadows leaned into car windows. Hands slapped together as cash transactions were done. There were still men — and they were all men — emerging from cars and cabs and heading for the Champagne Room, in groups and alone. But there were many more little piggies who had simply come to market. And they were doing a roaring trade in the car park of the Champagne Room.

'A lot of buying and selling out here,' Billy said beside me, splashes of red and yellow neon on his face.

On the far side of the car park a cellophane package

caught the moonlight for a moment as it was exchanged for a fistful of notes.

'But all I see are drugs,' I said. 'This was meant to be Lee Hill's drop-off spot for his cargo. But I don't see any evidence of people smuggling.'

We watched the figures trading in the darkness. Eyes on faces hidden by beanies and hooded tops checked us out, in suspicion and anticipation.

'We can't park up here forever,' I said.

'Could all this go on without the nod from Steve Warboys?' Billy said.

'Maybe,' I said. 'Most club owners are happy to keep dealing out of the house. But it's harder to swallow that lorryloads of Afghans are being dropped off here without Steve Warboys noticing.'

'So are we going to have another word with him?'

'I'm going to have another word with him. You're going to stay in the car.'

I saw Billy's disappointment. It was so easy to hurt his feelings. He was such a gentle soul. And although I wasn't completely confident that he could survive another night in the Champagne Room without losing his trousers, the truth is that I was glad to have Billy Greene with me. He needed the air miles and I needed a colleague who made me look less obviously like a cop. Some ops work better with a man and a woman, and some work better with two men. Strip joints especially.

'I need you to watch the car park for me,' I said, smiling to take some of the sting out of it. 'And besides – you're too popular with the ladies.' Then I got deadly serious. I remembered the sight of Steve Warboys wielding his cricket bat and I suspected that he was stupid enough to raise it to a cop. 'If I'm not out in ten minutes, call it in and come and get me.'

I headed for the entrance, overtaking a group of City boys who were already reeling from some Liverpool Street pub.

Mahmud X was on the door. Standing on the far side of the little velvet rope, guarding the Champagne Room's ridiculous patch of red carpet.

He held up his massive hands to block my path. I felt my blood rising at the realisation that he was actually going to try to stop me coming in. Who did these Essex hoods think they were?

They had held me back once. They were not going to do it again.

'Don't,' I warned him.

But he did.

Even though I had specifically told him not to.

The big doorman stepped forward over the little velvet rope to stop me and I remembered something about him now from when he was heavyweight prospect Peter Chivers, slowly moving around the heavy bag at Fred's gym.

He always kept his guard way too low, those great beefy paws held down by his hips. And that's perfectly fine if you can dance like Muhammad Ali. But it is not so good if you are a great big lump who moves in slow motion.

So I punched him in the heart.

Just one punch that started down in my shoes and rose up in a sliver of a second through my pivoting body – legs, hips, shoulders, arms – and ended with my knuckles slamming hard into his sternum, me having to reach up and aim almost diagonally because of his freak- ish height, the shock of impact running back up my arm as my fist connected with the bone and cartilage directly in front of his ticker.

It is a punch that doesn't always work.

The punch to the heart needs precision and a little bit of luck. It can very easily go wrong if you slip off a pavement or your target turns away or someone unfor- tunately comes at you from behind and hits you across the back of the noggin with a lager bottle.

But this punch was perfect.

Mahmud X reeled backwards, eyes wide with terror as his heart hammered in his chest from the shock of the blow, his hands grabbing at the front of his cheap tuxedo as he fell backwards over the velvet rope as if he was a falling redwood.

He came to rest on his butt, his mouth lolling open.

He could not quite work out what had happened to him. But he suspected he might be dying.

I bent down beside him.

'I told you to leave it, Peter,' I said.

'Orders,' he gasped. 'To keep you out.'

'Breathe deep,' I said. 'You'll be all right.'

I patted him on the back of his Crombie and went inside, standing stock-still for a moment as my eyes adjusted to the darkness and my ears attuned to the noise. I saw men in suits and ties and women in night-wear and heels. No sign of Steve Warboys.

But Bianca appeared out of the darkness.

'I'm sorry,' she said.

I had no idea what she was talking about.

'I was going to lie about you,' she reminded me. 'I was going to say that you had a Southend shoeshine when you did not have a Southend shoeshine.'

I laughed.

'Don't worry about it. You were just doing your job.'

She seemed stunned that I wasn't angry with her. She was a woman who was accustomed to men becoming angry with her.

'You need to get out of this place, Bianca,' I said. 'This is a bad place. These are bad people. I don't know quite how bad. But if anything happens – if you see anything – if you're ever in trouble – then you call me.'

I slipped her my card. She gasped as if it was a bouquet of roses, clutching it to her small breasts.

'Thank you,' she said, her eyes half-closed.

Then Steve Warboys was there, incandescent with
rage at the sight of me.

'We picked up a lorry driver,' I told him.

'And what's that got to do with me?'

'A fat man with a West Country accent,' I said. 'Lee
Hill. I thought you might know him. We pulled him not
far from here. He had a lorry full of Afghan migrants.
That ring any bells?'

He was struggling to keep his temper.

'What am I meant to do with a lorryload of unwashed
Afghans?' Steve Warboys demanded. 'Stick them in a
thong and shove them up a fireman's pole?'

'This lorry driver was meant to drop them off in *your*
car park,' I said.

He shook his head and sighed.

'The Champagne Room is on one of the busiest
motorways in the country,' he said. 'I'm only responsible
for what goes on *this* side of that little red rope.'

'So you don't know anything about this lorry?' I said.
'You weren't expecting a delivery from this Lee Hill?
It's got nothing to do with you?'

Steve Warboys looked at me levelly.

'I should give you a good hiding, Detective,' he said.

He jabbed a finger at me. 'Because you – I believe – are trying to *stitch me up*.'

'You're really not that stupid, are you, Steve? Give me a good hiding and the next policeman you see will be pointing a Glock in your fat ugly mug.'

'Where the fuck have you been?'

Mahmud X was at his side. Steve Warboys was a large man but the giant doorman loomed above him even as he cringed with embarrassment.

'We've got a problem,' Mahmud said. 'A big problem.'

And then we saw him.

The Middle Eastern man with the neat beard was standing at the bar, sipping a fruit juice through a straw, each of his arms in a sling.

Steve Warboys stared at him with disbelief.

'Him?' Warboys said.

'No,' Mahmud X said. 'Them.'

And then we saw the rest of them.

The friends of the man with the neat beard, filing slowly into the Champagne Room, dressed far too casual for this place, all baggy jeans and sagging basketball tops, staring at the near-naked girls as if they could not quite believe their hungry eyes.

A carload of them at first, and then more, another carload, most of them young and bearded like the man sipping fruit juice through a straw, but a few older men among them, until there were more than a dozen of them lined up with their backs to the bar.

'Do you know what I dislike about them?' Steve Warboys said, and I couldn't work out if he was speaking to me or himself. 'The Pakis and the Iraqis, the Somalians and the Eritreans and the Syrians? It's nothing personal. They were all wiping their arse with their hands last year but that's not their fault, is it? But these are people from brutalised societies, Detective.'

Mahmud X handed him a cricket bat.

Steve tested his swing.

'They have experienced war, poverty, mass rape, slave markets – things that the average person in this country thinks will never touch them,' he said. 'They have been *changed* by these things. And then we invite them in. Or – like your Afghans – they come in hidden in the back of a lorry and we can never send them home because it violates their human rights. Or because it's dangerous where they come from. Or because some senile old judge thinks it would violate their right to a family life. Or some such old bollocks. So now we have all those people with a *direct experience of horror* in Lagos and Baghdad and Eritrea and Kabul knocking around Ilford and Southend and Brentwood and Croydon, and even if they're picking their dinner out of dustbins, it's *still* like a lottery win compared to what they left

behind. And then we wonder why our country is changing.' His bat swished through the air. 'Know what I
mean, Detective?'

I watched the men with their backs to the bar and I
thought it was very likely that someone would die in the
Champagne Room tonight. The man with each arm in
a sling had finished his fruit juice. Another man who
could have been his younger brother took his empty
glass and casually hurled it at the rows of bottles behind
the bar.

Women screamed in the sudden shower of broken
glass.

The men at the bar fanned out in a wave of
destruction.

Steve Warboys waded into them, his cricket bat connecting with neatly bearded faces. Mahmud X grabbed
two men by the scruff of the neck and brought their
skulls together. A half-full bottle of sparkling wine flew
through the air and hit a half-cut City boy in the centre
of his face. His companions howled with rage and threw
themselves into the fray. Soon the Champagne Room
was full of flying fists and broken glass. The music never
stopped. Something about taking me to the sky above.
One of the good old songs.

I slipped outside.

Billy Greene was standing by the X5, his phone in his
hand. He was calling it in. I held up my hand and he

stopped. Because the secret truth is that we are never in a mad rush to stop two groups of villains from doing serious harm to each other. Vehicles were streaming out of the car park, suddenly anxious to be elsewhere.

'You had a message from the boss,' Billy said.

I waited.

'DCI Whitestone heard from your CI. Lee Hill? He's in Dunkirk with his lorry.'

I expected the usual diet of jam tomorrow that these Criminal Informants feed you, the promise of a major breakthrough that's going to be happening the day after tomorrow.

The usual baloney.

But Billy surprised me.

'The scar-faced man who brought the girls in,' Edie said. 'Mr Click-Click? Lee Hill has found him.'

13

Late next morning I stood under the big blue lamp outside 27 Savile Row, watching Edie Wren's breath make
steam in the freezing air. She was wearing a red Rab
winter jacket that was too padded to reveal she was
pregnant. She saw me looking at her.

'It's too early to show yet,' she said, and I turned
away, my face burning.

'Here he comes,' I said.

An unmarked squad car with Billy Greene at the
wheel was coming down Savile Row and as he pulled
up outside West End Central you could see that every
possible corner of the vehicle was stuffed with winter
coats that we were planning to take to the camp in
Dunkirk.

'You sure you're up for this?' I asked Edie. 'I can
always take Billy.'

She shook her head and tucked a stray strand of red
hair under her beanie.

'This op works better with a man and a woman,' she

141

said. 'And besides – you must be tired of babysitting Billy.'

I smiled. She was right, of course. I didn't have to worry about Edie in the same way I worried about Billy.

He began pulling coats out of the car.

'I went to Oxfam, Cancer Research and British Red Cross,' he said. 'I couldn't get any more in the car.'

'This is great, Billy,' I said, and the three of us took the coats out of Billy's squad car and loaded them into my BMW X5. There were coats for men, women and children. They were in good nick. Londoners in May-fair, Marylebone and Soho don't wear a winter coat until it falls to bits. They wear it until they get tired of it.

I paused, looking at Edie over the high bonnet of the big BMW, giving her one last chance to change her mind. I was torn. There was nobody I would rather have by my side than Edie Wren but her pregnancy changed everything. I wanted her to be OK. I wanted the baby to be OK.

'I don't know, Edie.'

'Trust me,' she said. 'It will work better with us.'

So we drove to France.

We saw the riot cops before we saw the camp.

The CRS, the general reserve of the French National Police, swaggered across the A16 in their helmets and boots, their semi-automatics held at a 45-degree angle.

One of them raised a hand from his weapon. I stopped and he stuck his head inside the car. I could see the scratches and scuff marks on his visor. He held out a leather-gloved hand and I gave him my driving licence.

There was no point in showing him my warrant card. We had no authority down here.

I watched him stare at the image on the driving licence and then back at me.

The CRS are often called riot police but in fact they exist to maintain crowd control. They don't smile much. This one glanced at the dozens of winter coats stuffed into the back of the car then gave me my licence back and stepped away without a word.

The drive had taken us just over three hours. Through the grey of south London, then the bleak winter fields of southern England, through the Eurotunnel and then on to the A16 motorway that runs along the north coast of France. Just over 160 miles. Dunkirk felt very close. But as we got closer, the camp at Grand-Synthe felt like it was on another planet still reeling from a war that nobody had won.

The motorway became a road, and then the road became a country lane that led to the camp at Grande-Synthe and we saw the trash piled in ditches, and then the bright colours of the tents showing through the sparse winter trees. As we drove closer we saw that the tents were all wrong for this place in this season.

They were thin tents for camping out under summer skies, not for living in, not in freezing mid-winter. They were the kind of tents that are abandoned after a music festival.

Then we saw the men.

They watched us drive slowly by, all these ragged figures with impassive eyes that stared through me and settled on Edie.

They stared at Edie and I was suddenly aware of my breathing.

And then we saw the mud. The mud went on forever. The mud was what the camp was built on. It was a sea of mud, a world of mud, and I had never seen anything like it outside of black-and-white photographs of the First World War.

In places the mud was full of frozen water, and in others some scrap of tarpaulin was stomped into the mud, and thin strips of corrugated metal traversed the mud in a parody of streets, pavements and civilisation.

It was like a camping site in hell.

Beyond the tents there were prefabricated cabins being built, wooden structures that looked like a village of portable toilets. Slogans were written on the side.

NO BORDERS – NO NATIONS and AIN'T NO BORDER HIGH ENOUGH and KILL THE BANKERS NOT THE POOR and WE ARE ALL EARTHLINGS and THE KING OF NOWHERE.

But what you noticed most was the mud and the men.

There were children playing outside tents and women with their heads covered by scarves. Smoke rose from their fires, leaving a low bank of fog drifting across the camp, as the women cooked and huddled for warmth.

But mostly this was a place of men.

And I knew with total certainty that, no matter what looked best for a cover story, I had been dead wrong to bring Edie Wren down here with me. I cursed my self-ishness. I knew that she was the best person for the job. But I now knew that it had been a rotten call. This place reeked of danger.

I turned to look at her.

'It's going to be all right, Max,' she said.

I shook my head. It was too late to stop now.

As I bumped across the mud towards a dozen parked vehicles near the treeline, a man stepped into my path and flagged me down with a gesture of authority that could have been learned from the CRS.

A rat the size of a neutered tom scampered across the boggy wasteland with some nameless prize in its mouth.

The man stuck his head in the car. Young, bearded, English, hair hanging down in matted blond dreadlocks.

'What you got?' he demanded.

'Coats,' I said.

'Just coats?' He grinned and nodded, showing a mouth

full of tobacco-stained teeth. 'Coats are good,' he said, and I smelled the skunk on his breath. 'You wouldn't believe the crap that people bring with them. Books and shit. You need to check in first. See that building?'

Beyond the miserable huddle of brightly coloured tents and just before the wooden cabins began, there was a ramshackle shack built from wooden pallets.

'You go in there and you ask to see Troy,' the blond dread said, indicating the shack. 'And if Troy approves your load, then you can start to distribute it.' He indicated the cars near the trees. 'Park over there.'

'Troy?' I said. 'What's that? First name, family name or nickname?'

A blank stare.

'He's just Troy.'

'And how will we know Troy?' I said.

A secret little smile split his face. His small teeth were the colour of weak tea.

'Oh, you'll know Troy,' he said.

Edie leaned across me and gave him a friendly smile.

'And are you and Troy working for some NGO?' she said.

His face twisted with distaste, as if it was unseemly for us to be asking all these questions.

'We're here until they take down the borders,' he said, stepping away and slapping the roof.

I bumped across the mud towards the parked cars,

thinking that it was still not too late to turn the car around and go home. But in my rear-view mirror I saw the men gathering in the road, cutting off any possibility of retreat, staring at our car, and so I drove on and parked where the blond dread with the skunk breath had told me.

I locked up and we walked towards the shack built of wooden pallets. There was a stencilled sign above the door:

NO BORDERS
NO NATIONS
NO FLAGS
NO PATRIOTS

'Who are these people?' Edie murmured.

The shack looked like a house found in the shadows of a forest in a fairy tale. But instead of gingerbread, it was built of all these wooden pallets hammered together with six-inch nails. A house of scraps. The doorway was a barrier of multicoloured PVC strips. A small, sharp-faced woman with matted dreadlocks stood before it. She briefly lifted her chin, her eyes narrowing as they flicked from me to Edie.

'Yeah?'

'We have coats,' Edie said, and I saw suspicion in the woman's eyes.

Coats were perfect. Perhaps coats were too perfect.

But the woman lifted her chin again and pulled back the rainbow-coloured PVC strips.

'See Troy.'

We went inside the shack of wooden pallets. A thick-set black man with short, dirty red dreadlocks was conferring with a man, maybe Afghan or Pakistani, who wore a Union Jack hoodie. They turned to look at us and as he took a step from the shadows I saw that the man with the dreadlocks was not black. His white face was stained black with swirls of tribal tattoos, curved shapes and spiral patterns piled on top of each other until only thin worm-like stretches of white skin were visible.

He stared at me hard, as if daring me to be repulsed by his face.

It looked like the end product of a tattooist who had gone insane.

'Troy?' I said.

'What do you have?' he said softly.

The accent was rough south-east English grafted on to one of those schools that cost Daddy five grand a term. Every pound-store radical I ever met was down-wardly mobile.

'Coats,' I said. 'We thought—'

'Hanif will help you distribute them,' Troy said, cutting me off and indicating the man in the Union Jack hoodie.

Troy showed none of the suspicion of the woman on the door. But as we turned to go he held out his hand.

'We ask for a donation to the camp,' he said.

'Who's we?' Edie said.

I lightly touched her arm.

'How much?' I said.

He was staring at Edie.

'A grand,' he told me, still not turning his illustrated face from her. You could tell that he was used to his features inspiring horror and fear. And that he liked it. But it didn't work on Edie Wren. She was still waiting for an answer. I took a breath. I knew the gang in the house of scraps had to be Imagine, although they were not quite the collective of well-meaning hippies and pious anarchists that I had been expecting.

'I don't have a grand,' I said. 'We've just brought some clothes that we thought—'

He finally turned to look at me.

'You can't ease your Western conscience with a few handouts,' he said. 'These people are desperate. These people want to go to England. These people are not human garbage for you to leave out for capitalism's bin men.'

I took out my cash and held it out. He took it and stuffed it into his pocket without counting. Then he gestured at the man in the Union Jack hoodie, who indicated that we should follow him.

Troy's voice stopped me at the rainbow-coloured strips that covered the doorway.

'You should unload the gear and go home,' he said. 'Don't hang about for a bit of sightseeing.' His hideous face grinned in the half-light of the wooden shack. 'Because – no offence – you smell a bit too much like pig.' His grin grew wider. 'And they're not big on pig around here.'

We followed Hanif to the BMW.

A group of men had edged towards the car but they seemed to know not to get any closer. They stood there, waiting for time to pass. In the distance I could see the children playing and the women in their headscarves, preparing their meals. But only men gathered around the car.

Everywhere you looked there was something that had been used up and tossed aside, resting in the mud. An abandoned car, an abandoned shopping trolley, abandoned people. Near the thin summer tents, a female photographer was taking a picture of a tiny girl who was clutching a doll.

I opened up the BMW and Hanif rummaged through the pile of coats until he found what he was looking for – a Giorgio Armani overcoat with a dark stain on one arm, possibly from a full-bodied Burgundy. Hanif slipped it on over his Union Jack hoodie.

'Looks good on you,' Edie said.

Hanif whistled and the rest of them came running.

Men and boys. A pack of them, more than twenty, and more were arriving every moment from the muddy track that led to the camp, from the coloured tents and the wooden cabin, their boots pounding across the metal walkways. The ones at the front reaching out with muddy hands to grab as many of the coats as they could carry, then spinning away as more hands reached out to rob them of their prize, the voices raised in furious Arabic.

We stood to one side of the car as Hanif smoothed the front of his new coat. Within minutes the coats had been torn from the car. Fists were thrown, curses were hissed and men yelled in each other's faces.

'Take it easy!' I shouted.

A man on the edge of the pack bared his yellow teeth at me. He raised his hand from his jacket just enough for me to see the weak sunlight gleam on his knife.

'They're all carrying blades, Edie,' I said.

'They're all front,' she said.

I didn't think so. What stops most people from committing crime is what they have to lose. And this crowd had nothing to lose.

On the far side of the crowd two men each held an arm of a light-grey Hugo Boss coat that I had been half-tempted to keep for myself. One of them was a large overweight man with a bushy beard. He towered over his rival, a smaller, leaner figure with his face almost totally covered by a balaclava.

But the larger man was the one who seemed afraid.

The man in the balaclava raised his free hand, the hand that did not claim possession of the Boss coat.

And he clicked his fingers.

Click-click.

Just once. It was enough.

The large man with the beard relinquished the coat.

The man in the balaclava put it on. It was a few sizes too big for him. He was heading towards the road out of the camp.

Edie was already following him.

Hanif was watching her. She turned to glance back at me and he saw the look that passed between us.

Hanif stiffened in his new Giorgio Armani coat, staring hard at me, as if seeing me for the first time. I jogged after Edie. There was nothing else to do.

'It's him,' she said.

'They're on to us,' I said.

'I swear to God it's him, Max.'

'I know but listen to me, will you? They've twigged that we're cops.'

'No,' she said, but without much conviction.

By the side of the BMW X5, Hanif was addressing a group of men in their nearly new coats. A boy in an oversized Berghaus was sprinting towards the shack of wooden pallets. Troy appeared in the doorway, his tattooed face grotesque in the sunlight. The boy pointed in our direction. We couldn't go back.

'Let's get the bastard,' I said.

'What's the plan?'

'ID our man. Apprehend and arrest. Then call Europol.'

'And if they refuse to hold him?'

'Then he's coming back in the boot of the car.'

She looked at me for a moment and saw I was not joking.

'It's not going to come to that,' I said. 'The driver of the lorry with twelve dead women in the back is on every Europol watch list.'

'What about the CRS?'

'I don't trust them.'

'Me neither. He's clocked us, Max.'

The figure ahead of us broke into a run.

We did the same, sprinting by the side of the muddy country lane, the ditch beside us overflowing with garbage. I felt the sweat trickle down my back. A bottle exploded on the road behind us. Something thudded into one of the trees.

The men from the camp were coming for us.

Then Edie slowed and stopped.

'You go on,' she said.

I stared at her incredulously.

'I'm not leaving you!'

'I'll be fine,' she said.

She reached into her coat pocket and pulled out what looked like a blue handgun with a bright yellow cartridge. A Taser X3. The X3 is compact, light and capable of firing three shots before it needs reloading.

'What happens after you've shot three of them?' I asked.

'I'm not going to have to shoot that many,' she said, and I hesitated for just a moment. She was right. When they saw one of their number twitching on the muddy road with involuntary muscular spasms, the rest of them were likely to find the fight draining out of them.

So I left Edie Wren and I went on alone.

I was running faster to keep up with the figure jogging ahead of me. I was hot now and he must have been hot too. Because, without breaking his stride, he removed his balaclava with a flourish, like a magician pulling a rabbit from a hat, and when he looked back at me I saw the ragged ranks of scarring that ran down one side of his face.

Mr Click-Click.

Then he was leaping across the trash in the ditch and sprinting into the winter woods.

I looked back at Edie. The mob had stopped twenty metres away from her. She held her gun hand in the air, the blue-and-yellow Taser clearly visible, but I knew her voice would be calm and rational and making it clear that she would prefer not to dish out any neuromuscular incapacitation today.

I felt a surge of fierce pride in her.

Then I jumped across the ditch and went into the woods, losing sight of my man, but hearing the roar of the traffic ahead and knowing that he must be heading for the road. I caught sight of him again, moving nimbly through woods that he must have known well. He was getting away from me.

I slowed on the uneven ground of the woods, and I stumbled over the tangled roots and dead leaves and brightly coloured trash that was scattered everywhere, and I found that I could not keep up with him. Ahead, the road was a torrent of traffic, all three lanes booming with giant lorries heading for the port, and when I finally reached it he was already standing on the hard shoulder of the other side.

We stared at each other like two men on different banks of some mighty river that looked impossible to cross.

There were other men on either side of the road, all of them looking up speculatively at the lorries, all of them desperate for England, all of them waiting for a chance to cadge a ride. But the lorries moved too fast, the drivers casting wary looks at the packs of men by the side of the last road in France as they rumbled by. On the far side of the road, I saw that scarred face smile at me.

The lorry that hit him came out of nowhere.

It was moving at twice the speed of the traffic on the motorway, barrelling down the hard shoulder at a good sixty miles an hour, and it went through Mr Click-Click as if he wasn't there. The force threw him into the air and into the middle lane of the motorway. The traffic skidded, slowed and finally stopped in a cacophony of angry horns.

And the men on both sides of the road went wild.

A cry of disbelieving joy went up at the sight of this miracle – the lorries on the last road out of France, stopping as if to pick up passengers. As they ran into the stationary traffic I stumbled after them, still trying to understand what I had seen.

Mr Click-Click on the far side of the road.

The lorry speeding on the hard shoulder.

Then the sickening impact of tons of steel colliding with flesh, blood and bone, and tossing him into the air as if it all weighed nothing.

But I could not see any sign of the lorry that had hit him – it had not slowed down, let alone stopped with the rest of the traffic, it had just kept on speeding down the empty hard shoulder – and I could see no sign of Mr Click-Click or whatever was left of him. I walked among the motionless lorries, still spilling their diesel fumes, the drivers with their windows down and voices from a dozen nations, but mostly the accents of London and Liverpool and Glasgow, and I wondered if I had imagined it.

And then I saw the blood.

A long streak of it across the tarmac, so much of it that at first I believed it had to be something else, it could not all be from one man, but then I could smell it, that metallic tang of freshly spilled blood. I followed the trail to the back of a massive blue Scania lorry with the picture of some market town idyll on the side. VISIT LINCOLN CATHEDRAL, it advised, spires against a blue sky, and my eyes drifted from that scene of tranquil beauty to the mangled body of the man who had been thrown beneath it by the lorry still speeding away on the hard shoulder.

I watched it disappearing into the distance without even a blink of brake lights. And I stared up at the appalled face of the driver of the VISIT LINCOLN CATHEDRAL lorry, almost grey with shock.

And I saw that Mr Click-Click was roadkill now.

Everywhere men were climbing into the backs of lorries. Drivers were getting out of their cabs, but they were always one against many, and the men in the back of the lorries jeered and laughed openly at the useless baseball bats the drivers carried. Nobody was paying any attention to Mr Click-Click. It was as if I was the only one who knew he was there.

And then I was shoved roughly aside as two men

dropped to their knees and fell upon him. At first I thought they were his grieving friends.

But then they began to go through his pockets.

I joined them. They shoved me. I shoved them back. They were rifling through his wallet, examining a wad of what looked like euros, British pounds and Turkish lira.

One of them pushed me in the chest and shouted something in Arabic.

I pushed him in the chest and cursed him in English.

The dead man was wearing the Hugo Boss coat we had brought from London but the impact of the lorry had ripped it from shoulder to hem. One of the pockets was torn wide open and I could see two mobile phones. I picked them up and put them both in my jacket. The man who had pushed me shouted something in Arabic, and then grunted and dropped as a CRS cop hit him on the back of the head with his sidearm.

There were three CRS men. They were mean, scared and angry, cops who knew that the situation was running away from them. In every direction you could hear the lorry horns blasting and the curses of the drivers and the men declaring the greatness of Allah.

The CRS cops were screaming at us in French and pointing their SIFG Pro revolvers. The man who had been struck on the back of the head was face down on the tarmac, out cold, inches from what was left of Mr Click-Click. The other man was still on his knees, protesting his innocence in pidgin French.

I held up my hands and got slowly to my feet, my face a mask of docile compliance, nodding obediently at the cop pointing a pistol in my face.

'I am a detective with the Metropolitan Police and I am following your instructions,' I said. I indicated the dead man between us. 'I was attempting to apprehend this man for—'

The CRS man swiped the butt of his gun across my face.

Not hard. Croissants at ten paces. Not as hard as he could have, but hard enough to shut me up. He wasn't interested in anything I had to say. He wasn't open to debate. The polymer frame caught my cheekbone and whipped my face sideways.

I felt a warm trickle of blood ooze down the broken skin but I resisted the urge to move my hands. The cop screamed in my face.

'Allons-y! Allons-y! Allons-y!'

The man who was still conscious was dragging his friend away, who was semi-conscious now and groaning and rubbing the back of his skull, euros and Turkish lira spilling all around them. I looked at the CRS men. They did not want to arrest us because they already had their hands full. But they would do so if we gave them no choice.

'Allons-y, connard!'

I glanced down at the remains of Mr Click-Click.

And then I went looking for Edie.

14

Edie was standing where I had left her, the Taser 3 still in her hand. There was no sign of the men from the camp.

I felt as though I had been holding my breath since the moment I had left her. I exhaled as she turned to look at me.

'What happened to your face?' she said.

'I was born this way. What's your excuse?'

Her cool fingers traced the mark the CRS man had left on my face.

'Did we get Mr Click-Click?' she said.

'He's gone,' I said. 'He was on the hard shoulder and a lorry hit him. The lorry was driving on the hard shoulder. It didn't stop. It didn't even slow down.'

She frowned, struggling to understand.

'He's dead, Edie. And it's chaos down there. Nothing moving. The boys from the camp think they've won the Lottery. The CRS are going to need a lot of extra tear gas before they clear it.'

'Did you tell them who you are?'

'I tried. They weren't very impressed. They called me *connard*. Does that mean *respected detective*?'

'No, Max, *connard* means *shithead*.'

'That's what I thought.'

'Was it definitely him?'

I nodded.

'What happened here?' I said.

She laughed. 'They bottled it. They came close but in the end nobody wanted to take a hit for the team. I didn't fire a shot.'

She slipped the Taser into her pocket and we smiled at each other.

'Let's go home,' I said.

Then I saw her face twist with pain.

She collapsed into my arms, the pain suddenly replaced by panic, and I held her close, already knowing, my mind whirling ahead, wondering where the nearest hospital was, and how fast I could get there, and if it could possibly be quick enough.

I scooped her up in my arms and carried her towards the car.

When she spoke, her face pressed against my chest, the words were muffled by my jacket and choked with what sounded like bereavement.

'My baby,' she said.

* * *

They were very kind at the Centre Hospitalier de Dunkerque.

When they finally let me see Edie a few hours later, she was sitting up in bed in her own private room wearing a white smock, pale as a red-haired angel.

I sat on the bed and took her hand.

'I lost the baby,' she said, as matter-of-fact as she could make it. 'Apparently I'll have cramping for a day or two. Bleeding for a week. Is that too much information?'

I shook my head. I held her hand tighter. I had no words for her.

'The body heals quick, so they say.' Tears sprang to her eyes. 'No news yet on how long the heart takes,' she laughed, making a joke about something that tore her apart. She pulled her hand away from me, wiping her eyes with the back of her hand. 'I made some calls. Someone's coming down for me. You can go home to Scout, Max.'

'I'll stay until he arrives,' I said, speculating how long it would take Edie's married man to make up an excuse to come to northern France.

'I feel so bloody sad, Max.'

'You'll have a beautiful baby,' I said. 'I know you will, Edie. And you'll never forget this baby. You'll never stop loving her.'

'Maybe I'm not meant to be a mother. I wouldn't know where to start.'

'You'll know when you the time comes. And you'll

have these feelings unlocked inside you that you never knew were there. This great store of unconditional love, Edie. That gets unlocked and that's what gets you through. A child changes everything. It's simple until they arrive. It's just men and women dealing with all the usual stuff. But after you have children, everything's got all these jagged edges. It's like life is holding you hostage. Because there's something in the world that you love more than yourself.'

I looked at the door as if expecting to see Mr Big walk in, removing his wedding ring.

'I know it's a mess,' she said, reading my face. 'And I know it's not easy. And I'm not so stupid that I think it will ever be easy.'

I said nothing.

'But he loves me,' she said. 'He loves me, Max. He does, I know it.'

Edie Wren was twenty-five years old. You might not have found her beautiful but I did. She was a small, feisty redhead, and probably the bravest person I have ever met. She made me laugh and she made me care. There wasn't much of her but it was all good.

I got up to go.

'Why wouldn't he?' I said.

I stopped for petrol halfway home.

Beyond the motorway, the chalk hills of the North

Downs stretched off into the distance, brown and green in the white winter moonlight and I stared at them as the big BMW filled up with diesel. I listened to the sound of the cars booming by and for a moment I hung my head and I thought about a baby who would never be born.

Then my phone began to vibrate.

WHITESTONE CALLING, it said.

'Did we get him?' she said.

I told her about the ID at the camp, the pursuit through the woods and what had happened on the hard shoulder of the road. I was still struggling to understand why there was one lorry speeding on the hard shoulder. It made no sense. But Whitestone did not care. She whooped with delight when I told her that I had two mobile phones recovered from Mr Click-Click.

'Good work, the pair of you,' she said. 'I'll see you first thing in the morning.'

So then I had to tell her the other news and why Edie would be coming back later than me.

Silence.

'One more thing,' she said finally. 'The Champagne Room burned down during the night.'

'It's got to be an insurance scam,' I said. 'Torching buildings for the insurance money is how Steve Warboys started out.'

'I don't think so, Max. Because Steve Warboys was

165

inside the Champagne Room when it went up in flames. They're still bringing the bodies out now and it looks like he was tied to a chair in one of the VIP rooms.'

We hung up and I walked to the service station to pay, suddenly noticing that the car was coated in the mud of northern France. Something about the sight of it sickened me, and I glanced towards the service station's car wash.

OUT OF ORDER, said a sign, but there was activity there, men were milling about with buckets and brushes, and when they saw me looking they hurried towards me, perhaps a dozen of them and they could have been from Afghanistan or Syria or Iraq, they were so similar to the men that I had seen at the camp on the other side of that narrow sea.

I shook my head and waved them away. I had heard too many horror stories about what these hand-wash merchants use to clean your car. There was a big fleshy Englishman at the till who took my money for the diesel without a smile.

'What happened to your car wash?' I asked him.

'We got shot of it,' he said, handing me my change. 'People are cheaper.'

PART TWO
Shadow People

15

It felt like the world was on the move.

As Scout and I walked past the men of Smithfield meat market, there were new languages among the old London voices that I had not heard here before – Korean and Russian and Arabic and Chinese, and not the Hong Kong Cantonese of London's Chinatown but real mainland Mandarin.

And I could sense the world on the move among the builders on their way to work at the huge developments of luxury apartments that were going up by the Thames. There were Poles and Russians and East Europeans of every nation. And in Smiths of Smithfield when we had our breakfast, Scout slipping scraps of pancake to Stan at her feet, there were the young people of southern Europe, the French and Italians and Spanish, a generation made exiles by the unemployment queues of their own countries, although you would never guess it from their smiles.

And there were homeless bundled up in the doorways,

men with the same haunted faces that I had seen in the camp at Dunkirk – Syrians and Iraqis and Afghans. You saw those faces mirrored in the men who stood in the corner of Holborn Circus, one of the great junctions of the capital, five minutes from our home, where six roads lead to different parts of the city In the shadow of the great shining buildings of glass and steel men shivered inside their cheap sportswear and lifted their faces in hope every time a white van or a lorry slowed down.

'What are those men doing?' Scout said.

'They're waiting, angel.'

'What are they waiting for?'

'They're waiting for work, Scout,' I said. 'You've seen all the new places being built and all the old buildings been done up?'

Scout nodded, her gaze not leaving the waiting men. 'I guess so.'

'Well, those are the kinds of places they want to work,' I said.

'Do they get work every day?'

'Probably not every day.'

And I looked into those faces, too, but I never saw Hana Novak's kid brother, Nenad 'Nesha' Novak.

I never saw the boy.

Up in MIR-1 Billy Greene tapped his keyboard and a blown-up passport photograph appeared on the big

HDTV, every ragged scar a livid, larger-than-life furrow in that hard, empty face.

'Mr Click-Click,' I said. 'This is the driver of the lorry that we found in Chinatown containing twelve women – eleven dead and one dying. The French police have identified him from his passport as Zlatko Draganov.'

MIR-1 was silent as DCI Whitestone stared thoughtfully at the face on the screen.

'Nationality?' she said.

'Bulgarian,' I said.

'Can we trust the French ID?'

'Not really,' Billy said. 'According to the Bulgarian embassy in London, a Zlatko Draganov with the same date of birth died of lung cancer four years ago. Zlatko Draganov was Bulgarian Roma. From Vidin, on the banks of the Danube in north-western Bulgaria. It's where Bulgaria, Romania and Serbia all meet.'

'Mr Click-Click looked like he was from the same neck of the woods,' I said. 'But my guess is that the passport found on him originally belonged to a brother or an uncle or some kind of relation. This town Vidin is a major hub for the people smugglers and the Bulgarian Roma in those parts are the poorest people in all Europe. And they're off the books. They're not big on registering with the authorities.'

'But this guy would be on our books if he has ever

been arrested here,' Whitestone said. 'Can we run him through IDENT1? Have we got prints?'

IDENT1 is the UK's central database for storing the palm and fingerprints of anyone who is arrested or detained by the police. If he had ever been lifted, even if he had never been formally charged with a crime, then Zlatko Draganov – or whatever his real name was – would be on there.

'Our CSIs are trying with the fresh prints they took from these.' I held up two phones in evidence bags. 'But IDENT1 is a long shot as none of the prints lifted from the steering wheel of the lorry in Chinatown has been identified. Suggesting that we have no record of Mr Click-Click on any database.'

'Talk to me about the phones,' Whitestone said.

'This one is a burner.' I indicated the cheaper piece of black plastic in my left hand. 'Use it and lose it. The IMEI numbers are only six digits from the phone that Lee Hill was using.'

'So they were using disposable phones from the same batch,' Whitestone said. 'Anything on the burner?'

'Never been used,' I said. 'Presumably Draganov – I'll call him Draganov, shall I? – would have received GPS coordinates for the drop-off point after arriving in the UK.'

I held up the other phone, the latest model of some Korean smartphone.

'This is his personal phone. Everything has been wiped – calls made, calls received, calls missed – apart from the photographs. And they're worth seeing. Billy?'

Billy had pulled on some blue latex gloves. As he took the evidence bag containing the smartphone from me, my own phone began to vibrate. I read the message and looked up at Whitestone.

'Edie will be back in the country tomorrow,' I told her. 'She's talking about coming into work.'

I expected Whitestone to say something about taking the rest of the week off after the miscarriage.

But our SIO merely nodded.

'We could use her,' she said.

And that was it. I waited for something more but it never came. And I saw that something had changed in DCI Whitestone after her son had been attacked in a bar last summer. The assault had left her teenage boy blind and Whitestone had understandably been a mess of rage and grief. But now that anger had cooled into something hard and unforgiving that I had never seen in her before. Something had calcified in the heart of Pat Whitestone.

Because of what happened to her son, because of the boy's bad luck in being in the wrong place with the wrong people, because of the random madness of some little pound-store gangster putting a glass bottle across his eyes in some dismal little club on the Liverpool Road.

'I think Edie needs to take it easy,' I said.

Whitestone looked at me sharply.

'I think we need to find whoever put those women in that refrigerated lorry,' she said. 'And we need to do it now. Before they do it again. What's the story with this bunch of anarchists, Imagine?'

'Imagine are meant to be some kind of no-borders, imagine-no-possessions radicals. Troy – the leader – the one with the tattooed face – has about as much human compassion as a merchant banker, as far as I can see. We had to pay for the privilege of handing out coats.'

'So these hippies – radicals – whatever they are – are they for real or not?'

'Imagine run the camp in Dunkirk. And Troy runs Imagine. He rules that camp like a feudal chief. It may be a dungheap, but it's Troy's dungheap. And they certainly do a little freelance trafficking when they're not saving the world.'

'These are the photos on Draganov's personal phone,' Billy said.

He had rigged the smartphone to his workstation. A photograph appeared on the big screen. A man and a woman standing side by side, the man's scarred face smiling, the woman – thin, maybe early twenties, pretty in an exhausted sort of way – totally impassive. The man was Zlatko Draganov.

'We've seen her before,' Whitestone said. 'Her face

was in the stack of passports we found in the cab. One of the Turkish passports.'

'There were two Turkish passports,' Billy said. 'One in maroon – the standard Turkish passport – and one in green – which allows the bearer to travel visa-free to some countries. In the opinion of Ken, our Questioned Documents guy from Heathrow, both of those passports were false. But the young woman pictured here had the higher-status green passport, travelling in the name of Rabia Demir. But who knows what her real name might be?'

There was some kind of modest castle in the background, carefully maintained, its pale walls topped with red-brick parapets.

'That's Fort Baba Vida,' Billy said. 'Main tourist attraction of Vidin, Bulgaria. There are six more photographs, but I can't identify the other locations. And the one in Vidin is the only picture that's not a selfie.'

Billy began scrolling through the photographs. They told the story of a man and a woman, travelling across Europe, strangers who became intimates. It was only the first photograph that featured any attempt to capture a picturesque background. The rest of them seemed to be taken at a collection of petrol stations. But as the seven photographs progressed, the couple became more familiar.

'*Besser denn je!*' said a sign behind them in the last

image, with the woman calling herself Rabia Demir snuggling in the arms of the man travelling as Zlatko Draganov. Now they were both smiling.

'*Better than ever!*' I translated. 'So that's Germany or Austria.'

'And what happened to her, Max?' Whitestone said.

'He might have killed her,' I said. 'When he got to London and found he had a cargo of dead and dying in the back of his lorry because he was too stupid to think about controlling the temperature in a refrigerated lorry. Because he didn't know how the thermostat worked. Or because – my guess – it never even crossed his mind that those women were in danger of freezing to death until he parked in Chinatown and it was far too late. Rabia Demir – the girl who got to ride in the cab – was a witness. If she talked to the law she could put him away for a long time.'

'But only if she knew,' Whitestone said. 'And only if she saw. She was a passenger. A favoured passenger, no doubt about it, the passenger who got to sleep with the driver, but my guess is that she didn't know what was in the back of that lorry. Because why the hell would he tell her?'

We were all silent, weighing the possibilities.

'Whatever happened when he got to Chinatown, he was in a state of panic,' I said. 'If he killed Rabia and ran because she had seen too much, then her body would have been there.'

'It's possible he could have killed her and taken the body elsewhere,' Whitestone said.

'Yes, but my gut feeling is – they both ran,' I said. 'They got to Chinatown, he clocked what had happened in the back of the lorry, and all the plans went out the window. Draganov may have killed those women accidentally – he had probably never seen a refrigerated lorry before – but he killed them. He wanted to put as much distance as possible between himself and all those dead girls. So they ran. And they ran together.'

'Then she's here,' Whitestone said. 'She's the only woman who was in that lorry left alive.'

I nodded.

'She's out there now – the girl in the cab, the thirteenth woman, the only one who didn't freeze to death,' I said. 'Rabia Demir. The only one who survived the journey. Find her and we find the chain that leads all the way to the bastards at the top.' I looked at Billy. 'Can you scroll through the photographs again?'

The images began to appear.

The young pretty woman and older scar-faced man looking almost formal in front of Fort Vida. And as they made their way across Europe, the woman becoming more relaxed, smiling more, something like her true self.

'What do you notice?' I said.

'He looks keen,' Whitestone said. 'And she looks less keen.'

'Understandable,' I said. 'He's the one with all the power. He's in the driver's seat in every way possible. Until they reach their destination. Until they get to this country. Until they reach London. And then he feels all his power suddenly slipping away.'

We stared at the screen.

'They tell a story, don't they?' I said. 'These seven photographs. You wouldn't call it a love story exactly. But they tell a tale. It has a beginning, middle and an end. She was the prettiest girl in her village. He picked her up. He drove her here. At some point – quite early on, I reckon – he fell hard for her. Love, sex, obsession – label it how you like. But she rode up front in that lorry all the way across Europe because he wanted her and because she needed him. And when all those other women died because he forgot to press a button or turn a dial, she lived because she got to sit in the cab. And then they reached Chinatown.'

'And then she dumped him,' Whitestone said.

16

I stood outside a duck restaurant halfway down China-town's Gerrard Street and looked up at the small office on the first floor. The lights were on so I excused myself as I edged through the long line waiting for a table and went up a short flight of stairs to the white door with its small sign.

SAMPAGUITA
Social Introduction Agency

I knocked and went inside.

Ginger Gonzalez looked up from her copy of the *Financial Times* and stared at me coldly, still resenting me for coming to see her with Whitestone.

'Come to bust me, Max?' she said.

She mockingly held out her wrists to be handcuffed, displaying the tattoos that ran down her lower arms.

Never for money, said one side.

Always for love, said the other.

'Maybe later,' I said. 'Fancy some Chinese?'

She stared at me for a moment and then got her coat.

We went across Gerrard Street to a cavernous Sichuan restaurant. It was crowded but there was no line outside and an indifferent waiter grudgingly found us a table for two. At the back of the restaurant there was some kind of celebration. An endless procession of waiters and waitresses brought massive plates that steamed and sizzled.

In the middle of it all, an old Chinese man stared at his phone, checking his messages.

I felt I knew him from somewhere.

Ginger and I ordered spicy dandan noodles and Tsingtao beer and then I pushed a manila envelope across the table. Hard 8 x 10 inch copies of the seven photographs we had looked at in MIR-1. The oldest photograph was on top.

'The man is Zlatko Draganov and the woman is Rabia Demir,' I said. 'The names might be false but we know that first photograph was taken at Fort Baba Vida in Vidin, Bulgaria. And that Draganov was the driver of the lorry we found in Chinatown and Rabia was the only woman to survive.'

Ginger began to thumb through the photographs.

'And how did she manage that?'

'Because she wasn't in the back of the lorry. She was sitting in the cab with Draganov.'

The waitress brought our order. The dandan noodles were a beautiful mess of pork, vegetables and scallions on a bed of noodles and drenched in a sauce of chilli oil and Sichuan pepper so spicy that it brought tears to my eyes. I took a gulp of ice-cold Tsingtao and watched Ginger go through the photographs and then do it all again, slower this time.

'Even in strictly commercial transactions, affection can creep in,' she said, more to herself than to me. 'But sometimes – usually – that affection is only one way. It tends to be the one with all the power who starts getting that loving feeling.'

'Draganov is dead,' I said.

'Good,' she said.

'But Rabia made it to London. Our theory is that she dropped him once she got here.'

'Smart girl. Trading up from a people smuggler.' She stared at the final photograph with the cool calculation of a professional. 'Not a bad-looking woman,' she said thoughtfully.

'She would have been the prettiest girl in her village,' I said.

'Then they get to London,' Ginger said. 'And she finds there are a million others who were all the prettiest girl in their village. And suddenly the village feels long ago and far away.'

'We have to assume that she's working,' I said.

'And not as a nuclear physicist, right?' Ginger bared her white teeth as she sucked some dandan noodles from her chopsticks. The heat did not seem to bother her as much. 'You mean a working girl in London.'

I felt a stab of pain.

'I think that's what she'll end up doing. I don't know what her original plans were. Hana Novak — the one who was still alive — wanted to be a nurse.'

'That's a new one. It's usually models, actresses and dancers.'

'We don't think Rabia Demir is working as a nurse.'

'We don't actually *need* any more working girls here, Max. The competition is fierce enough already.'

'And yet still they keep coming,' I said. 'And some of them come to you, Ginger. Don't they?'

'What do you want to do, Max? Save her or arrest her?'

'I want to know how she found her way into that lorry. I want to find out who put those other twelve young women in the back and then let them freeze to death at the other end of this street.'

I pushed the dandan noodles away. I wasn't hungry any more.

'I want to find the men who put those women in that lorry, Ginger, and then I want to lock them up so they can never do it again. But I need your help. Where should I start looking?'

Ginger put down her chopsticks and picked up her beer.

'You should check the language schools,' she said. 'If she's here, she'll be trying to improve her English.'

'Are you serious?'

'A lot of these girls are into self-improvement. The smarter ones know that nobody gets very far in this country if they don't speak good English. If she dropped the driver after getting here, then she sounds like the aspirational sort.' Ginger smiled at me. 'You know, I was hurt that you came to me with that hard little woman.'

'No choice, Ginger. Twelve dead women at the end of your street. We have to pursue every lead we can find.'

'I know,' she said. 'But I'm still allowed to be hurt.'

The waitress took away our bowls and Ginger fanned out the seven photographs.

'Just to be clear. My girls — they're not trafficked, Max.'

'I know.'

She stared at the images without speaking.

'Some of them like this life. They like the money. They like the freedom. They kid themselves they're in some branch of show business. Or they are at that point in their life when they're lost. And then they give it up and go back to studying or working in an office or they get married and nobody ever knows.'

I said nothing.

183

'The point is – they don't all have knives held to their throat, Max,' she said. 'Though some of them do.'

There was a sudden flurry of activity at the back of the restaurant. The manager was fussing over the departure of the Chinese man I had almost recognised. His entourage had fallen into step behind him. And now I knew where I had seen him before.

Keith Li, the man who had found the lorry parked in Chinatown.

'Please don't stare,' Ginger said.

'Why not?'

She lowered her voice to somewhere below a whisper.

'Because that's Keith Li and he is the head of the Wo Shing Wo.'

The Wo Shing Wo are by far the largest Triad gang operating in the country, although traditionally their power base is in Manchester, while London's Chinatown has been run for fifty years by the 14K Triads.

I stood up as Keith Li passed our table. There was nothing remarkable about his appearance. He was shorter than average but looked fit and hard. He resembled countless other men in Chinatown who have spent a hard lifetime working with their hands and their back. His expression was somewhere between placid and blank. If you had seen him on Gerrard Street, you would have stared straight through him. But he was the king of these crowded streets. Two goons instinctively came towards me but the nondescript old man made an almost imperceptible gesture with his right hand, and they fell back.

I saw the recognition in his eyes.

'Detective Wolfe,' he said. 'You were very polite to me when I was helping the police with enquiries.' He still sounded like an announcer on the BBC World Service in the Fifties. 'As I recall, you were the only one who demonstrated any of that famous English civility.'

'I thought you were a teacher in China,' I said.

'I taught Wing Chun,' he said. 'I wasn't conjugating verbs.'

Wing Chun is the form of Kung Fu that most closely resembles Western boxing.

'You told me you were nothing here,' I said. 'But that's not true, is it?'

I watched him stiffen with pride. *Face*, they would have called it in Chinatown.

'Your colleagues made me feel that way.'

He looked at Ginger and nodded politely.

'This is my friend,' I said.

'We've met,' he said.

Nobody ran a business in Chinatown without the nod from the Triads, although they tended to keep their business among the Chinese community.

'Very nice to see you,' the old man said, and went to move on.

'I don't believe you,' I told him, and I felt Ginger

flinch. 'I don't believe you just happened to be passing and found that lorry. I think you got an early morning call from someone. I think someone else found the lorry and you received a call asking, "What do we do, Mr Li?" Either that, or it was your cargo.'

He stared at me calmly.

'I was told there was a problem. I believed it was best if I dealt with the authorities personally. Do you seriously think I had something to do with those young women being smuggled into this country?'

I shrugged. 'I don't know.'

'But you know Chinatown. You see my people every day. And sometimes you see people who are perhaps not completely legal. Shadow people, we call them. Waiters. Cooks. The girls who push the dim sum trolleys. The women who stand in the doorway of the Chinese Medicine places offering a massage. You see the shadow people, don't you?'

'What's your point, Mr Li?'

'What do you notice about the shadow people of Chinatown, Detective?'

'They're all Chinese.'

He nodded.

'We stay with our own. We deal with our own. We do business with our own. We take care of our own.'

'It still doesn't mean that lorry had nothing to do with you.'

'When you find the men responsible, you know as well as I do what they will be,' he said.

'And what's that?' I said.

'They will be some kind of white man,' he said.

And then Keith Li, head of the Wo Shing Wo, nodded courteously to Ginger and me before stepping out into the red-and-gold lights of Chinatown, his two body-guards always one respectful step behind him.

I walked into the darkness of the crematorium and looked around for somewhere to sit.

There was plenty of choice.

The thin crowd was a reminder that Steve Warboys had never made it out of the minor leagues.

Some arson for the insurance money. Some Southend shoeshines. A bit of dealing on the side, in drugs, stolen goods and whatever else they peddled in the vast car park of the Champagne Room after dark . . .

It was a lifetime of criminality.

But it was not the stuff of legend.

They make films and they write books about Ronnie and Reggie, Charlie and Eddie, Paul and Danny. But nobody was ever going to make a movie about Steve Warboys, the late proprietor of the Champagne Room.

Not fifty years from now.

Not five minutes from now.

Steve Warboys was a minor Essex wide boy, all

swagger and wind, whose major claim to fame was that his grandfather had strutted through London when gangsters were rock stars.

But that was a long time ago.

I took a seat at the back of that cold dark room and watched them file in. The heavy-set, crop-haired men and their gym-thin wives with their sunbed tans. And then, heralded by a whiff of cigar smoke, the parents of Steve Warboys, their faces tight with shock.

Barry Warboys was an expensively tailored sixty-year-old who had the fair complexion of all the Warboys, but that was where the family resemblance stopped.

Barry was every inch the prosperous businessman, expensively out of shape after decades of the good life, taking a drag on his cigar as he entered the crematorium, the tip flaming red in the half-light before he stubbed it out underfoot. His wife, Steve's mother, was in a wheelchair.

She was painfully thin and dressed in chic designer black, hunched up as if she were in some kind of shell. One of her hands reached up to touch her husband's fingers as he gently eased her chair into the front row.

And then finally in came Steve's famous grandfather.

Paul Warboys was a bull of a man in a long black coat, the remains of his hair dyed an unbelievable blond, his face made golden by the years of Spanish sun he had soaked up after coming out of prison for the last time.

Even in his old age he still had enough of an aura to make grown men smile weakly, trying to catch his eye.

Paul Warboys ignored them all.

The old gangster took a seat in the front row across the aisle from his son, and the two men never once looked at each other.

They cremated Steve Warboys on that shifting border where London meets Essex. The sparse crowd stood in silence as the curtain came back and the coffin of Steve Warboys rolled into the flames.

Steve's mother and father had the stunned look of parents who were living the ultimate nightmare of burying their child. They stared unblinking at the flames as their heat crept into that freezing room.

But it was only the grandfather who wept.

17

I sat at the wheel of the BMW X5, the big car still caked with the mud of northern France because people are cheaper than machines, and I watched the man walk through the burned-out ruins of what had been the Champagne Room.

Now Barry Warboys was ready to show his grief.

Now he looked like a man who had lost everything.

Now – unlike the previous afternoon at the crematorium, surrounded by people who believed him to be a far weaker man than his famous father – he allowed himself to weep.

He staggered across the black sodden ruins of the roadside bar, still oozing smoke three days after the fire that burned it to the ground, and his step was so uncertain that it seemed he must surely fall under the weight of his pain. He stood in the ruin, absent-mindedly puffing on a cigar the size of a Cornetto.

There was still a squad car on the scene to keep back the curious and the ghouls but the two uniformed officers inside sat chatting because nobody came, nobody cared, only the man with a sorrow that seemed to buckle his knees.

But I was not the only one watching him.

A uniformed chauffeur stood by the open door of a Bentley and kept a protective eye on Barry Warboys as he stood in the ruins of the burned-out bar. Both of our cars had the engines running, as if we might have to make a quick getaway from this place of death.

My phone vibrated. WHITESTONE CALLING, it said.

'How can we have had a major Triad in an interview room and nobody noticed?' she said.

'Because we had twelve dead women that morning,' I said. 'And because for thirty years the Met have kept an eye on the 14K and assumed the Wo Shing Wo never come further south than Manchester. But things have changed.'

And because mistakes happen, I thought.

I heard her sigh.

'You buy the story that Keith Li was a concerned citizen who happened to be passing by?'

I told my boss exactly what I had told the head of the Wo Shing Wo.

'Keith Li was there because it's his patch,' I said. 'Somebody clocked the lorry, knew something was badly wrong and called the law. And for a lot of people in Chinatown, the Triads are the law and not the Met.'

'And what did he tell you?'

'That his community takes care of their own.' I watched Barry Warboys bend to pick something up from the smoking debris. It was a woman's high-heeled shoe, the kind with the red soles. Christian Louboutin. My ex-wife loved those. Barry Warboys looked at it with something approaching wonder. He hung his head and began to sob silently.

'So we should chalk him up as another totally innocent criminal who happened to be passing by,' Whitestone said. 'Just like your friend, the Filipina madam with her social introduction agency.'

'We can give Keith Li a tug if you want,' I said. 'But I think it's a dead lead.'

'Just keep one eye on the smooth little bastard,' Whitestone said, hanging up.

I got out of the car and the cops in the squad car and the chauffeur all watched me walk towards Barry Warboys. I thought the driver might make some token gesture of putting himself between me and his boss, if only to save face, but he wasn't that kind of chauffeur.

So he simply stood there by the open door, looking like a driver from some black-and-white film about the gilded rich a hundred years ago. He was even wearing gloves.

'Mr Warboys?' I said, holding out my warrant card. 'DC Wolfe of West End Central.'

He wiped his eyes with the back of his hands. I could

see his father in him but Barry Warboys was a milder, meeker version, with none of the teak-hard leanness of his old man. He looked like what he was – a prosperous businessman made soft by the good life. He dropped the shoe and politely shook my hand, a strong, firm hand-shake that did not attempt to crush my fingers, the handshake of a man who had made his life in business.

'I'm sorry for your loss,' I said. I hesitated for a moment and added, 'I can't imagine what it must be like to lose a child.'

He nodded in acknowledgement.

'Stephen was hardly a child,' he said. 'But of course they never stop being your children.'

His accent had none of the Cockney diaspora vowels of his father and son. Barry Warboys had an accent shaped not by class or city or region but by money and education – an accent posh enough to read the news but not so upper class that it would grate on anyone's nerves. He was what my grandmother would have called well-spoken.

He glanced over at his car and for the first time I noticed his wife huddled deep in the back seat, her face hidden behind dark glasses, and so impassive that she could have been sleeping or dead.

'I should go,' he said. 'My wife. The doctor gave her something and . . . Look, I don't wish to be rude, but I've already spoken to one of your colleagues.'

'I'm not here about the death of your son,' I said. 'That investigation is being conducted by detectives from Essex Police. I'm part of an ongoing investigation into a smuggling operation that led to the death of twelve young women.'

He looked genuinely shocked. He dragged on his cigar and then grimaced with distaste.

'Stephen was a petty criminal,' he said. 'I am well aware that he was no angel. But do you really think he was involved in something like that?'

It was a genuine question. And a novel experience for me. In the criminal world, what you usually hear are protestations of innocence. You hear men with blood up to their elbows swearing on their dead mother that they would never harm a fly. So I was shocked to hear Barry Warboys even consider the possibility that his son had been in the people-smuggling business.

'It's one lead we're following,' I said. 'We know of at least one lorry that was due to drop off its cargo of illegals in this car park.'

He thought about it. Then shook his head, dismissing the idea.

'Stephen was not some criminal mastermind,' he said.

'Neither were the people who smuggled those girls,' I said. 'They were stupid, vicious little villains.'

Just like your son, I thought, as he looked at me sharply. Then he softened.

'No,' he said. 'I just can't believe it.'

'Any idea who would want to burn this place down?'

He did not smile but some black brand of humour flickered for a moment in his eyes.

'I think the obvious candidate is Stephen himself,' he said. 'What's the expression? *He had form.*'

'You think this was an insurance scam? The usual idea is that you torch the building but not yourself.'

He looked at me with real anger. And then it faded. Anger did not come easily to him and he did not relish the feeling. Perhaps he had seen too much of it growing up with Paul Warboys as his father.

'I don't know what happened. None of it makes any sense. And, to be frank, finding out the truth will not bring my son back.' He looked over at the car. 'With you in a moment, Mr Doherty,' he said, and the chauffeur slipped into the driver's seat, his leather gloves at ten to two on the steering wheel. Then Barry Warboys turned back to me.

'I can't help you with your investigation. The Champagne Room – smuggling migrants – it's not my world. The criminal life is not my life. That was my father. And that was my son. But it's not me.'

'You run care homes, is that correct?' I said.

A flicker of irritation. I saw the pride in him, the hard-earned pride that he felt in stepping out from the long shadow of his father and making a fortune without even having to break the law.

'Golden Years is a chain of *retirement communities*,' he said, stiffening with the thin-skinned vanity of the self-made man. 'They are not care homes.'

'How did you get into that line of work, Mr Warboys?'

He softened, comfortable with a question that he had answered many times before.

'I was close to both of my maternal grandmothers during my childhood. I think it began with them. Being the recipient of such kindness from the elderly. And wanting to give some of that kindness back.'

I nodded. I knew what that felt like. My grandmother raised me.

'And was your son close to your father?'

'Stephen *idolised* my father,' he said with a wry smile. 'Didn't it show? But the feeling was mutual – my father had that unconditional love that is probably only possible for a grandparent to feel. I always think that parents are too close to their offspring. As a parent, you can't miss the fact that your child – whatever their age – is just one more flawed human being, same as everyone else on the planet. But I don't think that grandparents ever feel that way.'

He looked at the wreck of the Champagne Room.

'My father owned this place,' he said. 'Not my son. My father set Stephen up in business. Were you aware of that?'

'We know the lease is held by a company that was in your late mother's name.'

'Then perhaps you should be talking to my father.'

'I will,' I said. 'And what about you, Mr Warboys? Are you close to your father?'

Another look towards the car. I thought of the photograph I had seen in the Black Museum, of Paul Warboys and the laughing hardmen looking down at the timid little boy in his oversized boxing gloves. I thought I could see the ghost of that scared little boy in this sixty-year-old man with the forgotten cigar in his hand.

'Close? I wouldn't go that far,' he said. 'I don't talk to my father, Detective. Not any more. We were not close when I was a child – he was away, of course, for many years and it was my mother and my grandmothers who really raised me. And we were not close after I grew up. We were civil when we had to be. Unavoidable family gatherings and so on. But after my mother died, we finally stopped pretending.'

'Stopped pretending what?'

'That we liked each other. That we tolerated each other. That we had any desire at all to spend even one moment in each other's company.' He shook his head with a bitterness that he would carry to the grave. 'You see, my father did not treat my mother well. And that's the real reason why there's no way back for us.'

'You mean he had an affair?'

Barry Warboys laughed.

'He had lots of affairs?' I said.

'Worse than that,' he said. 'The ultimate betrayal is not having sex with someone else, Detective.' He waited for me to fill in the blank.

I shook my head.

'It's having a child with someone else,' he said. 'I was still a boy. It must have been before my father got sent away. Because I can remember my parents screaming at each other when the woman turned up on our doorstep with her baby.'

'Who was the woman?'

'The woman doesn't matter a damn.'

We stood in silence.

'I saw a picture of you with your father,' I said. 'You were very small – three or four. In some boxing gym.'

I saw him flinch at the memory.

'I remember the day,' he said. 'The boxing gym – I suppose it must have been in Hammersmith. I remember the smell of the men. The flunkies my father called friends. They reeked of cigarettes and aftershave, alcohol and sweat. And I remember how heavy those gloves felt on my hands and my father telling me to hit him.'

'I don't think I've ever seen a child look more afraid.'

'My father wanted me to box,' Barry Warboys said. 'He wanted to *teach* me to box. I preferred books. I preferred sitting quietly in my grandparents' home. It was a bone of contention between us. One of many. My business was another one. Cleaning bedpans in death's waiting room, my father once said. I was a bit of a disappointment to dear old dad, as you can tell. I always have been. But it probably started in that boxing gym. And it happens, doesn't it? There's nothing remarkable about our estrangement. Do you talk to your father, Detective?'

'My dad died a long time ago,' I said. 'How long did your father try to make you box?'

Barry Warboys thought about it.

'It felt like a lifetime,' he said.

18

The old gangster moved slowly now.

But a lifetime on from when Paul Warboys and his brother Danny were as notorious as the Krays and the Richardsons, the old man did not look diminished. In his late seventies now, he was conserving his energy for whatever he might have to fight in what remained of his days.

'So what's this then, Max? A spot of TIE, is it?'

Trace, Interview and Eliminate. He knew all of our acronyms.

'Just a chat, Paul,' I said.

'This is the bit where you say, "We can do it here or down at the station."'

We had a history. Our bond – such as it was – was based on the love of dogs, and the suspicion that we preferred them, on balance, to people.

When an old face called Mad Vic Masters had been found dead in a ditch on Hampstead Heath, I had

looked after Bullseye, his English Bull Terrier, until Paul
Warboys – Vic's former employer – could claim it.

I followed him into his new riverside apartment. It
was a ground-floor flat next to London Bridge, one of
the big apartment blocks that were sprouting all along
the banks of the Thames, block after block of glass towers in what had been a rough neighbourhood thirty
minutes ago. In the soft light of the early afternoon the
view from the ceiling-to-floor living room window
looked like a postcard of London, back in the days when
people still sent postcards to each other.

Tower Bridge. The Shard. All the gleaming spires of
the City. The last time I had seen Paul Warboys, the
night his wife took her own life, he had been living in
a house out in rural Essex that was the size of a small
Balkan country.

'Downsizing, Paul?'

He gave a cursory look around his apartment.

'The old place was too big for me after Doll died.' He
nodded, his eyes flooding with sudden tears. 'I was rattling around in that Essex gaff. And Doll dealt with
all – you know – *the staff.*'

He grinned at the irony of a celebrity gangster having
to deal with the gardener and the pool guy. Then his
face clouded.

'And now, Steve,' he said, his voice hoarse with grief.

I nodded and waited, in respect to all his loss – his wife, his grandson, a world that was slipping away. Bullseye padded into the room and I held out my hand to his gloriously sloping head. He checked out my scent and then curled up at the feet of his master.

'They allow dogs in these flats?' I said.

Pau Warboys shrugged. 'I never asked,' he said.

'Of course not.'

'I like it here,' he said, brightening. 'I like the history. I like being close to what was the docks. I like the thought of all those ships coming here from all over the world.'

'Your father was a docker, wasn't he?'

He nodded. 'Hardest bastard I ever knew. You didn't want to get on his wrong side when he'd had a few. You didn't even want to get on his wrong side when he was stone-cold sober. I can still feel his belt across the back of my legs.'

'I saw Barry,' I said. 'I saw your son.'

He nodded bitterly. 'Give him my best.'

'You don't talk.'

'The longer you live, the less people you have in your life. Some of them die. And some of them just wander away.'

'And why did Barry wander away?'

He thought about it.

'He was ashamed of me. Which is not nice. And

ashamed of his son. Which is unforgivable.' I watched the rage flare up in him. He had the ability that I had seen in many professionally violent men, the facility to turn their anger on and off like a tap. 'But all that father-and-son stuff is not easy,' he said. 'Every generation is softer than the one that came before.'

This surprised me.

'You really think Steve was softer than his father?'

'Steve wasn't as hard as he would have liked to have been. And he wasn't as hard as I would have liked him to be. If he had been, nobody would have torched his place.'

'But Barry's a legitimate businessman. These care homes he runs – Golden Years – are a big success.'

He shrugged, indifferent and unimpressed.

I smiled at him. 'You don't fancy ending your days in one of them, Paul?'

He didn't smile back. 'I hate all institutions,' he said. 'A life sentence does that to you.'

'I thought you might admire him.'

'Accountants. Lawyers. Legitimate businessmen. All pay their tax, do they? All keep it clean when their lovely PA is bending over to pick up her stapler? *Everybody's* bent, Max. We're all just bent in our different ways. Admire my son? What for? Because he made a couple of bob out of cheap care homes?'

'They're retirement communities, Paul. Tell me about

the Champagne Room. It was in Doll's name, under some shell company – so it turns out you're the owner of a bar that just burned down.'

Now he laughed.

'You like me for the fire that killed my grandson, Max? An insurance scam that went wrong – is that the theory in West End Central? Do me a favour!'

'We don't have a theory, Paul. It's not our investigation. Essex Police are running that one. But my mob is looking for whoever put those twelve dead women in a lorry we found in Chinatown. And we know all sorts have been dropped off in that car park behind the Champagne Room.'

'You know my theory? Someone in Savile Row wants a big scalp on their CV before I fall off my perch.'

I just stared at him. He knew me better than that.

'Maybe your SIO. What's her name? The four-eyed little bird. DCI Whitestone.'

'Come on, Paul. Enough of the hurt feelings. Steve had form and we both know it. I'm sorry for what happened to him, but he was hardly some innocent civilian.'

'He was a good boy. Trying to stand on his own two feet. Trying to show his dad he could make his mark in the world. That's why I set him up in his own little business.'

'Any idea who might have wanted to torch the place?'

'I'm making my own enquiries,' Paul Warboys said darkly. 'If anything comes up, I'll give you a shout.'

I almost told him not to take the law into his own hands, but I kept quiet. It would have been like asking Ronnie Kray to take a deep breath and count to ten before doing anything impulsive.

'This is a good flat, Paul.'

'I've got a lovely Polish lady that comes in twice a week. And it's handy for seeing some of my mates. Of course, most of the old faces are long gone now.'

'And how's your pension?'

A wolfish grin.

'You think I'm struggling for money? I invested my money wisely, Max. I didn't put it in stocks and shares. I didn't put it under the bed or in a bank. I put it in bricks and mortar. I didn't put it with any financial experts who would have pissed it all up the wall. I put it into London property. It's the reserve currency of the world, Max.'

'I'm happy for you. But you see my problem, Paul. I've got twelve young women who froze to death. And I've got a lorry driver with a bunch of Afghans in the back who is meant to be dropping them off in the car park of the Champagne Room.'

He folded his heavy arms, the gold chains rattling like new money, and his eyes got a faraway look. If there was one thing he knew how to do, it was wait.

Here was a man who had sat through countless police interviews, who had spent years of his life incarcerated. It was the stoic, Zen-like patience of a man who had served a life sentence – which is never the length of a lifetime but which is always long enough for your children to grow into total strangers – for sanctioning the removal of a former employee's tongue with the aid of a pair of bolt cutters.

Paul Warboys had the old con's genius for letting time pass by.

'So that lorry in Chinatown had nothing to do with you then?' I prompted. 'And nothing to do with your grandson – as far as you know?'

I think if it had been anyone else he would have just let the silence grow. But I kid myself that he actually liked me. He roughly scratched his old Bull Terrier on its head until it sighed in its sleep. And in the end he spoke.

'Why?' Paul Warboys said. 'Why would I have anything to do with these scumbag people smugglers?'

'For the same reason the world gets up every morning.'

'For money? You think I would do it for money? I *made* my money, Max. And I told you but you don't seem to believe me – I put it where it just keeps on growing. I don't need money.'

'You know what I've noticed about old faces and their money, Paul?'

'What's that, son?'

Whenever he called me son, I knew he was resisting the impulse to break my nose.

'The money runs out,' I said.

'You think I need one last score?'

'I think it's a possibility,' I said. 'You and your brother Danny made your money a long time ago, Paul. You're a dial-up gangster in a digital world. No offence meant.'

'None taken, son.'

'But you and your brother were not Bill Gates. You made a nice pile and even got to keep some of it after you'd done your time. But it was all a long time ago. And – while I don't doubt you made some sound investments in London property – I don't think all those Sixties strip joints and knocking shops earned quite enough to keep you for a lifetime. If you were rolling in it, you wouldn't be in a one-bedroom flat on the wrong side of the river.'

He leaned forward and placed his huge right hand on my arm. White scarring covered the knuckles of that suntanned paw, the souvenir of flesh that had been torn open time and time again.

He patted my arm with what felt almost like sympathy.

'If I wanted one last score, I wouldn't put a dozen tarts in the back of a lorry,' he said.

He looked at my face and laughed.

Because he knew I believed him.

'It's Chinatown,' he said, his tone almost paternal. 'You should be looking at the Chinks.'

19

In the freezing winter sunlight of Sunday afternoon, we gathered in Pat Whitestone's small back garden.

There were around a dozen of us in the garden, a mixed crowd of Whitestone's work colleagues, who spent all hours together but rarely socialised, and a scattering of her friends from the neighbourhood.

I had half-expected Edie Wren to turn up with Mr Big, but it wasn't her married man who walked into the little garden holding Edie's hand. It was Lil, Edie's grandmother, a woman who had exactly the same taste in hats and handbags as the Queen.

Lil was one of those tiny old Londoners who had survived economic depression, the Blitz and years of austerity. What you noticed first about her was the unforced affection she seemed to feel for the entire world.

'Hello, darling,' Lil said to me, although she had never met me in her life. 'Hello, sweetheart,' she said to Scout. 'Who's this handsome lad then?' she said, peering down at Stan as she rummaged in her handbag. She removed a pack of Werther's Originals and offered them around, urging them on the assembled guests, as though they were capable of healing all wounds.

Edie grinned at me. 'My nan,' she said.

Billy Greene had brought his fiancée, Siobhan, a dark-eyed beauty who was one of the civilian staff at West End Central, and they hung back a little from the rest of us, sharing smiles and whispers and a sausage roll the way young lovers do.

But we were all a little uncertain of the mood, and despite the snacks and small talk, there was an air of anxiety for reasons I could not identify.

We were waiting for a dog. And not just any dog.

'Dasher,' Scout said, her voice hushed with wonder. 'A two-year-old Labrador-Retriever mix.' She threw a tennis ball studded with teeth marks towards the end of the garden and Stan flew after it. 'It's the best breed for a guide dog,' she told Edie's grandmother.

Lil lightly touched Scout's solemn face.

'Such a clever little girl,' the old lady said. 'How do you know all this, darling?'

'It's all online,' Scout said, slightly bewildered. 'Dasher loves his toys and treats. I can show you.' Scout held out her hand to me. 'Give me your phone, Daddy.'

I handed her my iPhone and her tiny fingers flew across it like a concert pianist banging out some Beethoven. She stared intently at the screen as she absent-mindedly snuggled into Lil's arms and I saw the old lady melt, shyly holding Scout as she scrolled through the images of Dasher's life.

'Look here,' Scout said. 'Dasher going down the slide . . . Dasher playing in the garden . . . Dasher with his puppy walker . . . Dasher and his trainer . . . Dasher training in harness . . . Dasher smiling.'

'Good old Dasher,' said Lil, hugging Scout.

'There's a film I could show you later,' Scout said 'It's called, *Dasher is off to a flying start*. It's very informative.'

'That would be lovely,' Lil confirmed.

Stan returned with the ball, reluctant to relinquish it, growling when Scout pulled it from his teeth.

She tossed it to the end of the garden and this time the pair of them raced after it, looking like a warm-up act for the man and the dog we were all waiting for.

Pat Whitestone appeared in the open doorway to the kitchen with her son, Justin's face immobile behind dark glasses yet at the same time conveying the message that he would prefer to be anywhere else on the planet.

I understood why Whitestone wanted this day to be a time of celebration and hope, and why she wanted to mark it with this modest party. But I was far from sure that it was what her son wanted.

Edie sat in an old garden chair, a blanket wrapped

around her legs and a mug of hot chocolate in her hand. I wondered where Mr Big was today, and assumed he was home with his family. All the regular excuses – a meeting, stuck in the office, darling, working late – must be harder to pull off on a Sunday.

I felt a visceral loathing for this man I did not know rising in my blood.

'What?' Edie said.

'Nothing,' I said. 'You need anything from the kitchen?'

A small buffet of sandwiches and cakes was set up in the kitchen, most of it hardly touched.

'Stop fussing,' Edie said, the words softened by her laughter, and I turned away with my face burning just in time to see Scout suddenly stop dead in her tracks.

Whitestone's house was at the end of a terrace and you could see the street from the back garden. A car with a large yellow dog in the passenger seat was slowly coming down the quiet road.

The dog glanced our way, as if he was checking the house numbers. The car stopped and a middle-aged man emerged with the dog. It looked glad to be alive.

'Dasher!' Scout cried. 'They're here!'

Whitestone said something to her son and she went off to answer the doorbell. Justin stood there for a moment and then disappeared into the house. When Whitestone returned with Dasher and his walker – to cries of delight from our little party – her son was not with her. I looked up at the first floor and heard music drifting from one of the bedrooms.

'Oh, *Dasher*,' said Scout, weak with love at first sight, and when she scratched his ears you saw the good nature and intelligence of the dog, and his endless hours of training, and his total readiness to perform his new role. We gave the walker a paper plate of sausage rolls and a cup of tea and we all watched Dasher and Stan shyly performing their tail-sniffing introductions.

But although we waited and waited, Justin White-stone did not emerge from the house. And when his mother went in to get him, we were not surprised that she returned alone, shaking her head, and holding back the tears.

'That poor kid,' Edie said to herself.

But Dasher brought real joy to the little garden.

Even after Dasher's walker had said goodbye, the man choking back an unmistakable sense of loss, the mood was buoyant. Dasher seemed delighted to meet every-one, and he capered with Scout in his good-natured wake, with Stan trailing behind the pair of them, until they were all panting for breath and exhausted by the undiluted joy of it all.

It was only when darkness began to creep in that the truth hit us.

Dasher was a guide dog with nobody to guide.

The friends from the neighbourhood began to drift away. In the end, there was only our mob from West End Central, plus Edie's grandmother and Scout.

'Just is still getting used to the idea,' Whitestone said, casting an anxious look at her son's bedroom window. 'I'm sure that after a bit . . .'

Her voice trailed off. She stared at Dasher.

'My son doesn't want him,' Whitestone said eventually, something hard and fragile in her voice.

We all looked at Dasher and he grinned back at us, his mouth open and a glint in his eyes.

'He can come home with me,' Edie said.

Edie Wren lived in a one-bedroom apartment above a shop on the wrong side of Highbury Corner. It looked like a single woman's flat – her clothes, her records, her books, all without the imprint of another life. But she wasn't living alone because there was a camp bed taking up most of the tiny living room.

Edie's grandmother shuffled off to the bedroom, followed uninvited by Dasher and Stan. Knitting and an emergency pack of Werther's Originals sat on the bedside table.

'Lil's staying with me for a while,' Edie said, lowering her voice. 'She hasn't been doing great since my granddad died. She's a hearty old thing, but sometimes she has these gaps in her memory. So I'm on the camp bed.

Don't look like that, Max. It's more comfortable than it
looks.'

Scout came out of the bedroom, frowning at the
flat.

'What's wrong?' Edie said.

Scout looked at me.

'You tell her,' I said. 'It's OK to be honest, Scout.'

'Well,' Scout said, not wanting to be rude. 'Your flat,
Edie – it's very nice and all, but it's, well, it's a bit . . .
little.'

Edie looked around her single-girl flat.

'For Dasher,' Scout said. 'For a young Labrador-
Retriever.' Dasher was roaming about the flat, his nose
twitching at all the new scents. Stan was curled up on
the bed with Lil. 'These dogs love human company,'
Scout said. She closed her eyes and remembered the
words. '*Labrador-Retrievers are a healthy, happy breed but
they need regular human contact and a responsible amount
of exercise.*'

Edie was staring at Scout.

'She sounds like . . .'

'She sounds like the Internet,' I sighed. 'I know. But
Scout's right, Edie. It's not going to work.'

'It's a good place, Edie,' Scout said, with the
heart-tugging diplomacy that comes naturally to the
children of divorced parents. 'But it's too small for a
two-year-old Labrador-Retriever mix.'

215

'Dasher would tear this place apart if you left him home alone,' I said. 'I know you want to help, but he will have trashed the place before you get to the office.'

'Clos . . .' said Scout, struggling to summon the word. 'Clos . . . clos . . .'

'Claustrophobic,' I said.

So Dasher came home with us.

Scout was in raptures.

Stan was less keen.

Scout raced across the great empty expanse of the big loft – a space large enough for even a big boy like Dasher to wear himself out – as our Stan settled in the classic Cavalier King Charles Spaniel pose, his head resting on his front paws, casting anxious looks towards Scout and the newcomer.

I scratched the tuft of white fur on Stan's ruby-coloured chest.

'You'll get her back, old Stan.'

Whitestone called. I was expecting to be told to bring Dasher over immediately, but it was nothing to do with the dog.

'I've sent you a link,' she said. 'Watch it and call me back.'

The link took me to YouTube footage that was filmed by the side of a busy road. Above the noise of a constant stream of heavy lorries, I could hear the voices of excited men in French and English and sub-Saharan languages that I didn't know.

The camera panned briefly to a sign above the road.

GRAND PORT MARITIME DE DUNKERQUE

There was a date stamp in the corner of the screen. It took me a moment to realise that it was the same day that Edie and I went to the camp in Dunkirk and this was the road to the port from the direction of Grand-Synthe. The camera bounced between the faces of the men – mostly African faces, all young and male, all wrapped up for a bitter north European winter – as they merrily threw large branches of trees into the busy road. They were laughing and I could tell that it was not the first time they had attempted to slow down a lorry for long enough to clamber into the back.

They were not having much luck. The giant lorries barrelled over the scraps of trees they tossed into their paths. Sometimes I heard a lorry driver cursing the men as he tore past, and the men by the side of the road cursing the mothers of the lorry drivers.

And then, as the men paused in their efforts, the camera's eye settled with mild curiosity on a man standing alone further down the road, just above the hard shoulder, on the slope of the dead grass that led up from the motorway.

The man's face was stained with multiple tattoos, and he pressed a phone to his ear as he looked towards the oncoming traffic.

Troy.

And fifty metres beyond Troy, there was another dark figure, also alone, but standing much closer to the roaring traffic.

And I saw that it was Zlatko Draganov standing on the hard shoulder, staring across the road at something.

Staring across the road at me.

Then Troy abruptly stepped back.

And the men who had thrown their branches into the road were screaming, and scrambling away from the road, running for their lives, and the camera swung wildly, veering to the sky and the ground and swerving somewhere between, and when it finally regained control of itself it followed the path of a lorry that had roared past on the hard shoulder and narrowly missed the men throwing branches into the road.

The vehicle seemed to accelerate as it closed the short distance to Zlatko Draganov. It was on him in a broken fragment of a second, smashing into him with a force that hurled him into the air and into the thick of the traffic.

The lorry did not stop. The driver – whoever he was – did not even touch his brakes.

And then the traffic stopped and the riot began.

At first the camera dangled forgotten in the hand of the anonymous cameraman, until his colleagues began climbing into the back of a stopped lorry and he recorded this historic moment, the happy grins of men who looked as though they had just won the lottery.

When the cameraman was safely tucked up in the back of a lorry, his friends chuckling contentedly all around him, the view switched to three CRS men giving a beating to a man on the ground between the back of one massive truck and the front of another. The man holding the camera screamed at them in his schoolboy French.

The screen went black.

I watched it all again, feeling sick.

The men happily throwing branches in the road.

Troy standing alone with a phone in his hand.

The sudden appearance of the rogue lorry on the hard shoulder.

I paused the YouTube film here, and saw that the lorry's registration plates were smeared with the mud of northern France, a simple but effective way to hide a vehicle's identity.

And finally the brutal death of Zlatko Draganov.

It no longer looked like a road accident.

219

DIE LAST

It looked like an execution.

Then I called Whitestone. The cold Sunday afternoon seemed far away, the cheese-and-onion crisps in a back garden in Islington, the sandwiches and teacakes, the dogs running after the tennis ball. Now there was only the work.

'They took him out,' I told Whitestone. 'Troy and whoever he works for. They used a lorry instead of a gun, but someone knew that Zlatko Draganov was about to be lifted by the law. They knew that we had identified Draganov as the driver of the Chinatown lorry and they knew that, sooner or later, he was going to be in a cell and telling us what he knew.'

'What happened to the driver of that lorry?'

'The driver's in the wind,' I said. 'Maybe he got on board a ferry. More likely he kept going. He would have been in Belgium or Holland by the time the French cops got the alert out. Did you see what they did to the registration plates?'

'Yes,' she said. 'So just to be clear – the death of Zlatko Draganov was no road accident, was it?'

I could hear DCI Whitestone breathing at the other end of the line. She was waiting for me to confirm what she already knew.

'His death was a hit,' I said.

20

Early next morning Lee Hill sat in MIR-1, surrounded by our team. He was happy and relaxed, sipping the mug of builder's tea Billy Greene had made for him. If there had been any chocolate digestive biscuits, we would have offered him one. We made sure he was sitting comfortably. Then we began.

'We need you to make another run to Dunkirk,' DCI Whitestone said.

The lorry driver exploded.

'That wasn't the deal! The deal was I fingered the driver with the messed-up face! That was the deal we had!'

'What you do is you drive to Dunkirk and make contact with Troy of Imagine,' Whitestone said calmly, completely ignoring his protests. 'Your old radical comrade with the tattooed mug. Then you bring another load into the country. And then you tell us where the drop zone is and then you're done.'

'But last time I was down there I told them I was too

scared to try another run,' he said, sloshing tea on to his jeans. 'Oh bugger.'

'Tell them you changed your mind,' I said. 'Tell them you need the money.'

'Tell them whatever works,' Whitestone said. 'Tell them whatever you like. But – look at me, Lee – you *are* doing another run.'

'In your dreams, copper. That was never the deal.'

Whitestone looked at me. I knew she was thinking that we should have had this conversation in an interview room or a holding cell instead of MIR-1. Somewhere with locks and a metal grille on the door. Somewhere with not even the possibility of a chocolate digestive biscuit.

Doing it in a room that wasn't locked had lulled our bent lorry driver into a false sense of security.

'There was never any deal, Lee,' I said. 'You agreed to help with our enquiries instead of facing charges for facilitating the entry of illegal immigrants. Remember?'

'What do I get out of it?'

'Freedom,' Edie said.

He snorted with derision.

'You call this freedom?'

Whitestone nodded at Billy. He hit his keyboard and the YouTube footage from the road by the Dunkirk camp began to play on the big screen.

We all watched it in silence.

The men throwing their branches on to the busy motorway. The brief glimpse of the man with the tattooed face standing by the side of the road, the dark phone pressed to his ear almost invisible against his inked features, staring towards the oncoming traffic.

Troy.

And Zlatko Draganov in the last seconds of his life before the oncoming truck annihilated him.

'They killed him,' Whitestone said. 'Troy and those caring revolutionaries from Imagine. All those humanitarians with rings in the noses and bells on their toes. They knew we had ID'd the driver of the lorry in Chinatown. So they took him out. He was going to be given a tug, so they murdered him. Or they did it on the bidding of their masters.'

'Nothing to do with me,' Lee Hill said.

'Everything to do with you,' Whitestone insisted. 'Those dead women in Chinatown could have been in your ride.'

He shook his head furiously.

'I never wanted anyone to die. Look – I only brought those people in because I couldn't stop them. Nobody can. You have no idea what it's like for the drivers down there. Look at those jungle bunnies chucking trees into the road! They're going to be in the back of my lorry if I get paid for it or not. So why not get paid for it?'

223

Edie scrunched up her eyes.

'Because when you get nicked you do hard time – the kind of hard time that lasts long enough for your parents to die, your children to grow up and your friends to forget you. How about that for a good reason?'

The lorry driver grimaced with frustration.

'And what do I get if Troy thinks I'm ratting him out?'

'Troy's not going to think that,' I said. 'You were never arrested. Most of those Afghans you were bringing into the country were never collared. The ones that were haven't been anywhere near West End Central. Nobody knows you're here with us.'

He covered his face with his hands, not buying it. I felt for the poor bastard. But this is how it works with CIs. We suck the juice out of them in return for not locking them up.

'When would I go?' he said.

'Now,' Whitestone said. 'We would like you to go immediately. Make contact today. Make the run back in the next day or so.'

'I don't have a rig.'

'We've got your lorry out of the pound,' Billy said.

He held up a set of keys.

Lee Hill reluctantly took them.

'And when does it end?'

'When I say it ends,' Whitestone said.

* * *

Lee's lorry was waiting outside the great subterranean car park of West End Central, which is round the back on Old Burlington Street.

Billy walked him down.

'But he already failed to make one delivery,' I said when they were gone. 'Even if most of them got away. You don't think it looks like he's been turned?'

'Maybe,' Whitestone said. 'But he's all we've got.'

Edie was staring at her phone. All of her attention was suddenly somewhere else.

I recognised that look.

It is only our family who can make us feel that way.

We searched for Lil all day. In the markets and the shops and the parks of Holloway and Islington and Highbury, from the old Arsenal stadium all the way to the Angel. But as the sun faded on another bitterly cold day, we realised we were looking in the wrong part of town.

'I know where she will be,' Edie said.

Her grandmother had gone looking for her old neighbourhood deep in the East End.

But that neighbourhood was long gone.

The streets Lil knew, the terraced house where she grew up, the shops and the school and the people – it was as if none of it had ever existed. It took us two hours to find her.

'There she is,' Edie said.

Lil was standing outside a brand-new block of apartments, talking to a porter in a dark suit with the tribal markings of West Africa on his face.

'I'm looking for Harry,' Lil explained.

'Harry's not here,' he said. 'Is no Harry. Please go.'

Edie took her grandmother's arm, laughing.

'Come on, Nan, let's go home. Went for another wander, didn't you?'

Lil looked confused.

'Molly?'

'It's Edie. Your granddaughter. Remember?'

'Edie. Yes. Of course. That's quite right. *Edie*. I knew that.'

A dog walker emerged with half a dozen dogs. She looked askance at Lil.

'Excuse me,' the old lady said to the dog walker. 'Have you seen Harry? He's – what? – must be sixteen by now.'

The dog walker moved quickly away.

The porter had his arms spread wide, ushering us out. Edie put her small body between the porter and her nan.

'We're going, pal,' she said very quietly. 'But don't rush us.'

She gently led Lil to the street, holding her close, softly whispering to her.

'Harry's gone, Nan. Remember now? Harry went a long time ago. Harry was your brother, wasn't he?'

Lil became suddenly tearful.

I stared at the street. Building work was happening everywhere. The cranes loomed over the city as if they were the masters now. On the far side of the street a queue of men were being given hard hats and hi-vis jackets.

And that was when I saw Nesha Novak.

He was carrying bricks in a wheelbarrow. Almost running with them, as if it was some kind of grim new sport. I gave Edie the keys to the BMW and told her I would meet her at the car.

Hana Novak's kid brother looked at me as I brushed past the queue of men. But he carried on working, racing his load to the massive hole that was the centre of the site. Now that London was close to capacity, most of the building work was going underground.

Russian voices were everywhere. Men with shaven heads, cigarettes jammed between their lips and, among all the ragged sportswear, there were hoodies that looked as though they had been bought from a tourist shop on Oxford Street. There were more Union Jacks than the Last Night of the Proms.

I found the foreman.

'See that kid with the wheelbarrow?'

'What about him?'

'He's sixteen.'

'So what?'

'He's in this country illegally.'

The foreman smiled. He said something in Russian to his mates. Everybody had a good old chuckle.

'So what?' he repeated.

I took out my warrant card and showed it to him.

'So I can have you all deported so fast that your human rights won't touch the ground,' I said. 'Want me to make a call to my colleagues at Border Control, the tax office, immigration?'

His smile faded. He called Nesha over. The boy reluctantly set down his wheelbarrow, now empty, and approached us.

'Go,' the foreman told Nesha.

He hesitated for a moment and then handed in his hard hat and his hi-vis jacket and followed me silently.

There were two middle-aged women coming down the road, pulling suitcases on wheels, and once upon a time they would have been friends off on holiday but now I knew they were more likely to be foreign housekeepers or cleaning ladies returning home after working in one of the East End's new luxury apartment blocks.

The women saw me coming with Nesha trailing reluctantly by my side, every inch the policeman with his suspect, and quickly crossed the street and hurried by on the far side of the road, as if I was bad trouble just waiting to begin, and as if they were a long way from home.

When we reached the car, Lil smiled at Nesha brightly.
'Hello, sweetheart!' she said. 'Hello, Harry!'
'Hello,' said Nesha.
'Where's all your kit?' I asked him.
He directed me to a nearby industrial estate where a
dozen dead cars were lined up in the shadow of a giant
carpet warehouse. The dead cars were inhabited by perhaps twice as many men. Nesha was staying on the back
seat of a Vauxhall Corvette that had lost its wheels many
years ago.
The men – and they were all men – stood around a
fire in an old oil barrel, trying to get the chill out of
their bones, and they watched us without fear or interest
as Nesha collected his things. There wasn't much. He
filled half a black bin bag and he was ready to go.
Lil leaned into Edie. 'Is that our Harry?' she said.
'Harry's dead,' Edie said.

We dropped Edie and her grandmother back at her flat
and then I drove back to Smithfield and parked on Charterhouse Street.
I needed to talk to Nesha Novak.
'We got him,' I said. 'The driver of that lorry. The
one who drove your sister and those other women to
London. As far as we can tell, his name was Zlatko
Draganov. He was Bulgarian Roma. He made a living
out of people like Hana and now he's dead. Because we

got him.' I thought about it. 'Well – we didn't get him. Someone else did. But they got him because we were closing in on him.'

The boy traced a finger over his face to indicate scarring.

'That man?' He clicked his fingers twice. 'That man is dead?'

'Yes. But now we need to catch his bosses. The people who paid him to drive that lorry. So, for us – for the British police – it's not over. But he is dead now. And I thought that you would want to know.'

He nodded.

I could see that he had believed the death of the man who drove the lorry in which his sister died would bring him some peace.

But it didn't seem to be working.

He stared at the lights coming on in the meat market, not seeing them. I looked at my phone.

DEJAN JOVANOVIC – SERBIAN EMBASSY, it said.

My thumb hovered over the call button but I did not press it. My plan had been to turn the kid in and let his embassy ship him back to Belgrade. But I found that I didn't have the energy. I slipped my phone into my jacket.

'I've got to pick up my daughter,' I said. 'I've got to walk my dog. And before I do any of that I have to go to the gym because if I don't go to the gym then I will not sleep tonight.'

He shook his head.

He didn't understand what I was saying.

'Go,' I said, sounding like the foreman in charge of that two-million-pound hole in the East End.

'Go where?' he said, as we got out of the BMW.

'I don't know, do I? Go somewhere better than the back seat of a car with no wheels.'

Smithfield was the perfect place for an insomniac. This was, more than anywhere in the city, the neighbourhood that never slept. Young women and men were queuing outside the clubs on Charterhouse Street. The white lorries were arriving for the night shift at the meat market. It was a good place to find whatever you needed. But when we got out of the car, Nesha Novak followed me all the way to Smithfield ABC, keeping one hundred metres behind.

Fred was waiting.

'You're so lucky to be training,' Fred grinned, as I headed towards the lockers. He nodded in greeting at Nesha, who had sat down on a bench.

Then we went to work.

One of Fred's legendary circuits, guaranteed to possibly help you live forever and definitely get a good night's sleep. Twelve rounds. Three minutes three times each on the heavy bag, the speedball, the upper-cut bag and the super-heavyweight bag. Ten burpies and ten press-ups during the minute break between rounds. No stopping, no rest.

'Recover while you work,' Fred said.

James Brown on the sound system. Fred punching the bags by my side, his old black gloves whipping against the Lonsdale leather with blinding speed as we were watched from the wall by Joe Frazier and Sugar Ray Leonard and Muhammad Ali and Jack Dempsey and Jake LaMotta. Fred's hall of fame.

The sweat pouring, the blood pumping, the exhaustion that you pass through to the reserve energy supply that you did not know was inside you, and then beyond that secret fuel tank to the real exhaustion where the sickness is in your stomach and your muscles are twitching with the build-up of lactic acid and your eyes sting with sweat, the place where you are not aware of the music, not aware of time passing, not aware of anyone watching. The red leather of my heavy eighteen-ounce Lonsdale gloves shining with sweat.

The buzzer sounded.

'Time,' Fred said. 'Good. You'll sleep well tonight.'

I grinned at my trainer. It was true.

Everyone else had gone home now.

But Nesha was busy picking up towels.

'Is he thieving?' Fred said.

'I think he might be clearing up,' I said.

Fred nodded, impressed.

'What's his story?'

I told him. All of it. The whole tragic mess. From saying goodbye to his sister in Belgrade to living in a dead car in the East End.

Nesha Novak had his arms full of sweaty towels.

He stared at us.

'He's not afraid of hard work, is he?' Fred said.

21

The uniforms were doing something wrong.

They had been touring the language schools with the photographs of Rabia Demir in the company of the man who called himself Zlatko Draganov, but they were coming back with nothing.

So we tried it my way.

'There are hundreds of English language schools in this city,' I told Billy Greene as we weaved our way through the early morning crowds on Oxford Street. 'Some of them are fully accredited places of education. And some of them are fronts for visa scams.'

'You really think she'll show up at a language school?' Billy said.

I shrugged.

'If not for her language skills, then maybe for her visa. If she is registered with a language school, it's easier for her to get a student visa. Let's try this place.'

There was an open doorway between an old denim store and a new coffee shop. A young man – early twenties, Somalian or that neighbourhood – was leaning against the wall next to it, a stack of glossy leaflets in his hand, half-heartedly offering them to the indifferent crowds. I held out my hand and he stirred, sort of sliding up the wall, and warily gave me a leaflet.

Oxbridge International Language School
Learn English with the elite.
Low low prices!
Help with accommodation, work permits and visas.
Excellence guaranteed!

The border of the leaflet was adorned with the flags of twenty nations. I nodded to Billy and we went up the stairs.

The Oxbridge International Language School had an unmanned reception desk and, beyond it, a tiny classroom with half a dozen desks. It was empty apart from an overweight man in his forties, vaping furiously, and a couple of exhausted-looking Asian women in their twenties. When they are not conjugating verbs, most of these language students are out working long hours for low pay.

'You speak English?' I asked the man, showing him my warrant card.

'That's a bloody strange question,' he said.

'How many registered students do you have on your books?' I said.

'I would need to check online.'

'Ballpark figure.'

I watched him hesitate.

I indicated Billy.

'PC Greene here would be happy to check your records, if you find your mind's gone blank.'

The man licked his lips.

'One thousand, nine hundred and twenty-seven,' he said.

I looked at Billy and then back at the man.

'So the Oxbridge International Language School has nearly two thousand students on its books?'

He nodded, studying the floor.

'Look at me,' I said.

He looked at me. I gestured at the handful of desks and chairs.

'What happens if they all show up at once?' I said.

'Well,' he said. 'It gets rather crowded.'

'I bet they all have a student visa, right?'

He looked hurt. 'Of course!'

I took out my phone.

'Look at this woman,' I said.

I showed him the photographs of Rabia Demir and Zlatko Draganov. While he was studying them, I glanced at Billy and I saw that he got it.

This was the way our people had to play it with these language schools. Show them that their cosy little student visa scams would abruptly end unless we got some help with our enquiries.

'Beauty and the beast,' the man said, attempting a smile. Trying to bond with me.

'Just concentrate on the woman,' I said. 'Forget the man. The man's dead. Have you seen her?'

He studied the face in the seven photographs. I gave him the phone and he scrolled through the images himself, more slowly this time, trying to recall.

'What's her name?'

'Rabia Demir,' I said.

'Turkish,' he said. He handed me back the phone and shook his head. 'We have some Turks but they're mostly men. And she's not one of the women.' He smiled weakly. 'I think I would remember Rabia.'

I gave him my card.

'If she shows up, you call me. And if I don't hear from you, my colleague here will come back to work out how you manage to squeeze two thousand students into a classroom the size of a telephone box.'

He took my card and nodded obediently, but I saw the doubtful light in his eye and I knew exactly what he was thinking.

There are ten million people in this city.

And I was looking for just one woman.

Keith Li called me as we were going down the stairs.

'There's a lorry,' he said. 'It's been abandoned in Colindale. The place that was Oriental City. Do you know it?'

On either side of the millennium, Oriental City had been a massive Asian shopping centre located at the suburban end of the Edgware Road. Some people had called it the real Chinatown.

'I know it,' I said. 'But I thought they tore that place down.'

'The lorry is on the top floor of the old car park.'

'Why are you telling me, Mr Li?'

'It is the same vehicle that was recently parked outside the back of West End Central.'

Lee Hill's lorry.

'Who told you it was in Oriental City?'

'Some friends.' I could hear the impatience in his voice. 'I am doing you a favour, Detective.'

But I didn't feel like being grateful.

'Why the hell did they call you instead of the police?'

Now I could feel him smiling at the other end of the phone.

'They wished to speak to someone they can trust,' he said.

Nobody could mistake what had once been Oriental City for the real Chinatown any more. It looked like the world's forgotten shopping centre, a vast sprawl of empty parking spaces, abandoned shops and a food court where nobody had eaten in years.

'What was this place?' Billy Greene said.

'It was an Asian shopping mall. Japanese-owned and then Malaysian. There was a supermarket. Some great restaurants.'

In a dreary corner of North London, it had once been an outpost of East Asia. My mouth watered at the memory of all the Thai, Vietnamese, Chinese, Korean and Japanese food that I had eaten here.

Keith Li leaned forward from the back seat. I had insisted on his presence and he hadn't resisted.

'Top of the car park,' he said.

We drove to the top floor of the two-storey car park. Skateboarding kids scattered when they saw us coming. The lorry stood all alone in the far corner.

'That's Lee Hill's ride all right,' Billy said.

I looked at Keith Li in the rear-view mirror.

'You're never far away when a lorry gets dumped,' I said.

'Lucky for you,' he said.

Billy Greene got out of the BMW and we watched him as he walked towards the lorry.

'This has nothing to do with Chinese people,' Keith Li said. 'Whoever does these things, they don't look like me.' He nodded at my face as I glanced at him in the rear-view mirror. 'They look like you.'

'Maybe they don't look like either of us,' I said.

Billy Greene stepped up to peer into the cab.

He got back down again and shook his head at me.

Nothing.

I took out my phone and called Lee Hill's mobile.

'There was a *spoof* on the Internet,' Keith Li said, savouring the word *spoof* as if it was one of his all-time favourites. 'A picture of road signs supposedly in the north of England in both English and Arabic.' His eyes twinkled. 'Oh, people were very angry! I like this expression — *make the blood boil*. Wonderfully descriptive! All that cold English blood boiling hot! The signs said, "*Five miles — Rotherham*", in English and Arabic. "*Ten miles — Leeds*", in English and Arabic. And so on.' When he relished a phrase in English, he would pause to enjoy it. *And so on*. He liked that one, too. 'Many people were very upset to see English signs also in Arabic.'

I got out of the car. He got out, too. I smiled at him.

'But it wasn't real,' I said. 'The signs in Arabic and English were all fake, right? Yorkshire does not have road signs that are in English and Arabic.'

He nodded.

'Very good, Detective. It wasn't real. None of it was real. It was all Photoshopped. This *spoof*. To cause mischief, shall we say? But in Chinatown — in the heart of London, not Colindale or somewhere similar, not out here in *the sticks* — street signs have been written in English and Chinese for fifty years!'

I stared at my phone as it called Lee Hill but I was remembering the street signs on Gerrard Street,

Newport Place, and Lisle Street – those few short streets that made up London's Chinatown. Keith Li was right. They were all in both English and Chinese.

'The bilingual street signs in Chinatown are not Photoshopped,' he said. 'But nobody cares! And why not, Detective?'

Lee Hill's number began to ring. I began walking towards the lorry. Billy Greene was trying the back door.

'Because no Chinese ever put a bomb on the London underground,' Keith Li said, keeping pace with me. 'Because the Chinese mind our own business. *Because we take care of our own*. And that's why they call me instead of you.'

Billy Greene was staring at the back of the lorry.

And from inside the vehicle, a phone was ringing in answer to my call.

'Bust it open!' I said.

Billy stood there helplessly for a moment and then picked up a half-brick and threw it, quickly jumping backwards when the brick bounced off the lock.

I cursed and ran back to the BMW, removing a pair of forge steel bolt cutters from the boot. An unmarked squad car pulled into the car park just as I was snapping the big metal lock on the back of the lorry.

Edie Wren was driving. Whitestone was in the passenger seat.

They were getting out of the car as the lock snapped open and Billy threw back the doors.

Lee Hill was suspended from the roof at the far end, hanging from a meat hook that was buried in the underside of his jaw. He had been a large man, and the metal roof sagged and creaked with the weight of his body.

I felt the bile rise up in me and even after I fought it under control, I could taste it in my mouth. It was more than shock. It was the bitter tang of guilt.

We all stared at the body of Lee Hill.

My boss broke the silence.

'We're going to need another driver,' DCI Whitestone said.

22

'Slip and rip,' Fred said, his face between the pads he held on his hands in a high guard.

I threw a jab against his left pad, moved my head out of the path of his right cross, threw a right upper cut against his right pad, slipped his big right. We repeated the drill endlessly, until the only thing in my head was Fred's mantra – *slip and rip, slip and rip* – until your body knew exactly what to do even before it received the order from your brain, embedding the knowledge in blood and bone and muscle.

Then I banged the bags.

Three minutes on the speed bag followed by ten burpies and ten press-ups in the minute break and then straight on to the heavy bag.

'Good,' said Fred, nodding with approval.

I worked until the air was gone from me and I pushed through that invisible barrier to find the air that was on the other side, the air that the body stores for emergencies. And I worked until my eyes stung, blinded by sweat, and muscles in my legs and arms twitched with involuntary spasms and the sickness came, the feeling that you get on the edge of genuine exhaustion.

But I could still see him.

I could still see Lee Hill.

He was still there hanging on the end of that meat hook, the metal roof moaning and sagging in protest.

A buzzer sounded.

'Time,' said Fred. 'Have a drink and then do your stretching.'

Nesha Novak walked past carrying a load of white towels for the washing machine.

After that first night, he had taken to living at the gym, his sleeping bag unfurled on top of a couple of yoga mats, paying his way during the day by doing whatever was needed to keep Smithfield ABC running smoothly.

He nodded at me as I was stretching my abductors, one leg flat on a bench and the other on the floor, feeling the hamstring lengthen and relax.

'There's a man to see you, Max,' Nesha told me.

Barry Warboys was standing by the ring, watching two young pros spar, an unlit cigar in his fist. The boxers in the ring only had a handful of fights between them. One of them, the tall rangy black kid, already had a loss on his record. The other one, a white kid who was smaller but wider and stronger, was having trouble with his hands. Their careers, in the hardest of professions, were under threat before they had really begun.

So they sparred furiously, loading up with heavy punches, trying to knock the other guy's head off, both of them aware that they would know very soon if they were going to make a living at boxing, or if they were going to have to put the dream away forever.

I went over to Warboys, noticing his driver – Doherty – standing by the entrance to Smithfield ABC, still impeccably suited and gloved, magnificently out of place in a boxing gym.

Barry Warboys was watching the sparring with a horrible fascination. I stood by his side, remembering the photograph I had seen at the Black Museum, that black-and-white photograph of Paul Warboys in all his grinning pomp, posing in a boxing ring with a small boy wearing box-fresh shorts, vest and a pair of boxing gloves that were larger than his head.

I remembered the way the man and the boy both had their fists raised as if they were about to start fighting. I remembered Paul Warboys' leering amusement. But most of all I remembered the terror on the face of his son, Barry.

'This is the last place I expected to see you,' I said.

Barry tore his eyes away from the sparring fighters.

'I wanted to talk to you,' he said. 'But I didn't want to come into your place of work. I trust that's not a problem?'

'Go ahead.'

'You asked me about my father's finances. And I couldn't give you an answer because I didn't know. But now I do.' He looked back at the ring. 'My father's money has gone, Detective. He may have made a fortune with his brother, but it's long gone.'

'How do you know?'

'Because the bar my son ran owed everyone money, from the tax man to the company who supplied the beer. The Champagne Room was mortgaged to the hilt but that was only the start. My accountants are still going through the books, but I have seen a summary of the debts and they are in the high six figures.'

'And why have you suddenly seen these figures?'

'Because I'm the executor of my son's estate. My father wasn't Stephen's next of kin. I am.'

I thought about it. 'Do you know what long firm fraud is, Mr Warboys?'

'No.'

'There's no reason why you would. Long firm fraud is when a company is set up for fraudulent purposes. An apparently legitimate business establishes a good credit record and then, out of the blue, everyone gets stiffed. Goods are bought on a massive scale with no intention of ever paying for them.'

'But what's the point in that?'

I could not help but smile at his innocence.

'The goods get sold elsewhere, Mr Warboys. It's how the criminal mind works. It's a scam that was perfected in the Sixties. The big family mobs loved the long firm. Reggie and Ronnie Kray. Charlie and Eddie Richardson.'

He looked at me.

'And Paul and Danny Warboys,' I said. 'A long firm takes time and money to set up but it can be massively profitable. It ends with the business run into the ground and the owners long gone. Sometimes they burn the place to the ground before they do a bunk.' I watched his face carefully. 'Do you think your father burned that place down?'

He shook his head.

'No,' he said. 'Because my father would never do anything to hurt my son.' And then a look of doubt came over his face. 'At least, not deliberately.'

'I've seen your father's new home. It's an apartment in a luxury block by the river. It's not big, but he doesn't look as if he's struggling to get by on his state pension.'

Barry Warboys laughed bitterly.

'My father is broke, Detective. The last of the money was in that Essex house. My father couldn't sell it while my mother was alive. It was in her name – it had been in her name for forty years, ever since he went away for his life sentence, ever since it seemed the authorities might seize it. But as soon as my mother was gone, there was nothing to stop him putting it on the market.'

I thought of Paul Warboys alone in the soulless luxury of his riverside apartment block and I remembered something my grandmother used to say. *Fur coat and no knickers*. Meaning a public show of luxury and a private reality of poverty. Was that what the old gangster had come to?

'Why are you telling me this?' I said.

'You asked me about my father's finances,' he said. 'And now I'm telling you. I don't believe he burned down the Champagne Room. I don't believe that he – or Stephen – had anything to do with those women in Chinatown. But I do not want to keep anything from you. This is not easy for me, Detective.'

'I appreciate that,' I said. 'If he needed one last score, what do you think your father would do?'

His voice was soft as a prayer and I could hardly hear him over the slap of leather hitting flesh and bone and the groans of pain coming from the ring.

'My guess would be – anything,' he said.

We watched the boxers for a while without speaking. They were both very tired now.

'A room in one of your homes,' I said. 'How much would something like that cost?'

'Retirement communities,' he said. 'We have several financial packages that we find suit most incomes. Did you have a guest in mind?'

'You call them guests?'

'Yes.'

'And do you take people who are unwell? You know – struggling to remember things?'

He leaned on the side of the ring.

'We take anyone,' he said. 'Is this a member of your family?'

'The grandmother of a friend,' I said.

Barry Warboys gave me his card.

Golden Years
Residential and retirement communities
Elderly care for every pocket.

There was a personal mobile number on the card.

'Tell your friend to call me,' he said.

The black boxer bounced off the ropes and walked straight on to a hard right cross that caught him on the point of his chin. He was unconscious before he hit the floor. The white boxer stared at him, dumbstruck with shock.

Then Fred was in the ring, kneeling over the floored fighter, pulling out the gumshield to stop him swallowing it, shouting for Nesha to call an ambulance.

I saw that Barry Warboys was trembling.

'Will he be all right?' he said.

'He'll be fine,' I said. 'But that ring is not for everyone.'

He nodded.

'I know,' he said. 'And if it's not for you, then it's the loneliest place in the world.'

23

The white ten-ton truck came hurtling towards us, the morning sunshine turning the windscreen a solid block of molten gold, the growl of its diesel engine growing louder as it picked up speed in the wide-open space of the landing strip.

The abandoned aerodrome was on the north-west edge of London but it could have been the middle of the countryside. There was a lake on one side, shimmering with a thin film of ice, and nothing but flat fields on the other side, all edged with trees that grew close enough together to keep out prying eyes. The big engine howled like a trapped animal as the driver changed gears. The truck wobbled in protest but kept coming towards us.

'Where's this one from?' asked the bespectacled man standing with us, his eyes never leaving the truck.

'We seized it from a crew who were bringing in counterfeit money inside kitchen appliances,' I said.

'Not the vehicle,' the man said. 'The driver.'

The sun was suddenly gone from the windscreen and

Billy Greene's face appeared behind the steering wheel, holding on as if it might possibly fly from his grip.

'PC Greene is one of our detectives,' Whitestone said.

'Better stand back a bit,' said the man.

Glenn was a driving instructor for the Met. Mostly based at Hendon, the twenty specialist courses he taught included anti-hijack protection driving, tactical pursuit and containment, advanced car, advanced motorcycle, off-road, high-speed response and – Billy's lesson – driving a heavy goods vehicle.

Glenn ushered Whitestone and me off the tarmac and on to the scrubby grass as Billy slammed on his brakes.

This end of the landing strip had a wide circle of tarmac, big enough for a light aircraft to make a complete turn before heading off to the hangars that had been falling down for the last thirty years. Billy was meant to be practising his turn on the circle but he came in too fast and executed his turn too abruptly. The three of us jumped back as the truck went up on its left wheels, hovering dramatically for a long sickening moment until the airborne side came down with the crash of ten tons of steel.

The lorry screeched to a halt.

Billy buzzed down the window and wiped the sweat from his face on this freezing cold day.

Glenn looked up at him and smiled.

'Good,' he said mildly. 'The main mistake that people

252

make when they first drive an HGV is that they go far too slow. You're not making that mistake. But you're still struggling with the dimensions of the thing, aren't you?'

'Sorry, sir,' Billy said. 'I—'

Glenn held up his hand. 'You're doing fine. But it's not a squad car. It's an ocean liner. Whatever you ask it to do, please give it plenty of warning. Now let's go again.'

Billy nodded gamely and the truck took off, picking up speed as he headed for the far end of the landing strip. Glenn walked back towards us and exchanged a look with DCI Whitestone.

'Any other candidates?' Glenn said.

Whitestone indicated the truck roaring down the tarmac.

'Billy is it,' she said. Then she looked at me.

'It seems possible that old man Warboys was running a long firm at the Champagne Room,' I said. 'If that's the case, then it would have been in collusion with his late grandson, Steve Warboys, although I have no idea if they were partners or employer and employee.'

'Why the element of doubt?'

'It's also possible that it wasn't a long firm and that Steve Warboys was just lousy at business. The Champagne Room was mortgaged to the hilt and owed money to everyone. But it doesn't necessarily follow that all the debt was criminal activity. It could be incompetence. I met Steve. He was no businessman.'

Whitestone laughed grimly.

'But his grandfather invented the long firm,' she said. 'Sounds like Paul Warboys was topping up his pension. These old faces never change.'

'I still can't see him involved in people smuggling,' I said.

Whitestone looked at me with something like anger.

'Why not, Max? The Warboys brothers were the biggest pimps in London. That's what Paul and Danny *did*, Max. Not Reggie and Ronnie Kray. Not Charlie and Eddie Richardson. *Paul and Danny Warboys*. The Warboys brothers were into the flesh trade. And although the world gets all misty-eyed about these old celebrity gangsters, there was no romance in it. Not then, not now. The Warboys firm peddled girls in Soho and if the girls answered back or were too tired to work, then they lost their front teeth. So don't be fooled by this sweet old man.'

We were silent for a moment.

'So you want to bring in Paul Warboys?' I said.

'I want the old man watched. But I want to bring in this Chinaman for another interview.'

'But if you like Paul Warboys for this, then why are we sweating Keith Li? He gave us the lorry with the dead girls and the lorry with Lee Hill. Keith Li led us to them.'

'Exactly. We're being led around by the head of the Wo Shing Wo, Max. It stinks.'

I shook my head but said nothing.

At the far end of the landing strip, Billy was attempting to reverse but the rear wheels were up on the grass verge and struggling to gain traction on the icy ground.

Glenn began running towards him, waving his hands to stop but Billy kept his foot pressed down on the metal, his wheels screaming in protest, the ten-ton truck going nowhere.

I had a bad feeling about all this.

'Billy's not ready,' I said.

'He has five more days' intensive training with Glenn,' Whitestone said. 'He will be ready by the end of it.'

'I'm not talking about the driving. I know he can be taught to handle an HGV. I'm saying that he's not ready for an operation this dangerous.'

'Billy's no canteen cowboy. He's got a heart on him.'

'I'm not doubting the size of his heart. He's just too raw to go into that migrant camp alone. He hasn't got the miles on the clock.'

Whitestone turned to look at me. The low sun blazed on her glasses and I could not see her eyes. But her voice was full of ice.

'He's been in the field with you, hasn't he?'

'An Essex strip club? A language school on Oxford

Street?' I could feel my blood rising and I struggled to keep my voice under control. 'It's hardly the same thing as that camp in Dunkirk.'

I thought of Billy in the field. How easy it was for a couple of strippers to play him. How he tried to open the back of the lorry containing Lee Hill's body by chucking a brick at it.

And I felt sick to my stomach.

Whitestone and I watched the lorry at the far end of the runway in silence. Glenn was giving Billy a wide berth as he called out instructions and Billy slowly eased the giant truck off the icy grass.

'Billy's going to France,' Whitestone said quietly, and I exploded.

'The guy's used to sitting behind a desk in West End Central!'

'Don't raise your voice to me, Detective.'

'Ma'am,' I said, almost begging her now. 'These people operating out of Dunkirk, they have already murdered two men. They saw that Zlatko Draganov was going to be lifted and they turned him into roadkill. They knew — or maybe they just suspected — that Lee Hill had been turned by the law and they lynched him.' I remembered Troy's hideous face leering at me, warning me not to hang around because I looked too much like pig. 'If they have any suspicions at all that Billy is not what he claims to be, then they will kill him,' I said.

'They will never know he's a cop.'

'They'll know it the moment they look at him! Jesus Christ, doesn't that matter to you?'

'You want to know what matters to me?' We were shouting at each other now. 'Those twelve dead women in the back of a lorry in Chinatown. How many more women have to die, Max? Because if we don't nail these bastards, then I promise you it will happen again.'

My phone began to vibrate.

EDIE WREN CALLING, it said.

'We've got another lorryload of girls,' Edie said.

I felt my stomach fall away.

I remembered the touch of Hana Novak's icy hands as she reached out and touched my wrist, too cold to be of this world. I remembered the terrible stillness we had found in the back of the truck in Chinatown.

'And this time they're alive,' Edie said.

24

There was a small but growing crowd outside West End Central, kept back from the entrance by two uniformed officers, their placards bobbing in the grey light of Savile Row.

REFUGEES WELCOME HERE said some. NO MORE BORDERS said others. IMAGINE said one, and I expected to see that it was being held by a young man in dreadlocks with his face blackened by tattoos. But it was not Troy. The IMAGINE placard was held by an elderly gentleman with a wispy white beard and a sensible corduroy jacket and a lifetime of polite activism behind him.

I eased my way through the crowd, nodding at the two young uniforms, a young female PC – the Met no longer calls them WPCs – and an even younger black officer. It didn't seem like much in the way of crowd control but the protest seemed peaceful enough.

The women were on the top floor, spread out across Major Incident Rooms 1 and 2, all in their late teens and early twenties, all wrapped in blankets as they sipped hot drinks, and all quietly terrified as detectives and immigration officers moved among them with their questions.

'We found the lorry parked in a motorway layby just outside of Maidstone,' Edie told me. 'The driver ran out of petrol and did a runner. Left this lot to stew.'

'What road?'

'The M2 motorway. Northbound.'

'The road from Dover to London,' I said. 'Anything in the cab? Passports? Phones?'

'Not a sausage.'

'Have we talked to the women?'

'They're about to be shipped out. Immigration wants them to have a medical before we do any formal interviews.'

A woman with frizzy hair and an iPad blinked at me furiously behind her spectacles.

'These women are not criminals,' she said. 'They need health care, rest, fresh clothing—'

I wasn't going to argue with her. I wasn't going to point out that they might have information that could help us catch real criminals. I knew how it worked.

One of the women had the pale-skinned, dark-eyed look of Hana Novak. They were probably not even the same nationality but they could have been sisters. Nobody was talking to her. They had either processed her already or they hadn't got around to it yet. I walked over to her. She looked at me warily.

'What will happen to me?'

She had good English. I decided to tell her the truth.

'A big coach will come here soon and it will take you to a reception centre. From there you will go to some kind of accommodation that will either be a small hotel or house.' I looked around the room. 'It's likely that some of these women will be with you.'

I didn't tell her that the accommodation would be privately run and that it was in the interest of the private contractors to keep costs at rock bottom. I didn't tell her that she would be sent to one of the poorest areas in the country – the dumping grounds of the faraway towns, hundreds of miles from the big London houses of the politicians and the protestors down on Savile Row with their pious placards. I didn't tell her any of that.

Instead I got her a fresh cup of tea.

She sipped it and pulled a shocked face.

'What is this drink?'

'Tea,' I said. 'Boiled water, two sugars and a bag full of leaves. Is it all right?'

'Yes. Thank you. Am I in trouble?'

'You'll either be allowed to stay in this country, in which case you will have the same rights as everyone else, or you will be sent back to your country of origin. Where was that?'

She hesitated.

'Didn't you have a passport when you set off? Did someone take it away from you?'

She shook her head.

'We were told to destroy our papers when we reached Zagreb in Croatia. I did not want to destroy my papers. We were told we must.'

'That's because having no papers makes it easier to stay in this country. And easier to claim asylum. And easier to say that you come from a place where there is a war. Even if you don't.'

I waited.

'Tirana,' she said. 'My home is Tirana.'

'Albania,' I said. I held out my hand. 'I'm Max,' I said. 'May I know your name?'

The immigration officer was suddenly by my side, barking with fury.

'You do not have the right to interrogate this woman! You make me ashamed to be British!'

My hand was still there.

The young woman shook it.

'Aurora,' she said. 'My name is Aurora.'

'Nobody's going to hurt you in this country,' I said.

She nodded.

The women were filing out of the room.

'The coach is *waiting*,' bristled the woman from immigration who was ashamed to be British.

'And what did you do in Tirana, Aurora?' I said.

We both stood up. It was time to go. But we smiled at each other.

'I was a nurse,' she said.

A roar came up from the street. I went to the window and stood by Edie's side. As we looked down, a crowd of protestors surrounded a large white coach. A bottle bounced off the massive windscreen. A brick shattered it. I heard a cheer that chilled my blood. It was the sound of a mob that had just got its first scent of blood.

'Christ. Where did this lot come from?'

'There's a march in support of refugees from Hyde Park to Trafalgar Square,' Edie said. 'Some of them must have gone for a wander. I don't see any coppers down there.'

'There are only two of them,' I said.

We headed for the lifts, hit the call button a few times and then decided to take the stairs. They were full of our people running down to the street. Uniformed and plain clothes, all floors and all ranks.

Some of them had already made it out of the double glass doors that mark the entrance to West End Central but they had not got much further because the protestors were everywhere, swarming around the waiting coach and all over the nine stone steps that lead from our front door to the pavement. The steps are divided

by a metal railing and as the crowd surged for the coach
it buckled and collapsed, taking police and protestors
down with it.

And then I saw him.

Troy was forcing his way up the steps, his illustrated
features twisted with something like pleasure, steadily
elbowing his way through the mob as if he planned to
enter West End Central.

But that wasn't his target.

He had seen the two uniformed officers go down
among those that fell with the metal railing.

A gap suddenly appeared in the crowd, one of those
inexplicable gaps that are made for extreme violence, to
give it the room it needs, and I saw the young black
copper on his knees, holding a gash on his forehead,
uncertain of where he was or what had happened.

And I was hammering against the glass doors of West
End Central, pushing against the screaming tide of
humanity that pressed up against them, preventing me
from going anywhere, leaving me helpless to watch the
vicious kick to the face that put the young copper on his
back.

And then Troy was standing above him, the gap in
the crowd getting bigger, so that Troy could take a step
forward, his tattooed face seething with a pious fury and
his boot stamping on the young policeman's face, rising
and falling, again and again, the hate without end.

25

I watched from one of the loft's giant windows as Mrs Murphy came back from walking Stan and Dasher.

It wasn't easy.

Freed from the role he had trained so long and so hard for, Dasher had good-naturedly decided to do his own thing. And water was his thing; the filthier the better. The muddy puddles that surrounded Smithfield meat market were his favourite habitat and I watched as he eased his hefty two-year-old golden body into a muddy puddle as if it was a Jacuzzi. As Mrs Murphy did her best to persuade him to get out, the Labrador-Retriever grinned at her, his pink tongue lolling, and rolled around, just to make sure he was completely mucky.

Stan had the Cavalier King Charles Spaniel's allergy to water. He craved human contact as much as Dasher craved a muddy Jacuzzi. So while Mrs Murphy did her best to persuade Dasher to rise from the dirty water, Stan stood on his hind legs, scrabbling at her coat, bug eyes gleaming as he demanded her full and undivided attention. It was the dog walk from hell.

Dasher finally emerged from the puddle and began to furiously shake off the excess water as both Mrs Murphy and Stan recoiled with disgust. They had almost made it to our door when Stan spotted a pristine poodle on the far side of Charterhouse Street and attempted to throw himself into the oncoming traffic so that he could find true love, or at least have a sniff of it.

Mrs Murphy reeled him in, breathless with the trauma of it all.

As she struggled into our building with the wayward dogs under her feet, my face was hot with shame.

Every lone parent needs a network of support to help raise their child and Mrs Murphy was my network of one.

On too many nights, it was Mrs Murphy and not me who made sure that Scout was fed, read and put to bed. On too many mornings, it was Mrs Murphy who walked Scout to school. I could not imagine our lives without her hard work and kindness.

I knew she would do anything for our little family.

But two dogs were too much.

I walked Stan and Dasher to Smithfield ABC and let them off lead.

Stan made a beeline for Fred, a lifetime dog lover, knowing he was assured of a warm welcome. Dasher sniffed around the gym with shy good humour, a gleam in his eye and that irresistible Lab grin on his face.

Nesha was wiping down the weight machines. He held out the back of his hand and Dasher gave him a sniff, and then another. Nesha whispered to him in Serbian. Dasher acted as if he understood every word.

'Do you like dogs, Nesha?' I asked him.

'My grandfather had dogs to guard his cattle,' he said.

I thought about that for a bit as he scratched Dasher behind the ears. The kid had a reserve with the dog that I liked, as if he understood that the canine sense of decorum is at least as refined as any human's.

'I need someone to walk the dogs,' I said. 'I'll pay.'

'That's me,' he said.

Fred and I went out to the street to see the boy walk off with Stan and Dasher.

The big yellow dog and the small red dog trotted contentedly by his side as Nesha stared down at them, not talking too much because it is not necessary to talk to dogs when they are walking in their world of scent, but watching them carefully, walking with a loose lead, murmuring a few words when they stopped for a traffic light.

'How's he doing?' I asked Fred.

My trainer flashed his pirate's grin.

'Nesha's at that awkward age when you're not sure of the way forward,' said Fred. 'When you're lost and

wondering what you can do that the world might want.'
He gestured at the figures of the boy and dogs. 'Maybe
this is it,' Fred said. 'Maybe this is the thing he can do.'

We watched them until they were out of sight.

Then we went back inside Smithfield ABC, put on our
gloves and spent the next hour hitting the pads, the speedball, the heavy bag, the upper-cut bag and each other.

Seven days had gone by since the riot. It was all quiet
on Savile Row now. The famous old street was empty
apart from a young blonde woman waiting on the nine
stone steps of West End Central. She had a depleted
beauty that made you think that good looks are a finite
resource that can get used up just like anything else. It
took me a moment to recognise her from the Champagne Room. It took me another moment to realise that
she was waiting for me.

'Bianca,' I said.

She smiled at me as if this was all a beautiful
coincidence.

'Hello, Max. Do you have time for a coffee?'

We walked across to the Bar Italia and she told me
she would have what I was having. I ordered two triple
espressos.

I thought she wanted to tell me about the night the Champagne Room burned to the ground with Steve Warboys
inside it. But that wasn't what Bianca wanted.

'It's so good to see you,' she said.

I nodded. 'Were you at work the night the bar burned down?'

'Night off,' she said.

I stared at her, wondering if I believed her.

'Night off?'

'Horrible,' she said, shuddering. 'I'm at a bar in *Ilford* now.' She made Ilford sound as exotic as the Serengeti. 'But the manager is a pig.'

I shook my head. I still didn't understand. Then her fingertips reached out and touched my face.

And finally I understood.

I was not flattered.

I felt like a mark, like another man who walked into another bar where the girls get paid to make you feel like a bigger man than you really are.

'*Frumos*,' she sighed. 'You know that word in Romanian? *Frumos*, Max? It means handsome.'

I downed my triple espresso in one shot.

'I know another word in Romanian,' I said. '*Rahat*. You know that word, Bianca?'

She chuckled good-naturedly.

'*Rahat* means bullshit. Very funny! But it's not bullshit, Max. You're very *frumos*.' Her face grew serious. 'I wanted to see you because I'm not going back there to *Ilford*. They are not English gentlemen in Ilford.'

'I thought you might want to tell me something I don't

already know, Bianca. Steve Warboys died when the Champagne Room was torched. Whoever killed him is still walking the street. We believe they may be the people who brought in that lorryload of dead girls.'

'I *know*, Max.' She ran her fingers through wispy yellow hair that had been dyed cheaply too many times. There was a touch of the drama queen about Bianca. 'I know these things but I want to forget them. *Fires* and *dead women*.'

She touched my hand. I pulled it away. She looked hurt.

'But what did the other girls say about the fire? You must have talked. Did you hear anything? Steve Warboys had done time for burning down his own places for insurance money. Did you hear anything about that? That Warboys might have started the fire?'

'I heard nothing,' she said.

'Did you ever see a man at the Champagne Room whose face was covered with tattoos?'

I watched her mouth tighten with what looked like fear.

'I don't mean a black teardrop under one eye,' I said. 'I don't mean a dolphin on his neck. This guy – his name is Troy – has tattoos over every inch of skin on his face. Did you ever see him?'

She said nothing.

'You would know him if you saw him,' I said. 'It's kind of hard to mistake Troy for someone else.'

'Once,' she said. 'One night I saw such a man. Before

you came for the first time. The other girls told me to stay away from him. Because he likes to hurt people. It gives him pleasure, they said.'

'He talked to Warboys?'

She shrugged. 'They were in the VIP room. I stayed away from them. And then he was gone. He just disappeared.'

No, I thought.

Someone who does that to their face can never disappear.

After the riot in Savile Row, and the assault on the young uniformed officer, Troy's description was on every police Most Wanted list in the land.

How the hell do you hide an ugly mug like that?

By running off to Dunkirk, I thought.

And crawling back under your rock.

Bianca was smiling at me now, lowering her chin as she shyly peered up at me.

'I thought about you so much,' she said.

She placed her hand on my face and now I was embarrassed. They know me in the Bar Italia. I gently took her hand away.

'Bianca,' I said. 'If you've got nothing to tell me then what the hell are you doing here?'

'I want to *work* for you,' she said. 'I can do anything for you, Max. Clean. Cook.' She lowered her voice. 'Take care of you.'

I felt a stab of anger.

'I don't need you to do anything for me,' I said.

She looked crushed.

'But . . . you told me to come and see you.'

'I told you to come and see me if you had any information.'

'You told me to come and see you if you could *help*.'

Is that what I told her? Maybe it was.

'You don't need me,' she said.

I made my voice go hard.

'That's right, Bianca. I don't need you.'

'That's all right,' she said. 'Men say things they don't really mean all the time. I understand.'

My phone was vibrating with new messages. It was time to go.

'Aren't you going to finish your coffee?' I said.

'I don't like coffee,' she said.

We stood together for a moment outside the Bar Italia and I could feel her disappointment. Had I really given her the impression that I was interested in her as something more than an informant? All I had done was show her some respect and kindness in a place where there was none.

And perhaps that was enough.

'You have somebody else,' she said.

'I have an Irish lady who lives nearby who looks after my daughter, my dog and my home.'

I didn't even know why I was telling her this stuff. Somehow I felt I owed it to her.

'That's not what I mean. You know what I mean. You have somebody else.'

I laughed at the idea. But she wasn't laughing. She smiled sadly and I felt a flood of sympathy for her. She was trying to be a decent woman in a universe that was only interested in her when she was wearing a thong.

'Where will you go, Bianca?'

'Not Ilford!'

I held out my hand and she shook it, and that was when I saw the livid red marks on her wrists. Now she tried to take her hands away from me. But I would not let her.

'Are they cigarette burns, Bianca? Who did this to you?'

She pulled her hand away, shaking her head.

'No,' she said. 'No more white knights. No more pretending you will save me.'

'Bianca—'

'*No.*'

She turned up her collar and began walking north towards Soho Square. Already she looked like someone I had never met in my life. But then I had never seen her in daylight before.

I knew immediately.

I knew because MIR-1 was crowded with officers

from every department in West End Central and they all had that look on their face.

It could have been me.

Here was the reminder of the knowledge that every police officer lives with, the terrible knowledge we do our best to ignore – the awareness that you might not actually be going home at the end of your shift, but to a hospital bed or a stainless steel slab in the morgue.

So I knew, and I felt that knowledge as a physical knot of grief and rage inside me, as real as a tumour, and it was in my gut and growing as I pushed my way into MIR-1, pushing too hard so that some of them looked up angrily and then looked away quickly when they saw it was me.

And I knew because I saw that DCS Elizabeth Swire was there, the Chief Super from New Scotland Yard, that this was big enough and bad enough for her to clear her schedule and come over from Broadway to Savile Row, and she was going to say something because somebody always has to say a few words when one of us is killed.

But I knew already, I didn't need anyone's meaningful words, I knew even before I got to the workstation where Edie Wren covered her face in her hands and I touched her red hair at the back of her neck and she looked at me and shook her head, and I knew long before the woman standing next to her, DCI Pat Whitestone,

273

looked at me dry-eyed and impassive, her voice far calmer than I believed it had any right to be.

I knew everything already but she said the words anyway.

'We lost Billy,' DCI Whitestone said.

26

You could smell the sea.

I stood in the fast lane of the empty motorway and inhaled deeply, tasting the salty tang of it, sensing the wind on the open waves, feeling the sea but not seeing it or hearing it. The only sounds were the DO NOT CROSS tape flapping in the wind where Kent police had shut the road and the quiet voices of the CSIs as they worked around the lorry on the hard shoulder.

But the air was different here. I closed my eyes, breathing in, and I wondered if Billy Greene had smelled the closeness of the sea before they killed him.

A burly, white-haired sergeant from the Port of Dover Police had been given the job of briefing me. I was aware how hard it was for him.

'According to port records, TDC William Greene arrived in Dover on the ferry from Dunkirk, cleared customs just after 10 a.m. and must have been forced to stop before he got far on the motorway.' He hesitated. 'Were you close?'

I didn't know what to say. 'I feel like I watched him grow up.'

'So he was a friend?'

I nodded. 'Yes,' I said, my throat closing on the words, my eyes suddenly blurring with tears. 'Billy Greene was my friend.'

'Your friend put up quite a fight. He fought them all the way. But there must have been multiple assailants. And they knew he was coming.'

'How did you know to call West End Central? He wasn't carrying any ID on him.'

'Didn't you know? He has four numbers tattooed on his chest. Just above his heart.' The sergeant tapped his chest. 'Four plain, simple numbers. Nothing else.'

I almost smiled. 'His warrant number,' I said.

The sergeant nodded.

'Those four numbers wouldn't make any sense to most people,' he said. 'Unless you knew what a Metropolitan Police warrant number looks like. That was the only way we knew he was one of us.'

'Somebody else knew without ever seeing his warrant number,' I said.

I looked across at the lorry. The back doors were open and I could see the blaze of dazzling lights that make every crime scene look like a low-budget film set. As I watched, a body bag was eased out of the back doors, and the tenderness and care of the paramedics who had never known Billy Greene clawed at my heart.

'What was he like?' the sergeant said.

I remembered Billy Greene as a young uniformed officer, overwhelmed at the sight of his first murder victim. And I remembered him overcoming his fears, and his natural-born mildness of manner, and I remembered Billy putting himself in harm's way for total strangers. I remembered the scars on his hands.

I coughed, clearing my throat.

'He was all right,' I said. 'He was a good lad.'

I saw a car blazing blues-and-twos pull up at the perimeter. Pat Whitestone and Edie Wren got out. Edie held up a hand in salute but I looked away.

'I want to see him,' I told the sergeant.

He stared at me. This was not my investigation. I was not Billy's next of kin. The Port of Dover sergeant had every right to tell me to go away.

'Of course,' he said.

We walked towards the lorry, towards the convoy of squad cars that surrounded it with their almost festive blue lights, towards the body bag resting by the side of the road.

The other side of the motorway was still open, heavy traffic steaming south for the coast, not moving fast and slowing further with that ghoulish instinct to observe tragedy. Their hand-held devices covered many of the faces at the windows of the cars and the lorries, and I wondered what possible reason anyone could have to want to look at this scene ever again.

The sergeant nodded at the paramedics and something passed between them, giving me access to my friend without need of explanation, and I knelt by the bag and inhaled deeply, not tasting the sea any more, just the diesel fumes of the motorway and the dead winter fields beyond.

We don't call it a body bag. We call it an HRP – Human Remains Pouch – and although the movies like to show them as heavy black rubber jobs, the reality is different. The HRP that held Billy was white plastic with webbing handles and a black zip running the length of it, which I pulled down briskly before I had a chance to think about it too much and change my mind.

His face was marked with scuffs and bruising where he had fought for his life. There was a red mark around his neck, as vivid as a lynching, and I pulled the zip down to his chest so that I could see the four numbers tattooed above his heart for the first time and the last time. It still looked like him. It is the elderly that appear changed by death, and it is the sick that seem changed by death. The young dead – the dead robbed of the fifty more years of existence that they are owed – look unchanged, as if they have not yet finished with life.

There was a single knife wound just under the tattoo

of his warrant number. He fought them with everything, but death, when it came, would have come quickly.

I gently patted his face twice and zipped up the HRP.

When I stood, DCI Whitestone and Edie were there. Beyond the heads of Whitestone and Edie, I could see the traffic slowing down to look at Billy.

'They knew,' I said. 'They let him bring in another load, but they knew he was a cop. And they knew from the moment they first looked at him. The moment he drove into that camp. The moment they looked in his eye.'

'We don't know what happened to Billy,' Whitestone said, for once in her life sounding uncertain.

'I know he was nowhere near ready,' I said, the sadness stronger than the anger now. 'He had basic training to drive that lorry. He had no training at all at working undercover. Billy had never even worked as a Surveillance Officer.'

'He was our best bet,' Whitestone said.

'It was a suicide mission,' I said. 'But you can replace him, right? We can get another TDC in from Hendon. All these young kids are good with computers. No problem replacing Billy, right?'

'You're angry with me. I understand.'

'You don't understand a damn thing,' I said. '*Ma'am*. I'm angry with myself. I should have told him to walk away. From West End Central. From this madness.' I lifted my chin at DCI Whitestone. 'From you.'

'Billy would have ignored you,' she said.

'You should have sent me,' I said.

She exploded. 'Now you're talking like a child! They *know* you in that camp!'

She got a grip on herself and looked at the sergeant from the Port of Dover Police. 'Did they give him a phone? Did he have a burner on him?'

'If they did, they must have taken it with them on this side,' he said. He gestured at the fields beyond the motorway. A long dark line of officers from the Specialist Search Team were making their time-consuming way across the field, on their hands and knees on the frozen earth. 'But if your man ditched a burner before they took him, we'll find it.'

'Nothing in the back of the lorry?' Whitestone said.

I felt Edie touch my arm. It didn't change a thing.

'Only the usual,' the sergeant said. 'A bucket that was used for a toilet. Remains of food – some of it looks like it was bought back in the Balkans. So your man brought in a load, but they were long gone by the time we found the body. But I'll get my SIO to have a word with you, ma'am.'

The sergeant climbed into the back of the lorry. Whitestone and Edie watched the HRP being loaded into the ambulance. The traffic on the other side of the motorway had ground to a complete standstill. People were getting out of their cars. A crowd had gathered on the central reservation, phones held in front of their faces, bright white lights shining, collecting their souvenirs.

I began walking towards them, my fists clenched by my side, feeling my throat choke with rage and grief.

Here were the members of the public that Billy Greene had served. Here were the ordinary men and women that we are sworn to protect without fear or favour. Here were the good honest citizens who would call us in the middle of the night if someone was kicking down their front door.

I realised that I had wondered for a long time if they were worth it. And now I had my answer.

'Max?' Whitestone said, and began giving me instructions about liaising with the Port of Dover and Kent Police.

But I was not interested.

I kept walking towards the ghouls in the middle of the motorway.

I was done.

'You're early,' Mrs Murphy said. 'Everything all right?'

I was unsure of what to say, unsure how to explain it, unsure of what would happen next in my life. I felt I had lost my moorings, as though I had been cut adrift from the only thing that I was ever any good at.

Stan padded across the loft towards me, his tail

wagging his pleasure at my unscheduled appearance. I crouched down beside my dog and let my fingertips run through fur that was softer than silk. He looked at me with a love that I did not deserve.

'I just wanted to be home,' I said.

That was it. That was all. That was everything.

Mrs Murphy nodded.

'Best place for you,' she said. 'The policeman on the news down there in Kent – was that your colleague?'

I nodded, not looking at her, my hands on Stan. Dasher had been sleeping in Stan's basket and he stirred himself to greet me with his saucepot smile.

I pressed my face against the Labrador-Retriever's beautiful golden head. He grinned at me as if it was a wonderful life.

'A terrible thing,' Mrs Murphy said. 'I'll put the kettle on, shall I? Then I'll be off to pick up our Scout.'

'I'll come to the school with you,' I said.

Mrs Murphy looked at me steadily, as if understanding that something had changed.

Then she smiled.

'That would be grand,' she said. 'We've got time for a nice cup of tea. Sit yourself down.'

I could hear Mrs Murphy making the tea and Radio 2 turned on low coming from the kitchen. There was an old Luther Vandross song playing. 'Give Me the Reason'. It was strange to be home so early in the day. But it felt good and right. And it felt peaceful. That was the best thing of all. I had a glimpse of a different life.

What would I do now? I had seen that there were private security guards appearing all over London. Some of them had no qualifications beyond a shaven head and big boots, but some of them were serious men – ex-British Army Gurkhas, small and smooth-skinned Nepalese who never raised their voice but who would not be beaten in any physical confrontation unless they were killed. Maybe that was a road I could take. If I did not want to be a real cop any more, then someone might pay me to be a different kind of cop. Right now, I didn't care what I did.

I just knew that I had had enough.

But the police is what you know, a voice said. *And it's the only thing you know.*

Nesha buzzed up to walk the dogs and Mrs Murphy decided that Scout would approve if the whole gang of humans and dogs were waiting for her at the school gates.

So we all walked to the school, Nesha with both the dog leads, proudly demonstrating his dog-handling skills as we passed through the market and Stan and Dasher caught the scent of all that fresh meat, Mrs Murphy smiling to herself as she hummed that old Luther Vandross song. And I felt how far I had travelled from normal life, the life that carried on in all its decency and dignity while I stood on the hard shoulder of a taped-off motorway.

At the school gates there were parents chatting, people who saw each other every day while I was at work, and there were more fathers these days, and then a distant bell rang and the children were streaming out and home, and one face among them shone like the brightest star.

'Daddy!' Scout said.

We were not the most physical father and daughter. But she touched my arm and I smoothed Scout's shining bell of hair and it meant as much to me as any hug. We smiled shyly at each other.

'You got home from work *early*,' she noted, and she took my hand and did not let it go, not even when we waved off Nesha and the dogs as they headed to the park. Scout held my hand all the way back to the loft.

And when she finally let it go, my phone began to vibrate and I fought the urge to throw the damn thing out of the window.

GINGER GONZALEZ CALLING, it said.

Her voice was soft and low and urgent.

'The woman in the cab,' she said. 'Rabia Demir. The one who lived, Max. She's sitting in my office.'

PART THREE
The Girl in the Cab

27

The lights were coming on all over Chinatown.

I drove as close as I could get, the blues and twos flaring and screaming, all the city making way for me. I left the BMW X5 on Gerrard Place but it was only when I saw the shrine of dead flowers that I realised exactly where I was parked.

For a long moment I stood under the red-and-gold awning of the dim sum restaurant, staring at the flowers that marked the spot where we had found the lorry with twelve women who died and one woman who lived.

And then I ran.

I ran through the dawdling late afternoon crowds on Gerrard Street to the doorway by the duck restaurant halfway down and then up the ancient wooden staircase three steps at a time to the bright white room on the first floor.

The door to Sampaguita was closed.

Low voices were coming from inside.

I went in without knocking and stared at Ginger

Gonzalez and a man I didn't recognise. He was not yet thirty, a clean-cut City type, lean inside his good suit, the kind of man who goes to the gym for a serious cardio workout before he goes to move money around in one of the big glass towers. He looked privileged but not soft. It was a look you were seeing more and more. He was smiling at Ginger as he moved slowly towards the door, about to make his exit.

I was about to knock him to the ground when Ginger spoke.

'Max, this is Kris. Max is a colleague of mine, Kris.'

He held out his hand, smiling politely, and I had shaken it before I knew what I was doing.

'Good to meet you, Max.' He turned to Ginger. 'I'll call you later.'

As he left, I stared at her wildly.

'Where is she?' I said. 'Where's Rabia Demir?'

'She's gone, Max.'

'How can she be gone? Where did she go? Have you got a number, an address? Why the hell didn't you keep her here?'

'I'm sorry, I tried, but Kris showed and she got spooked.'

'How long ago?'

'Fifteen minutes.'

I went to the window and desperately looked down at the crowds.

Then I banged my fist hard against the wall and cursed.

'You don't know where she went, Ginger? You let her walk out just because some john from Deutsche Bank shows up?'

Her face clouded.

'Kris is *not* a client, OK?'

I looked at her for a moment, long enough to work it out.

'That guy's your boyfriend?'

'Yes.'

I let it sink in.

'And he doesn't know, does he? He doesn't know what you do here.' I looked at the sign on the frosted glass of the door, the words inverted. Sampaguita – Social Introduction Agency. 'Don't tell me he really thinks you're some kind of dating agency?'

'Men believe what they want to believe.'

I stared at the door as if the girl in the cab might walk back in. But then I knew Rabia Demir was putting as much distance as she could between herself and this room.

I pulled up a chair and stared at Ginger.

'I'm sorry, Max. I did my best to stall her.'

'Talk me through it,' I said.

'This young woman shows up uninvited. It happens maybe a few times every day. Looking for work. Word of mouth. She wouldn't tell me who talked to her about what I do here. She claimed she didn't remember. And I get that every day too. But I didn't realise it was *her*, Max. You have to believe me. She was different from the photographs.'

I called up the photos on my phone and slid it across the desk.

'How was she different?'

Ginger scrolled through the photographs of Rabia Demir and Mr Click-Click, shaking her head.

'She didn't have – I don't know – the *spark* she has in these pictures. She was blurry. As if she was on something.'

'What?'

'Something bad and strong. And everything about her was wrong. She had a tattoo on the inside of her right wrist. There.' She showed me. 'You know I don't like tattoos. My clients don't like tattoos.'

'Yeah, I know they're a really discerning bunch, your clients. What kind of tattoo, Ginger?'

'A bar code.'

I thought about the reasons why someone would get a bar code tattooed on their wrist.

I could not think of a good reason. I could not even think of a bad reason.

I leaned back in my seat and sighed.

'So you turned her down,' I said.

'I didn't get the chance. She lost her temper with me. She told me she knew I operated on a fifty-fifty split with my girls but she wanted a better deal. I also get one of those every day – the kind of girl who thinks she can do a bit better than everyone else. Little Miss Special. And then suddenly I knew who she was.'

'The prettiest girl in the village,' DCI Whitestone said.

Whitestone was standing in the doorway. She nodded at me as she came into the small white room, followed by Edie. I had sent them a text message on my drive to Chinatown telling them that Rabia Demir was waiting for us up at Sampaguita.

'So where is she?' Whitestone said, apparently not surprised to find Rabia Demir long gone.

'She scarpered,' I said.

Whitestone leaned against the wall and folded her arms, staring at Ginger with undisguised contempt.

Edie sat on the desk.

'You got an address?' she asked Ginger. 'A number? Anything?'

'I'm not police, OK?' Ginger said.

'No,' Whitestone. 'You're a pimp, Miss Gonzalez. And for the life of me I don't understand why we didn't bust you long ago.'

Ginger looked at me, pleading.

'There was no way I could get her to stay. I called

you as soon as I knew, Max. But when I got back, Kris had arrived and he was talking to her.' I saw her face flush with embarrassment. 'Kris thought she was my PA.'

'And who the hell is Kris?' Whitestone said. 'Another lonely heart?'

'Boyfriend,' I said.

Whitestone shook her head. 'And I bet he doesn't know what you do, does he?' She glanced at her watch. 'I bet he doesn't have a clue, does he? The poor sap! One born every minute. Not married, is he? That would be par for the whore-mongering course.'

'Why don't we continue this interview at West End Central?' Edie said, easing off the desk.

Ginger ignored them.

'Max,' she said. 'Rabia was angry with me. I showed her my standard contract. My usual terms and conditions.'

Whitestone laughed scornfully.

'I pay my taxes!' Ginger said. 'And so do my staff!'

'Your *staff*!' Whitestone said.

'But Rabia said she had already had an offer of work somewhere else. She was raving. And she kept telling me how much more they would appreciate her at this other place. And she kept repeating the same thing about why it was a much better place to work. *No papers. No papers.* In the middle of this stoned rant about why she would be better down the road. *No papers.*'

'No papers,' I said. 'Meaning that if she worked for you, there would be forms to sign and taxes to pay and work visas required. But not at this other place.'

'Because they use illegals,' Whitestone said.

We waited.

Whitestone was staring hard at Ginger.

'What can you do for me, Ginger?' she said.

'I think I know where she's working. Rabia mentioned a name at the other place.' She hesitated. 'And it was a name that I know.'

We are used to being lied to in our job. It happens constantly. People will say anything to escape whatever is coming for them. But I believed Ginger was telling the truth, even as Whitestone and Edie looked forward to the moment they shut her down.

'There's a woman,' Ginger said. 'Madam Theresa.'

Whitestone stirred at the name.

'Madam Theresa was a pimp in the old days,' she said, her eyes still on Ginger. 'Started out in the Sixties and Seventies. When the rich and famous were hanging out with the Krays and the Warboys. Prostitution in the golden age of social mobility. Madam Theresa was meant to be French or Belgian, the black sheep of some European aristocracy. They said Madam Theresa Defarge could get you *anything*. Have I got the right pimp?'

Ginger nodded briefly. 'That's the one.'

'But I thought Madam Theresa died years ago,' Whitestone said.

'She's alive and working again harder than ever,' Ginger said. 'She made a comeback and now she's operating out of that big luxury apartment block on the south side of the river. The circular one directly opposite Big Ben.'

'The Hopewell Centre,' I said.

'When was the last time you saw this Madam Theresa?' Edie said.

Ginger shook her head. 'Years ago.'

'And when was the last time you spoke to her?' Whitestone said.

We watched Ginger Gonzalez bite her lower lip.

Whitestone pushed herself off the wall.

She came and stood between me and Edie, her eyes boring into Ginger.

'Let me explain how it works now,' Whitestone said. 'You're either with us or you are against us. You either play it straight with us or we burn you to the ground. What you *can't* do is play both sides. Do you get it?'

'I get it. The last time I spoke to Madam Theresa was a few weeks ago.'

'What did she want?' Whitestone said, and then answered her own question. 'She wanted women, didn't she? Of course she did.'

Ginger nodded.

'And I declined. Because I don't like what's happening

294

up there. At this Hopewell Centre. They're getting through twenty new girls a week.'

'Twenty new girls a week?' Edie said.

'I know a knocking shop has a high turnover of staff,' Whitestone said. 'But twenty girls a week is ridiculous. What are they doing up there?'

'I don't want to know,' Ginger said.

'If they're getting through that many girls,' Edie said, 'then it's not even some high-end brothel. It's a slave market.'

'And how do *you* know this Madam Theresa?' I asked Ginger.

It was full disclosure now.

'I worked for her,' Ginger said. 'When I first came to this country.'

I shook my head.

'That's not the story you told me, is it?'

The story I had heard from Ginger was that she had met a rich man – a very rich man, Victor Gatling, a property developer they called the Man Who Built London, and after that relationship had come to a natural end, with the money she had put aside she set up her business, picking up men in the bars of five-star hotels and putting them in contact with her ever-changing stable of college-educated, tattoo-free girls.

I should have known it was all a bit too *Pretty Woman* to be true. I should have known that it was a far harder climb from arriving here with nothing to running her own Social Introduction Agency from a room in Chinatown.

The kindness of one old big shot wasn't going to be enough.

'Was Madam Theresa before or after Victor Gatling?' I said.

'Madam Theresa was before Victor. In fact, she introduced us.'

I shrugged, not understanding.

'But why didn't you tell me the truth?' I said.

'A woman doesn't tell a man everything,' Ginger said, unsmiling.

Whitestone and Edie laughed out loud.

'And is that all she wanted from you?' Whitestone said. 'Fresh meat? Nothing else?'

'And new business. She told me that she would welcome a handful of personally vetted, trusted clients, preferably men I have known for years.'

'Who's pulling the old girl's strings?' Edie said, still grinning. 'She didn't set herself up in the Hopewell Centre with her pension, did she?'

'I don't know who she's in business with,' Ginger said.

Whitestone went to the window and thought about it. When she turned away, she had made up her mind. For the first time, Ginger Gonzalez looked genuinely frightened.

'So do you think you can get someone in there, Ginger?' she said. 'Do you think you can get someone inside the Hopewell Centre?'

I looked at Edie Wren and she looked back at me.

She wasn't smiling now.

'A client or a working girl?' Ginger said.

Whitestone stared at me.

'Are you still holding the line, Max?'

I thought of Billy and what they had done to him.

I thought of Hana and the life they had stolen.

And I felt the anger flare.

'This must be the place that Hana and those other women were being taken,' I said. 'So yes – I'm holding the line.'

'Good,' Whitestone. 'Because I never know with you these days.'

'Don't worry about me,' I said. 'Ma'am.'

'Who do you want in there?' Ginger asked again. 'A man or a woman?'

Whitestone looked at Edie Wren and me.

'Both would be good,' she said.

28

I dialled the number that Ginger had given me for Madam Theresa, but it just kept on ringing.

I shook my head at Sergeant John Caine as he brewed our tea in Room 101 of New Scotland Yard, the last stop before you enter the Black Museum.

'Maybe she changes her number every week,' John suggested, placing a mug of steaming tea before me. 'They're wary of phones in that game. Change them all the time. More paranoid than drug dealers. How old is the number?'

'A few weeks.'

'A few weeks is a long time in prostitution.'

'This Madam Theresa gave it to Ginger when she was fishing for girls to run. And clients. Maybe she doesn't need either of them any more. Business sounds like it's booming. What do you know about her, John?'

'Back in the day, Madam Theresa Defarge ran the slickest sex operation in London. A-list clients. A-list girls. She took prostitution off the streets and put it into prime real estate at a time when everyone thought sex should be given away. She claimed there was no such thing as free love. They say she invented the term 'call girl'. Discreet. Expensive. Exclusive enough for big names. A real beauty in her time. One of those Carnaby Street dolly birds, all black mascara and a skirt that was hardly there. She was supposed to have had a baby with one of her clients. But nobody ever saw the child. And that was all a long time ago. She dropped off the radar around the millennium. I thought the old girl would be pushing up daisies by now.'

'Any pictures of her?'

'I can goggle her for you,' he said, peering into the screen of his elderly computer, glancing up to see me smiling. He had said it once as a genuine mistake – *'I'll goggle it, Max, shall I?'* – and now he said it whenever he wanted to lighten my mood.

There were two pictures of Theresa Defarge.

Both were taken in a photographer's studio.

One showed a poster girl of London in the Sixties, a brunette, all panda-eye make-up and match-thin limbs, reclining on white satin sheets in a white baby doll night-dress. Her look was coquettish, inviting. She could have been a model for Mary Quant. The other photograph showed a woman in her late sixties, her hair that careful shade of white gold, wearing high black heels and a tight black basque against a pitch-black background, perched on what appeared to be a chair with a swathe of black silk thrown over the top. The look was challenging, defiant.

I could not tell that it was the same woman.

'But why did she do the photo shoots?' I said.

'Some of these old-school madams always kidded themselves that they were in a branch of show business,' John said. 'I heard that some Hollywood producer promised to film her life story, no doubt when he was in his cups and with his trousers around his ankles. I guess it got stuck in – what do you call it? – development hell.'

I tried the number again, running through my lines.

But nobody answered.

I rang off and sipped my tea.

'And what happens if you get in?' John said.

'Get positive visual ID on Rabia Demir and call it in for immediate response. The heavy mob will kick the doors down and come in with guns. If Rabia is in there – and she's working – then it's a trafficking case, enough to bust everyone up there. Human Trafficking, Smuggling and Slavery, the CPS will call it. Enough to put someone away for fourteen years.'

I saw a look of real concern in his eyes.

'Better get your call in quick. There will be some serious muscle up there behind all the canapés and small talk.'

'They're trying to get Edie Wren in there as back-up. Undercover. A new girl on her first night on the job.'

He raised his eyebrows.

'Edie can take care of herself,' I said, with slightly more conviction than I felt. 'And we're going to be in and out.' I realised how much I valued his call. 'What's wrong, John? Do you think this sounds like a suicide mission?'

'Edie will be fine,' he said. 'She knows enough not to take anything, right? A lot of these places have got the women on flunitrazepam – you know, Rohypnol, the date rape drug. Roofies. No odour, no taste, no chance. Keeps them quiet, keeps them pliant – the poor little cows. Because I bet not every man who pays for sex at Madam Theresa's is a movie star. Not back then and not now.'

I thought about Edie up there alone and pushed the thought aside.

'You think this Madam Theresa is fronting for someone?' I said.

'Trafficking doesn't sound like her style. But who knows? Maybe she moved with the times. Maybe she lived longer than her money lasted. It happens with these old villains all the time.'

'She never got busted?'

'Not until now.'

I tried the number again.

But it just kept on ringing.

I stood outside Broadcasting House, where the BBC staff and their guests wait for their cabs, the perfect place to loiter as I watched the Langham Hotel on the other side of Portland Place.

A black cab pulled up and two young women got out. The taller of the two, a brunette in glasses, looked like a London businesswoman with her pink *FT* and iPad tucked under her arm.

Ginger Gonzalez.

And the other a woman was a slightly built redhead with make-up that made her face almost ghostly in the lights of the hotel. When her winter coat fell open you could see legs beneath a short skirt and leather boots that came up to the knee.

My mouth went dry.

Edie, I thought.

They went up the short flight of stone steps on the left side of the hotel that led to the Artesian Bar. I watched the main entrance and I watched the steps to the bar. But I saw no sign of anyone who looked even remotely like Madam Theresa. After what felt like a hundred years, Ginger came out of the main entrance alone.

The staff hailed her a black cab.

Moments later my phone vibrated with a message from Ginger.

She is in.

I realised my hands were shaking. I felt sick. Fighting back my panic, I called the number yet again.

But the phone just kept on ringing.

It took me ten minutes to walk to West End Central, where DCI Whitestone was on stage in the first-floor briefing room. Our boss, the Chief Super, Detective Chief Superintendent Elizabeth Squire, stood behind her.

On the screen behind them was a picture of the Hopewell Centre and a map of the neighbourhood it dominated.

There was standing-room only in the briefing room. Uniformed officers in shirtsleeves. Special Firearms Officers in their black kit. Some plain-clothes men and women from SC&O 10, the covert policing department of the Met, undercover agents. With luck, the penthouse suite would not know we were there until the doors were kicked in and they had a Remington pump-action shot-gun pointing at their faces.

'The premises are located on the fiftieth floor of the Hopewell Centre,' Whitestone said. 'The penthouse suite. We will – we hope – have two undercover officers inside the building – DC Wolfe and DC Wren, both of West End Central. They will both be in radio contact.' She paused and made sure she had their full attention. 'When they have positive visual ID they will release a Grade A response code. You will have a target time of eight minutes to get inside, establish our authority and secure the building.' Whitestone looked at the Chief Super. 'Ma'am?' she said.

DCS Swire stepped forward.

'Human trafficking is a blight on the modern world,' she began.

The Chief Super was a good speaker. She would make our people think that they were a part of history. But I could not concentrate on her words.

Edie, I thought, slipping outside the briefing room.

I remembered the words of John Caine in Room 101, New Scotland Yard.

She knows enough not to take anything, right?

I fought down my nausea.

I dialled the number again.

And this time someone answered.

29

'Mr Dempsey?'

I looked up from my still mineral water. In the hour before midnight, the lighting was subdued in the Artesian Bar of the Langham Hotel. The man smiled politely in the expensive twilight. In his dark suit and tie, and with his air of calm efficiency, you would have mistaken him for a hotel employee.

I glanced at my watch. He was exactly on time.

'I'm Dempsey,' I said.

'Your car is outside, sir.'

I paid my bill and followed him through the lobby. Guests were returning from the theatre and dinner, discreet security guards watched from the corners of the lobby, ensuring all was well.

They did not look twice at the man I followed through the revolving doors of the Langham's main entrance.

A black Mercedes Benz was waiting outside. The man from the bar brushed past the Langham doorman and held the back door open for me. As I settled myself in the car, the uniformed driver turned to offer me a silver tray with a hot towel. The man on the pavement waited until we pulled away, acknowledging our departure with a small bow. The driver asked me if I was happy with the temperature in the car, told me about the Wi-Fi that was available and then fell silent as London glided by like a series of old-fashioned postcards.

Broadcasting House. Marble Arch. Park Lane. Buckingham Palace. All lit up to inspire awe in the passer-by. At this time of night, it took just twenty minutes to the river. The Hopewell Centre soared fifty storeys high on the far side of the Thames, a circular tower of glass and money.

The driver murmured, 'Five minutes,' into his headset as we crossed Westminster Bridge. Then we were too close to the building to see it. The Mercedes eased down into the underground car park where another polite young man in a suit and tie was waiting with an iPad.

'Mr Dempsey? This way, sir.'

We walked to a line of lifts. There was one that exclusively served the penthouse. The man with the iPad stood back as I entered, holding the lift door for me, and then stepped inside and swiped a key card. I wondered how our people would access the top floor without a key card, and then I stopped thinking about it as the lift rose above ground level and suddenly all of London was spread out below. We rose above the city so quickly that I felt the pressure in my ears.

The man with the iPad smiled at me.

The lift gave a discreet ping and the door slid open at the end of a long, hushed hall. A wider, larger man was waiting at the far end of the corridor. He rang the doorbell to the penthouse suite as soon as he saw me coming.

'Enjoy your evening, sir,' said the man in the lift, and the doors closed silently behind me.

Madam Theresa was waiting in the doorway.

'Mr Dempsey! How kind of you to join us!'

She had loomed in my imagination as some kind of giant. The two photographs I had seen of her, taken fifty years apart, had given the impression of broad shoulders and endless legs, a woman who had success-fully carved a career from the desires of men. But as I felt her fingers dig into my arm, guiding me inside, I saw she was barely five feet tall.

Her face, once as beautiful as any face in London, was withered by the years but she beamed up at me with a smile so porcelain white it would have looked out of place on a twenty-year-old.

She led me into what felt like a Victorian drawing room, so strict was the segregation of men and women, so rigid was the old-world formality fifty floors above the city. A line of young women sat along one wall, talking quietly among themselves and waiting to be approached. Edie Wren was not among them, a fact that I noted with a mixture of relief and dread.

There was a small bar in one corner of the room, served by a bartender with a shaven head and a bow tie, and a handful of men in suits with no ties stood around, quietly conversing in their own language as they clutched their drinks and measured the women. Beyond the windows and far below, London glittered like a box of jewels emptied by some careless god.

'Sit with me,' Madam Theresa said. She took my hand. 'How's our mutual friend?'

'Ginger's very well.'

'Your first visit to us,' she said, and called a waiter with a slight turn of her head.

He held a tray with a silver bowl.

'Adam will take your drinks order and – if you don't mind – your telephone. We charge it for you while you're here. And of course the absence of phones ensures the total privacy of other guests.'

Her voice lilted with a French or Belgian accent, but deep beneath it I felt I could detect the eternal, undying vowels of a council estate in a small town somewhere in the north of England.

I placed my phone in the silver bowl, my face impassive.

The waiter took it away.

Now I saw that the main room led to a corridor with a line of other rooms. A door opened and a man emerged with a tall black woman walking two places behind him. I recognised him as a senior politician. He did not look our way as he left the penthouse with the woman walking behind him. The waiter brought my water.

'Mr Dempsey,' Madam Theresa said, more business-like now. 'May I explain how our establishment works?'

I nodded.

And I tried not to stare as Edie Wren came out of one of the rooms. Rabia Demir was with her.

She appeared to have trouble standing. Edie seemed to be supporting her.

Edie nodded briefly without looking at me.

Now, she was saying.

Tell them now.

Code A.

Do it, Max.

But I couldn't do it. Because I had just placed my phone on a silver tray and watched it being taken away.

'Do you know what a bar fine is?' Madam Theresa asked me.

I forced myself to look at her.

'It's a south-east Asian convention,' I said. 'A bar fine is the fee I pay to the house if I choose to leave with one of your employees. The bar fine compensates you for the loss of their employment for the evening.'

She clapped her hands and smiled.

'A man of the world!' she said. 'And of course, after the payment of the bar fine, any arrangement you make with the girl is up to you and her.' She leaned closer. 'But if you would like a more permanent arrangement, then we can discuss terms.'

Edie had taken her seat with Rabia Demir. A man from the bar approached them. It was almost as if he was asking for a dance. Edie shook her head and indicated Rabia, who appeared to be struggling to stay awake.

I again forced myself to look at Madam Theresa.

'What does a more permanent arrangement mean?' I said.

'We can discuss the details later. For the time being, let's just say that none of our girls have to be home by a certain time.' Her eyes narrowed with something like hunger and she leaned close enough for me to smell the Chanel. 'Can you imagine the possibilities, Jack?'

'I think you're implying that none of them are going to be missed,' I laughed, leaning back. 'Because they're all in this country illegally.'

'Sound good?'

'Just what I'm looking for.'

Another man walked across the room and approached Edie. She again shook her head and indicated Rabia Demir.

I saw now that a number of the women had the same long drink in their hand. One of them sniffed it delicately, as if aware that she was possibly holding a cocktail of fruit juice and Rohypnol. The women all looked scared. They all looked as if they were in deeper than they ever planned to be.

A door at the far end of the corridor opened and a man came out muttering angrily in Russian. It was the first raised voice that I had heard in the penthouse.

'Excuse me,' Madam Theresa said, and went over to attend to the man.

I looked at Edie, but she was totally focused on Rabia Demir. As Madam Theresa placated the Russian, a young Chinese woman in an elaborate white wedding dress came slowly out of the room he had just left. She leaned against the bar, ignored by everyone, as Madam Theresa called across a hard-faced blonde in a red dress. As I watched her deftly handle this minor crisis I glimpsed the experience of more than half a century in the whoring industry.

Madam Theresa came back to join me, only slightly flustered.

'No more fruit juice for Precious,' she told the waiter, indicating the Chinese girl.

'You use bar names,' I said, and she smiled. I looked at her face, thinking of the men she had been linked with. JFK and Reggie Kray and Errol Flynn. Everybody's dead, I thought, everybody except her, and I wondered which one of them was the father of her child. I nodded at the Chinese girl as she attempted to climb on to a barstool.

'Her name's not Precious,' I said. 'Not outside of the Hopewell Centre. But why do you use bar names if nobody knows they're here?'

'Convention. Call me old-fashioned.' I felt she was beginning to lose patience with me. As if I was asking too many questions. I wanted to get my phone back and bring down all hell on this old crone. 'Have you made your choice yet, Mr Dempsey?'

'I like her,' I said. 'Precious.'

'She's a new arrival. I'm not sure we're going to keep her on, to be honest. Why don't you try someone else?'

'I like her,' I said.

She narrowed her eyes and gave me that blazing white smile.

'Of course you do.'

Madam Theresa clapped her hands and it sounded as vicious as a slap.

The Chinese woman came over, moving as if she was in a dream, the wedding dress trailing behind her. Madam Theresa took her arm, and I saw the girl flinch with pain as the old woman shook her like a dog with a dying rat.

'If you upset anyone else tonight I am going to be

very cross with you, Precious,' she said, turning to me as if we had exhausted all of our small talk. She could have been a market trader losing patience with a dozy customer. 'Do you want a room or the bar fine?' she said sharply.

'Room. Let's see how we get on.'

We stood up just as a door opened down the corridor.

Bianca from the Champagne Room walked out with two Korean businessmen. The men went to the bar, laughing among themselves, while Bianca stood there smiling at me.

I felt my stomach fall away as she came over. I had stopped breathing.

'Max!' she said.

I stared at Bianca while Madam Theresa stared at me.

'I think you're mistaking Mr Dempsey for someone else,' she said, not taking her eyes off me. 'Don't stand around with your pretty mouth open, dear.' She clapped her hands again, an edict that must be immediately obeyed. 'Your friends are waiting.'

Bianca joined the two Koreans at the bar, glancing over her shoulder at me, smiling uncertainly. Precious was talking to herself in Chinese.

'Room four,' Madam Theresa told the waiter.

'Follow me, sir.'

I took Precious's hand. She stared at me as if noticing

I was there for the first time. Her long slim body leaned into me as we followed the waiter to the room. There was a splash of red wine on the wedding dress.

'Please, sir,' she said. 'I want to go home.'

The waiter opened the door and Precious lurched inside.

I followed her and somebody hit me from behind with a hammer. It cracked across the back of my neck, hard enough to buckle my legs with shock and pain but not accurate enough to put my lights out.

So they hit me again.

The hammer struck the back of my skull this time and my vision immediately exploded into a billion tiny lights. I was suddenly down on my knees without having any idea of how I got there, and the sickness that comes with excruciating pain was rising up inside me. When my vision cleared, I saw that I was in a room with a large shallow bath and a single bed. The bath was empty. Precious was on the bed, the wedding dress hiked up over her thighs.

And Troy was standing above me – Troy of Imagine, who I had last spoken to in the Grande-Synthe camp and who I had last seen stomping on the face of the young uniformed policeman during the riot outside West End Central.

His tattooed face split with a delighted grin.

'Good evening, Constable,' he said. 'We've been expecting you.'

A CCTV camera fluttered its black-and-white images high on the wall behind him. I could see the Mercedes and the man with the iPad. I did not even need Bianca to betray me. They had seen me coming all the way.

'Get his clothes off and hand me that hammer,' Troy said.

30

The dreadlocked goon that I recalled from the Grande-Synthe camp tore off my clothes and rolled me into the shallow bath where I settled on my back, the pain in my skull radiating out through every limb in my body.

Without water, and with Troy's grotesquely blackened face hovering above me, moving in and out of my blurred vision, the bath felt like a shallow grave.

Precious was moaning a request.

'Please, sir,' she said. 'I want to go home now.'

Troy gestured at her, the hammer already in his hand.

'Shut that bitch up while I do the pig,' he said.

The goon moved towards Precious on the bed and after that she was silent. I closed my eyes and fought down the bile in my throat. When I opened my eyes, Troy was kneeling above me, perched on the edge of the shallow tub. Behind him, high on the wall, the CCTV revealed dark figures pouring into the lift to the penthouse.

I wondered if they would reach us in time or if this

was the night that I died. I thought of Scout, and I thought of Edie. If Troy and the goon saw me coming, did they also know that Edie was here? No, I thought. So that was one good thing to cling to.

'How's the revolution going, you ugly freak?' I asked.

'You dumb bastard,' Troy told me. 'You have no idea what you're messing with, do you?'

He lightly tapped the head of the hammer against the bridge of my nose.

Then Madam Theresa was in the doorway, peering through reading glasses at something in her hand.

'DC Max Wolfe, West End Central,' she read from the card I had given Bianca. Then she threw it at Troy. 'He's a police officer!'

'Yes, you old witch,' Troy said, nodding towards the CCTV. 'We clocked him the moment he got out of that Merc. We were on to him when your flunkies were still holding the door for him and kissing his arse.'

'The boss is not going to like it!' Madam Theresa shouted, her accent growing less Boulevard du Montparnasse and more Bolton with every second.

'I'm dealing with it!' Troy screamed back at her.

I chanced a look up at the black-and-white CCTV screen. The Mercedes was still parked by the penthouse lift but there were no signs of life.

I closed my eyes again. They had to be on their way up. Troy raised his hammer.

'Not in here, you abomination!' Madam Theresa said.

Troy sighed.

'Where would you like me to do it, you mad old bat?' He waved the hammer at the bath. 'I do him in here. We chop him up. Hands off, head off, teeth out. Take him out with the rubbish. Get a few of your tarts to give this tub a good scrub and it's business as usual.'

She thought about it, clearly a bit happier.

'Well,' she said. 'Mind my tiles with that hammer.'

'So how does it work?' I said, wincing from the pain in the back of my skull. 'You find these women in the camps? Or does it start much earlier? Where does it begin? Belgrade or long before that?'

I thought of Rabia Demir, the prettiest girl in the village.

'Tell me how it works, you ugly bastard,' I said, reaching up and lunging at his throat, wanting to tear it out.

He easily swatted my hands away.

'No more words,' he said.

He lifted the hammer high above his head.

Then he brought the hammer down.

I rolled on my side and the hammer smashed into the tiles of the tub, splintering them with a metallic crack. I lashed out with the heel of my foot, connecting with nothing, and he adjusted his stance, bringing the hammer down again.

Pressed up hard against the side of the tub, there was

nowhere left to roll. So I covered my head with my arms and brought my knees up to my chest as the hammer came down again, banging hard against my left elbow, sending an electric shock through my arm, and coming down again, smashing the tiles by my right ear.

There was a fleck of white froth at the corner of Troy's mouth.

The dreadlocked goon was shouting his name.

Troy had missed something.

He had missed the sound of the front door being kicked down.

But now we heard them out there. It was very loud and just the other side of the door. Women were screaming and men were shouting, there were cries of fury and pain, the unmistakable sounds of breaking glass and breaking bones.

The door to the room opened and a heavy-set Chinese man in his forties suddenly stood there. He hit the dreadlocked goon across the face with his forearm and the goon went down with his lights out before he hit the ground.

Another Chinese man entered the room, this one twenty years younger, tall and lean, and he bent over the girl on the bed, talking to her in Cantonese, the tongue of Chinatown.

Then Keith Li was there, moving slowly into the room as if he had all the time in the world, taking it all in – the young woman in a wedding dress on the bed, the unconscious goon, Troy with his hammer and me cowering naked in the bath, spitting fragments of smashed tiles out of my mouth.

There was a moment when everything seemed to stop, and Troy and I stared at Keith Li, neither of us understanding what he was doing here.

'Did Edie call you in?' I said.

'Nobody calls me in,' he said.

The head of the Wo Shing Wo moved as casually as if he was taking a stroll down Gerrard Street on Spring Festival, so relaxed that at first I did not notice the machete he held by his side.

He looked more carefully at the young woman on the bed and I saw his body stiffen with anger at the bruising around one eye and the splatter of blood across the shoulder of the wedding dress.

He barked an order in Cantonese.

The two Chinese men seized Troy's arms, and I heard the hammer clatter between my feet.

Keith Li murmured some brief instructions. The younger Chinese man shoved Troy's left arm halfway up his back while the older one slammed down Troy's right arm as if it was a roast duck going on the chopping block.

Troy's fingers flexed and tensed by my face.

'Now wait a minute,' he said.

Keith Li lifted his machete and there was a moment of total stillness in the room as he brought it down on Troy's arm at its thinnest point, removing the hand and perhaps three inches of wrist from the arm where the radial artery rises close to the surface.

It is exactly where you take a pulse, looking for signs of life, and now a bright arterial spurt of blood announced the end of a life, and Troy's scream seemed more of shock than pain.

Then I was scrambling away from the severed hand that had fallen inside the tub, unable to breathe, so much blood still flowing, looking at Troy's body twitching on the floor with his final scream still ringing in my ears. Keith Li had the girl in the wedding dress in his arms. The other Chinese men were already leaving, the younger one dragging the dreadlocked goon by his feet, still groaning, and the older one hefting Troy's lifeless body and throwing it across one of his shoulders.

Keith Li followed them, whispering something to the girl in the wedding dress, until my voice called him back.

'Don't go,' I said, desperately pulling on my clothes. 'There are other people who need your help.'

Keith Li shook his head. He didn't even turn to look at me.

'I told you,' he said. 'We look after our own.' A pause. 'Now perhaps you will believe me.'

'Keith, please – there's a woman who needs help out there.'

But he was gone.

I was expecting to find a war zone in the drawing room. But beyond the front door hanging from its hinges and a frosting of broken glass over the thick carpet, the room was untouched apart from a chair that appeared to have been broken over someone's head.

But everyone was gone.

I searched the bedrooms.

They were all exactly like the room I had left, these bleak little sex cells with a large shallow bathtub and a single bed. Rooms to seal the deal. In the room at the very end of the corridor I found Edie Wren bending over Rabia Demir. She was not moving.

'I just called it in on the landline,' Edie said. 'But I think it's already too late.'

'What's wrong with her?'

'The women in here are on a diet of Rohypnol,' Edie said. 'But they're been experimenting with Rabia. She's on something more powerful than Roofies.'

'Fentanyl,' I said.

Edie nodded.

'And it's killing her, Max.'

Fentanyl is one hundred times more powerful than pure, pharmacy-grade heroin. Fifty times more powerful than morphine. It is a painkiller so powerful that it can kill you without you caring very much. It is often called the most powerful drug in the world.

'Where are our people?' I said.

'Someone jammed the penthouse lift. They're using the stairs.'

'Fifty floors? The stairs are not going to be fast enough.'

'I'm going to try to get the lift working. Stay with her, Max.'

Edie left the room and I sat on the bed with Rabia Demir. I took her hand and she half-opened her eyes. They were the darkest eyes I had ever seen. In the distance I could hear sirens but they seemed to be coming from another world.

She tried to speak and I took both her hands in mine.

'No need to talk,' I said.

But she wanted to talk. There were things she wanted to say. And even in the middle of the Fentanyl fog that was killing her, she was aware that there was not much time.

'I am not a bad woman.'

'I know that, Rabia.'

Her mouth moved.

'You know my name. Not the name they gave me here. My real name.'

'Because I looked for you. I have been looking for you for a long time.' I felt my eyes flood with useless tears. 'I'm sorry I did not find you sooner.'

'I never wanted this life.'

'I know.' I could hear Edie shouting on the telephone in the main room. Then everything was silence. Even the sirens seemed to have given up.

'What did you want, Rabia?' I said. 'Why did you come here?'

'I am a nurse,' she said proudly, and then she closed her eyes, and I held her hands long after she had gone.

31

This was the ritual.

The day after we shut down the penthouse, Edie Wren and I drove to a small terraced house in Tottenham where the mother and the fiancée of our colleague TDC Billy Greene were waiting for us.

Mrs Greene and Siobhan had prepared tea and lemon drizzle cake for our arrival. It sat untouched on a coffee table between us as Edie began to talk. The ritual demanded that Edie speak to the bereaved first because she had known the deceased the longest.

'I knew Billy from Hendon,' Edie said, the name our people always use for the Peel Centre, the training centre of the Metropolitan Police College. 'You meet people at Hendon who are not sure if this life is for them. But not Billy. Being a policeman was all he had ever wanted.'

Her eyes drifted from the mother and fiancée to the family photographs on the mantelpiece, settling on the grinning, gawky figure of PC Billy Greene with his arm around his mother on the day he graduated from Hendon.

'Then we were in uniform at New Scotland Yard,' she said. 'And then he followed me to Homicide and Serious Crime Command at West End Central, where we both trained to be detectives.'

Edie paused, lost for words, aware that all this was sounding more like a CV than a eulogy. She wrung her hands, and then stopped and looked at me.

I picked it up.

'Billy was still in uniform when I met him,' I said. 'And there were people who didn't think he would make it because he was kind and decent. But these were the things that made him a great policeman. He was the bravest young man I ever met. Not because he was never afraid but because he always did the right thing, no matter how scared he was. Every day of his working life, he brushed up against the worst of people – cruel, violent men with all their lies and greed. And he saw people who were hurt and scared, innocent people, good people. In most of us, that leaves a hardness, but not Billy. He was not lessened by it as most of us are. He remained himself.' I shook my head at Mrs Greene and Siobhan. 'And I don't know what else to tell you.'

'But you got them,' Mrs Greene said.

I remembered Madam Theresa when they dragged her out from behind the recycling bins in the basement of the Hopewell Centre. And I saw Troy twitching as his lifeblood ebbed from him on the floor of that room with the empty bath and the single bed. And I also recalled how they ran, all of them, the clients and the women and the hired hands, how they couldn't get away from the penthouse of the Hopewell Centre fast enough.

'Yes,' I said. 'And it wouldn't have happened without Billy.'

There was a fierce pride in the face of Mrs Greene. But the fiancée was still poleaxed by the loss of all their plans.

'I don't understand,' she said. 'I still don't understand why Billy died.'

'Billy lost his life helping us to smash a people-trafficking network that was run out of the Grand-Synthe refugee camp in Dunkirk,' I said. 'Illegally bringing vulnerable young women into this country to work in the sex industry.' I thought of Rabia Demir, full of a killer dose of Fentanyl. 'It is quite likely that murder charges will result from our investigation.'

She shook her head, as if my words were meaningless.

And they were.

Because I knew what she was really asking but I had no answer.

Was it worth it?

We had our tea and cake, and my left elbow throbbed

like a beating heart where Troy had hit me with his hammer and we were not in that room for more than thirty minutes for there is never much that can be said.

'Billy's fiancée – Siobhan – will meet someone else,' Edie said when we were back in the car.

'I hope so,' I said. 'What is she? Twenty-three? She should meet someone else, shouldn't she?'

'But that will make it hard for her to see Billy's mum. The new man will not understand if she wants to stay in touch with Mrs Greene. He – the new man – will see it as clinging on to the past and he is not going to like it. So she'll lose contact and the old lady will be left alone. That's what it will be like, isn't it?'

'But that's what is meant to happen, Edie,' I said. 'You are meant to meet someone else.'

But not Billy's mother, I thought. The world was not big enough to fill the gap in her life.

Edie cursed, and wiped at her eyes with the back of her hand. And then we did not talk about it for a while.

And that was part of the ritual, too.

After a short drive across North London we sat in my car, a box of Milk Tray opened on Edie's lap as she removed all the chocolates that would be too challenging for her grandmother's teeth.

'Doesn't look too bad, does it?' she said through a

mouthful of Hazelnut Swirl, showing me the box. There were three or four missing chocolates. I nodded approval, my mouth full of Apple Crunch.

'She's still got her Strawberry Temptation, Orange Truffle and Caramel Softy,' Edie said, closing the lid.

We ate our forbidden chocolates in silence and stared out across the gardens of the Golden Years retirement community, Finchley branch. It was set on one of those winding, leafy backgrounds that make parts of North London look almost rural.

The building itself was a small manor house built for some local big shot at the turn of the twentieth century, a city house that dreamed of the countryside. Beyond the net curtains of leaded windows, white-suited nurses drifted like angels. Another nurse in white was walking carefully along a sanded garden path with an elderly woman, arm in arm, both of them laughing. The nurse pulled the old lady's collar up against the chill.

'Lil's settled in?' I said.

Edie nodded and I could see her relief.

Lil had a corner room on the first floor. The room was tiny – all the rooms at Golden Years were designed for a largely sedentary single person – and Lil was sitting in the room's only chair while a Filipina nurse in a pristine white uniform changed her bedding. They were laughing together as we walked in and I was struck by the genuine and easy affection between the residents, who were mostly women, and the white-suited staff.

Edie presented her grandmother with the chocolates.

Lil made her selection, ignoring the missing chocolates, and grinned at us through a Strawberry Temptation.

'My favourite young couple,' she said, and I felt my face redden.

'Wow,' Edie said. 'Now the old girl's really gone batty, hasn't she?'

Lil swatted a playful hand at Edie's head and thrust the Milk Tray at her nurse.

'Maria?'

'No thank you, Mrs Wren,' Maria said, as she finished making up the bed and helped Lil back under the covers.

'*Salamat po*,' I told her and she nodded, smiling at my Tagalog.

Edie sat on the bed and took her grandmother's hand.

'Happy, Nan?' Edie said.

'Best place I ever lived, sweetheart,' Lil said, her mouth full of Orange Truffle.

We drove to New Scotland Yard and went up to the first floor where Sergeant John Caine was waiting for us. There were no visitors to the Crime Museum today.

There is a glass cabinet in Room 101 of New Scotland Yard, a modest display dedicated to police officers who have perished in the line of duty.

OUR MURDERED COLLEAGUES

More than a hundred years of faces. The images of the nineteenth century almost grey with age now. All of them are official portraits but some of the faces are dead serious, as if aware of what violent fate was waiting, and some of them grinning with genuine amusement. There were only men in the older pictures but then, from the middle of the last century the faces of the women officers start to appear. Some faces were still in the flush of youth and some in their middle years. Most of them were unknown to me but I had heard about some of them. A few had been my friends.

DCI Victor Mallory. Age 50. Stabbed.

DI Curtis Gane. Age 29. Died of injuries.

All those dead coppers. They were in plain clothes and in the uniform of the Metropolitan Police, most of them long forgotten but some of them so famous that their deaths had been front-page news.

WPC Yvonne Joyce Fletcher. 17 April 1984. Age 25. Shot.

PC Keith Henry Blakelock. 6 October 1985. Age 40. Stabbed.

Rank. Name. Age. And cause of death.

All those policemen and women, I thought. All those different ways for us to die.

Stabbed. Shot. Run over. Killed by a blow to the head. Rammed by vehicle being pursued. Bludgeoned during arrest.

And yet they were not infinite, these ways to kill us. The same causes of death came round again and again and again, and they were no different now than they were when Queen Victoria was on the throne.

Shot. Stabbed. Run over. Shot. Stabbed. Run over. Kicked in the head. Kicked in the head.

John went to put the kettle on as Edie and I stood by the glass cabinet and stared at all those names, our eyes always coming back to the latest one.

'He's in there,' John said. 'He's with the rest of them now.'

'Thanks, John.'

Trainee Detective Constable William Greene, it said. *Age 25. Stabbed.*

The first warrant number in the Metropolitan Police – number one – was issued in 1829 and the first police officer to die in the line of duty was one year later – PC Joseph Grantham, kicked in the head while attempting to arrest a drunken man in Somers Town.

Knocking on for two centuries of our dead.

We thought about Billy.

We remembered him.

It is always cool and dark inside the Crime Museum, and although its prime function is as a teaching aid, when it is deserted, it is a place that seems built for remembering.

We thought about the sacrifice our friend had made for people who would never meet him, and we thought about the dangers that he faced every time he went off to work, we thought about the mother and the woman who loved him.

We thought about ourselves and all the luck we had enjoyed so far.

We had our tea.

Then we went back to work.

And this was the ritual too.

32

'So how did it work?' Whitestone asked.

Edie and I stood outside the interview room in West End Central, watching on the CCTV feed. Madam Theresa sat with her elderly lawyer.

'She's aged twenty years overnight,' I said.

'Then that makes her one hundred and ten,' Edie said. 'Someone should have busted her years ago. She's never going to live long enough to make it to the Old Bailey.'

Madam Theresa's eyes narrowed at Edie as we walked into the interview room.

'You could have done very well with me,' the old woman said. 'Juicy little thing like you. *Petite rousse chaude!* Hot little redhead! You could have had a great career on your back.'

Edie leaned against the wall and folded her arms.

'Until I overdosed on Fentanyl during my tea break,' Edie said.

Madam Theresa looked from Edie to me and laughed bitterly.

'I should have seen the pair of you coming,' she said. 'Slipping in my dotage. Letting my guard down. Becoming too trusting.'

'Yes, you're just an old softy at heart,' Edie said.

I sat next to Whitestone, staring across the table at Madam Theresa. I did not think she would be dead before she came to trial. If anything, she seemed energised by her arrest, full of rage and poison for those who had put her in this room.

'It was that little Filipina whore in Chinatown, wasn't it?' Madam Theresa said. 'The things I did for her when she was fresh off the banana boat! And she ratted me out! Turning up her nose at me and then sending me a pair of undercover cops. That little *bitch*. What does she get in return? I bet you all look the other way in Chinatown, don't you?'

Whitestone rapped her knuckles on the table.

'Look at me, you old crone. You are under arrest. You do not have to say anything. But it may harm your defence if you do not mention when questioned something you later rely on in court. Anything you do say may be given in evidence. I want to show you something.'

Whitestone's hand slapped down hard on the table.

When she took it away, Billy Greene's warrant card was there.

'Pick it up,' Whitestone told her.

Madam Theresa glanced at her lawyer, as if this was

another trap, and then reluctantly picked up the warrant card.

'Look at that face,' Whitestone said.

'I never saw him before.'

'And his mother's never going to see him again. And his girlfriend is never going to see him again.' Whitestone was trembling with anger now. 'And the baby she's carrying is never going to see him.'

I looked at Edie.

She nodded.

I had been so wrapped up in the ritual that I had not noticed Billy's fiancée was pregnant. I felt something flinch inside me.

'That's the warrant card of Trainee Detective Constable William Greene,' Whitestone said.

'The policeman who died,' Madam Theresa said. 'The one who was driving the lorry.' She pushed the warrant card away. 'It had nothing to do with me.'

Whitestone clenched her fists. 'It's *all* to do with you! This reeking mountain of misery. I've got a lorryload of dead girls in Chinatown. I've got a knocking shop that is using up twenty women a week. What happened to them? I've got a young woman whose name was Rabia Demir – whatever grotesque pet name you gave her – who was killed by an overdose of Fentanyl.'

'Wait a minute,' Madam Theresa said, desperately looking at her brief.

'My client wishes to cooperate,' said the old lawyer.

'Good for her.'

'But she can't answer questions about activities that she had nothing to do with. This lorry in Chinatown – Madam Defarge is not a people trafficker!'

'No,' Whitestone said. 'She's just a done old pimp.'

I recognised Madam Theresa's brief as a criminal lawyer from way back. I thought he had retired years ago. And perhaps he had and Madam Theresa never upgraded to a newer model. A common mistake made by the ageing villain. Whitestone was running rings around him.

'So how did it work?' I said. 'Who set you up in the Hopewell Centre?'

She looked at her lawyer. He nodded.

'I was semi-retired,' Madam Theresa said. 'Conducting some minor business to pay the bills. Making introductions. Giving odd jobs to foreign students who needed to pay their rent. Young actresses who were resting. Models who were not quite tall enough or not quite skinny enough or not quite pretty enough or no longer quite young enough. And then I received an offer to set me up in a new establishment. Someone was bringing large numbers of young women into the country and there was a surplus. The Hopewell Centre was where we would put them to work in a high-end, big-ticket environment.'

'But why bring them in?' I said. 'Why go to all that risk?'

'Makes for a passive, pliant workforce,' Whitestone said. 'This old pimp's just like every other corporate employer in the world. She prefers her workers to be terrified of losing their jobs.'

I did not quite buy it. Running illegals across borders still seemed like a lot of heavy lifting for an upmarket knocking shop.

Unless it was far more than that.

'Who was your sponsor?' I said. 'Who set you up in business? Troy?'

Her face twisted with genuine loathing.

'That abomination? *Fils de pute!* That son of a whore was just a hired thug under the delusion he was some kind of revolutionary. I remember Paris in 1968 . . .'

'Spare us the detours down memory lane,' Edie said.

'I am so sorry about what happened to you,' Madam Theresa said to me. 'I have always abhorred violence.'

I felt my left elbow throbbing with the memory of that hammer coming down.

'No harm done,' I said. 'Why were you getting through so many girls a week? What happened to the ones that disappeared? You boasted to me about residencies – as if I could buy a woman. Not for an hour, or a night, but forever. As if they were there to be bought and sold.'

She waved a dismissive hand.

'That was just sales talk,' she said. 'Women come and go in this field. Ask your little whore from Manila. Ask anyone. They get sick of it! They get a better offer! Some man with a soft heart and a hard cock takes a shine to them! *That's* why there was a large turnover.'

Whitestone looked at me and I shook my head.

The old woman was lying through her pearly white teeth.

Whitestone placed an empty notebook and pen on the desk.

'I want to know who set you up in the Hopewell Centre or I am concluding this interview.'

'I never saw my sponsor,' Madam Theresa said. 'I never met him. I never spoke to him on the phone. It was all conducted by some kind of factotum. A driver, I believe. I would know the driver if I saw him, but not his boss.'

'Not good enough,' Edie laughed. 'Nowhere near good enough.'

Whitestone grinned. 'But maybe it's true. Maybe there's nothing more you can tell me. And then there's really nothing you can do for me.'

'I want to help you!'

'I've got you on trafficking, manslaughter and living on immoral earnings.' Whitestone nodded at me. 'And I've got you on the attempted murder of this detective.

And you want to cooperate? I am going to watch you die inside with or without your lousy cooperation.'

'I'll tell you everything I know,' Madam Theresa said, suddenly desperate. 'Troy. The Grande-Synthe camp. The lorry drivers.' I saw her hesitate. 'And what happened to the women who left. But on one condition.'

Whitestone chuckled. 'There are no conditions!'

'Then I'll tell you nothing.'

Whitestone smiled, shaking her head. 'Let's hear it.'

'I have a son,' Madam Theresa said. 'He has . . . problems. There's some money put aside. I don't want the money confiscated. I want it to go to him.'

Whitestone laughed out loud. 'Every old lag inside has children! Every low-life scum doing time has a son or a daughter who has to queue up to see Daddy or Mummy with all the other poor little sods whose parents got sent down! You should all think of those innocent little children before you buy the ticket.'

'My son is not a child. He's a man. And he's in a home.'

'A home?'

'My son is a long-term resident at Summerdale.'

'Summerdale is a psychiatric hospital,' I said. 'How long has he been there?'

'Always. Since he was a small boy. He has learning difficulties. And now he is a middle-aged man.'

'What's wrong with him?'

'In the Sixties they called him *backward*.' There was

a lifetime of bitterness in the word. 'They would have other names for it today. They would be more understanding today. But fifty years ago there was no understanding. Fifty years ago there was only fear and shame and contempt.'

Whitestone mockingly touched her heart.

'So you did it all for your son! A tart with a heart of gold – my favourite criminal cliché.' She headed for the door. 'I am concluding this interview.'

'I'm not asking for your sympathy,' Madam Theresa said, her voice rising. 'I will take what's coming to me. But there's a little money put aside. I want to make sure that my son is properly cared for. In return I will cooperate as fully as I possibly can.'

Whitestone laughed out loud, and I saw the chip of ice that had been in her heart ever since the night that someone ruined her son. Whitestone would have listened to Madam Theresa once, I thought. There was a time when she would not have so casually dismissed a villain begging in the name of their child. That time had gone.

Edie was shaking her head.

'You should have thought about all this before you set up shop in that penthouse,' she said.

Whitestone left. Edie followed her. But I stayed where I was as Madam Theresa reached across the table and once again I felt those long bony fingers digging into my arms.

'Please,' she said. 'I never wanted you hurt. I never wanted those girls hurt. I did not want them pumped full of those disgusting drugs. I never did these things in the past. Ask your friend. Ask Ginger. It was that abomination and his paymasters. My son is blameless. And I'm begging you not to punish him too.'

I felt my elbow throbbing with pain, pulsing and straining against my skin, as if that hammer was still coming down and connecting with fragile flesh, blood and bone.

I shivered. Her hand felt as if it was seizing me from beyond the grave. I shook it off.

'Why should I give a damn about your son?' I said.

'Because you are a parent too,' she said.

33

I had been home for an hour when someone rang our bell down on Charterhouse Street. There was a tiny black-and-white screen by the intercom and the sight of DCI Whitestone jolted me. I buzzed her up, expecting her to tell me that the only thing she wanted from Madam Theresa now was to see her burn. But there was something else on her mind.

'We want our dog back,' Whitestone said.

'His name is Dasher.'

'We want Dasher back.'

I felt like shutting the door in her face. She had not asked about Dasher once. He was our dog now. I have no sympathy for anyone who gives up a dog, whatever the reason. But then I thought about all the time and money that someone else had lavished on Dasher, and of all the tests he had to pass, and the serious task that he had been trained for and I could not find it in me to send her away.

This wasn't about Pat Whitestone. This was about her son.

'You better come in.'

Whitestone had never been to my home before. She walked into our loft and stood there staring at all that empty space. That's what everyone does when they see our place for the first time. A loft is like a cathedral. It is built to inspire awe.

'Dasher's being walked with our Stan. They'll not be long.'

She nodded, still adjusting to the cavernous room. Mrs Murphy was laying out Scout's school clothes and I introduced her to Whitestone, seeing her face fall as I told her why Whitestone was here.

Mrs Murphy blinked back the tears, briskly folding Scout's freshly ironed school clothes as Whitestone wandered over to the window, her gaze drawn to the left and the great white dome of St Paul's.

Scout came out of her room.

'Scout, thank you for looking after Dasher,' Whitestone said. 'I've come to take him home, if that's OK with you.'

Scout thought about it, weighing it all up.

'It's really hard to become a guide dog,' she said, looking at me for confirmation.

'That's right, Scout,' I said. 'Guide dogs have to be aware of their environment but not overwhelmed by it. They have to be sensitive without being timid. They have to be confident without being too wild. It takes a lot of people to train a guide dog.'

Whitestone nodded, attempting to smile.

Then she addressed Scout.

'Justin – my son, Scout, who you met when you came to our house – he had some problems adjusting to his new life.'

'He's blind,' Scout said.

'That's right. So for all sorts of reasons we couldn't take Dasher at first. But now we can. I hope you understand.'

'Dasher's going to live with you and Justin now?'

'If that's all right with you, Scout.'

'I better draw a picture of Dasher,' Scout said. 'To keep when he's gone.'

'I'm sorry, Scout,' Whitestone said. 'I know you'll be sad to see Dasher go.'

Scout nodded briefly, dry-eyed but subdued, and went off to her room to get started with her drawing.

'What's wrong with your arm?' Whitestone said.

After that night at the Hopewell Centre I had developed the habit of flexing my left arm. The elbow pulsated and throbbed as if it was a living thing, filled to bursting with blood. Moving it seemed to ease the pain. I did it without thinking about it.

'Just a knock.'

'What exactly happened in that penthouse before we arrived, Max?'

'You were late.'

'The lifts were out. The CCTV was out. We had to walk up fifty floors. Who was there before we arrived? Some crew were there before us. Edie says she didn't know them.'

'Madam Theresa must have got on the wrong side of the wrong people.'

'It looks that way. CSI found a severed hand up in one of the rooms. They've run the fingerprints of the hand through IDENT1 but it doesn't ring any bells. Ten million fingerprints on IDENT1 but not this character. So you didn't clock who the crew were?'

'Whoever they were – God bless them. They saved my life.'

'You're still angry,' Whitestone said.

'What makes you think that?'

'You're angry about Billy. You're angry about the dog.'

'*Dasher.*'

'Dasher. And you're angry about the Hopewell Centre.'

I could feel my left elbow throbbing with too much blood.

'And you're angry about Edie being undercover in there,' Whitestone said. 'You think I've taken too many chances.'

'You're meant to be on our side.'

'I am on your side! That's why I sent you and Edie in there – to watch over each other. That's what the pair of you do. That's what the two of you are so good at.'

I shook my head.

'Edie didn't need to be there. I could have done it alone. There were women dying in there.'

'Don't let your personal feelings get in the way of the job.'

'I don't know what you're talking about.'

Whitestone stared at me.

'I'm sorry about everything, Max. I'm sorry you think I put Edie in danger. But she's a tough woman and it's a dangerous job. This is what she signed up for.'

'What about Lee Hill? What did that poor bastard sign up for? He was a bent lorry driver, but that's all he was. He didn't sign up for the risks we take, did he?'

'I'm sorry about Lee Hill – he had earned some hard time but he didn't deserve to die. And – please believe me, Max – I'm sorry about Billy.'

'Billy was never a field man,' I said. 'That's what was so wrong about sending him to that camp. It was insane. Troy saw right through Billy – and through Lee Hill, too. Troy was shrewd enough to know what side they were on and he was enough of a cop-hating psychopath to kill them.' I flashed on Troy stamping on the face of the young black cop in the riot outside West End Central. Some of them do not worry about how big our gang is – they just want to bury us. 'Yes, I'm sorry about Lee Hill, too. But Billy – that just breaks my heart. He was out of his depth and it killed him.'

'Billy was never a canteen cowboy. How does anyone become a field man, Max? Not by sitting in West End Central. Billy was brave, tough, resourceful. I never dreamed he wouldn't make it back.'

'You asked too much of him.'

She nodded, all the defiance suddenly gone, her mouth flinching with some emotion that I couldn't read.

'And now I have to live with Billy's death for the rest of my life,' she said. 'And it cuts me up, too – in a way that it will never cut up you or Edie. Because Billy's death is my fault and I carry that weight to my grave. OK?'

And I felt that she was not asking for my understanding or forgiveness but just the recognition that she was the one who had to make the call, the one who had to make all the hard choices, and she had to do it again tomorrow and then try to sleep with all the damage done.

I nodded, giving her that, not envying her job, and some ice between us began to crack at last.

'OK,' I said. 'Here they come now.'

Nesha was crossing the street with the two dogs. They were a striking pair. Stan's fur was that deep burnished red colour that you only see in dogs and Dasher was pale yellow and gigantic at his side, with all the calm intelligence and quiet strength of his breed.

'I'll get Dasher's things,' I said. 'There's a blanket he likes. And an old tennis ball.'

'Max?'

'What?'

She turned back to the window.

'Thanks.'

Everyone said their goodbyes to Dasher.

When I was down on Charterhouse Street with White-stone and Dasher, I looked up and saw Scout, Mrs Murphy and Nesha solemnly watching us from the window while Dasher was happily oblivious, wearing his big Lab grin, ready for his next adventure.

I drove Whitestone and Dasher to the terraced house in Holloway that already looked like his new home.

There were fresh boxes of Nature's Menu Country Hunter food – 'seriously meaty' – in the tiny kitchen, a silver bowl full of water and a collection of brand-new balls, toys and chewing sticks. Dasher padded off to give it all a good sniff. But there was no sign of the boy.

'Justin wants to talk to you,' Whitestone said. 'If that's all right.'

Dasher padded behind me upstairs to the boy's bedroom. I don't know what I was expecting. Nothing good. But Justin was calling Dasher's name before we went inside and he got down on his knees to wrap his arms around the Lab.

Dasher responded with excited licks of Justin's face.

'Do you shave yet, Justin?' I said.

'Of course,' he said. 'Twice a week now.'

'Dasher loves aftershave balm. It's like ice cream to him.'

'I thought he might be annoyed with me,' Justin said, easing into his chair by his desk. He moved with more confidence than when I had last seen him. It had not become easy. It would never be easy. But it was not quite the struggle it had been. 'Because of when we met,' he said.

'Dogs are endlessly forgiving,' I said. 'My friend Fred always says that if he locked his wife and his dog in the boot of his car for four hours, when he went back only one of them would be pleased to see him.'

We laughed, the boy's fingers in Dasher's fur as the dog settled at his feet.

'You sound as if you like dogs more than people,' he said.

'Whatever you give Dasher, he'll give it back a hundred times over. You don't find many people like that, do you?'

His face grew serious.

'I wanted to ask you something,' he said. 'About your work.'

'Why don't you ask your mother?'

'Because she'll tell me what she thinks I want to hear. And I think you'll tell me the truth.'

So I sat on his bed and I waited. Dasher sighed and closed his eyes. Justin's hand soothed his head.

'After what happened, everything changed,' he said. 'I felt like the future I was expecting had been taken away. That caused all those feelings. Depression. Self-pity. I know it's pathetic.'

'It's not pathetic.'

'But I've had a chance to think now. And I know I want to be like you and my mum – I want to do what you do.'

I did not speak.

'I want to make a difference,' he said. 'And I wanted you to tell me honestly – is that just stupid?'

I shook my head.

'No, Justin, it's not stupid. The Met has thirteen thousand civilians working with thirty-one thousand officers. They're all sorts of people, with all sorts of skills. What happened to you – that doesn't have to stop you. But first you have to get out of this room and out of this house. It's always going to be hard, Justin. It's already going to be harder for you than I can imagine. But that's why Dasher is here.' I didn't know what else to tell him. I stood up. 'OK?'

'OK, Max. And thank you.'

I went downstairs leaving the sleeping Dasher with him.

'Your son thinks we make a difference,' I told Whitestone.

'And you don't,' she said. 'Because you went to see

Billy's family and now you wonder if it's worth it. But we all wonder if it's worth it, Max. You have to stop thinking that makes you a bad policeman. It doesn't. It makes you human.' She gestured at my arm. 'Let me see that elbow.'

'It's all right,' I said.

She gestured impatiently. I rolled up the sleeve of my shirt.

My left arm was a mass of black and purple bruising from my bicep to my wrist. The point of my elbow had swollen up to the size of a ripe apple.

'Olecranon bursitis,' Whitestone said, prodding it. 'There's a little sac of fluid around the joints. The bursa. It helps movement. But it fills with blood if it has a trauma. That's what has happened here. It needs to be drained.'

She came back from the kitchen with a first-aid box, took out a disposable hypodermic needle and eased it into the livid red lump that was now my elbow.

'You think I've become a heartless old cow,' she said, as we both watched the needle fill with blood that was closer to black than red. The lump on the tip of my elbow began to shrink.

'That's a bit harsh,' I said. 'You're not that old.'

'And you're right, Max. I am changed from the woman I used to be. And the woman I wanted to be. And it's not because of what happened to Justin. It's not

352

because of what some mindless little thug did to him in some bar. It starts long before then. It starts when his father left us. I always thought that being a single parent would make me a better person. All that sacrifice and caring for someone who depends on you for everything. But it didn't make me a better person. It made me harder. I find I care less about the outside world. Sometimes all my compassion is reserved for my child. Maybe that's what's wrong with me. Do you know what I mean?'

Of course I knew what she meant.

I watched her dispose of the blood-gorged syringe.

'You need to walk Dasher,' I said. 'That'll cheer you up.'

I stayed to watch them prepare for that very first walk. I watched them put Dasher into his bright yellow harness with its blue Guide Dogs logo. I watched them double- and triple-checking that the lead was correctly attached to the collar, and that they had enough poo bags, hand wipes and dog treats for twenty walks. And I smiled because all those preparations would become second nature before they knew it. Then they stepped out into the quiet street, bound for the open pastures of Highbury Fields, Whitestone and Justin talking nervously as Dasher wore his reassuring grin between them.

By the end of the street, I could hear their laughter and I could see the spring in their step.

Dogs can break your heart. But they can heal it too.

Then I drove across town and picked up the motorway at Brent Cross, flexing my left arm as I followed the GPS to Summerdale Psychiatric Hospital.

It was feeling better already.

'Summerdale is increasingly focused on promoting mental health rather than simply responding to mental illness,' the hospital's Director of Nursing told me. She was a tall woman nearing the end of her career, and in her classless accent I could detect just a hint of Australia, the country she had left a lifetime ago. 'We want people to get well and stay well,' she said. 'We believe change is possible. But we also provide mental health care for long-term residents. Like Tommy Defarge.'

I looked out across the grounds. It could have been a private school, or a country hotel.

'So in the past, people would come here and stay here,' I said. 'But now they receive care and then they leave. Is that about right?'

She nodded.

'But the young man you're interested in – no longer so young, but then neither am I – is one of our long-term residents. You have to understand, Detective, that there was a stigma about mental health when Tommy Defarge was born.'

'He's never going to get better?'

'He doesn't have a disease. He has a condition. A life-long developmental disability.'

'Is he autistic?'

'He has AS – Asperger's Syndrome. It's on the autism spectrum. Tommy doesn't have problems with learning, or speech, but he has difficulty with social interactions, and understanding, and processing language. We know far more about AS now than we did when Tommy was born. He is a lovely man but he will be with us for the rest of his days. The fear his mother has – that he will be abandoned – is simply not going to happen. She has the understandable concerns of an ageing parent who wants to protect her vulnerable son. But we will take care of Tommy as long as he needs us. And he will need us forever. There he is now.'

Tommy Defarge, who must have been in his late for-ties, looked like a large boy, with a shock of fair hair and dressed in clothes that someone else had chosen for him. He moved slowly, holding the arm of the man who accompanied him.

'Who's that with him?' I said. 'That's not a nurse, is it?'

'That's his father,' she said.

And I saw it was Paul Warboys.

I walked across the grounds towards them.

Paul Warboys saw me coming, and watched my face as I stared at Tommy.

This close, Tommy was clearly not a boy but a man in his middle years. Yet he had a sly, youthful grin.

'Tommy?' Warboys said. 'This is Max.'

'Hello, Tommy.'

He hugged me in his powerful arms. I hugged him back, and then gently broke free of his strong embrace.

Then I looked at Paul Warboys.

'Fancy seeing you here,' he said.

And I felt that finally I saw the truth.

'So you've been topping up your pension plan, Paul. How could I have missed it? Madam Theresa was done. Finished. Retired from the game years ago. But she came out of retirement because someone had a job for her. And who better to bankroll her comeback than the father of her son?'

He laughed at me.

Tommy chuckled along with him.

'No,' said Paul Warboys. 'It was never business with me and Theresa. Not back in the day when this one here was born. And not now. Do you think I was ever interested in her because I thought I could make a few quid? Theresa wasn't always an old lady, Max. She was *beautiful*. They were all over her back in the day. Sniffing around. All those big names. Film stars, Max. Politicians.'

'I've heard all the names.'

'And she chose me,' he said, and half a century on his voice was still full of pride. 'A rough boy from Hammersmith.'

'A married man from Hammersmith,' I said. 'Your son – your other son, Barry – told me that you betrayed his mother and that's what the real problem is between the pair of you. Not that Barry wouldn't go into the family business. Not that he was too soft for your taste. Not that he was too straight for his dear old dad. And not even that you took one look at the dolly birds of Swinging London and decided that you wanted some of the action. Tommy,' I said, and the boy-man grinned at me, raising his eyebrows at the sound of his name. 'Tommy is the reason that Barry hates you.' And a deeper truth now seemed obvious to me. 'But Barry doesn't hate you just because Tommy was born,' I said. 'Barry hates you because you love him.'

There were tears in the old gangster's eyes but his mouth was twisted with violence. Not for the first time, I wondered what would happen if the pair of us went one on one. I would not fancy my chances unless I got in first.

'But I was never a pimp, Max. That's where you've got it all wrong, son. And I told you once before – if I wanted an extra couple of quid, I wouldn't stick a bunch of poor little cows in the back of a lorry.'

'I don't believe you.'

'I don't care what you believe. You know what I believe? I think you wanted my scalp all along.'

I turned away.

'I'll let you spend time with your son,' I said. 'But settle your affairs, Paul. Because I'm coming for you.'

34

We smashed down his door at dawn.

The time of pliant suspects in their pants, pulled from REM sleep with slow reflexes and the vulnerability that comes with all that naked flesh.

But Paul Warboys stood fully clothed in the narrow hallway of his docklands flat with a black sap in his hand.

Waiting for us.

'Come on, you cow sons,' he said, and it struck me that he still spoke the lost language of old London – only the oldest faces still said *cow sons* – and that some words die with their generation.

Then he brought the sap down on the head of the leading copper.

He was a big uniformed sergeant, one of mother nature's rugby players, as brave as they come, but he went down like a snowflake, his legs giving way the moment we heard the dull *thwaaack* of leather-clad lead on the thin crust of bone that covers the skull, out stone-cold before he hit the deck.

It was as narrow as Thermopylae in that hallway and Paul Warboys, a student of military history, was the Spartans. He was outnumbered and outgunned but fighting on ground that he had chosen. He had also chosen his weapon well. Civilians think that they can protect their homes and their family with a baseball bat. But you can't swing a baseball bat in a confined space. The baseball bat is not a close quarters weapon.

You can swing a sap in a telephone booth.

'Come on, come on,' he said.

We had made the mistake of sending the uniforms in as our vanguard, half a dozen officers pouring past the shattered door the moment the scarred red battering ram brought it down. They all had their batons drawn but somehow the old gangster had the element of surprise. The sap came down again and again, delivering massive impact with minimum applied force.

Warboys grinned at me above the heads of the fallen officers.

I threw myself at him, seizing him in a bear hug, pinning his arms to his side before he had a chance to open my head with that sap. We slammed hard against one side of the hallway and then the other, glass breaking as we collided with a watercolour of the Thames, and I could smell his sweat and aftershave and I suddenly knew that he had been waiting for us all night long.

He cursed me, straining against the bear hug, he tried to sink his teeth into my ear.

Behind us, I could hear the cries of pain and threat.

'You old bastard,' I said into the side of his face, feeling his strength as he raged against me, my arms losing their grip. 'If you're an innocent man then why are you fighting?'

He laughed out loud.

'Because you're in my home,' he said.

Then he threw me off and, as I bounced off the wall, aimed the black leather sap at the bridge of my nose.

I stumbled backwards, fell over a uniformed officer who was on his knees and felt the stubby black weapon slap hard against my bicep. In the broken doorway I could see the grey Kevlar body armour of the Authorised Firearms Officers, struggling to get inside, stepping over the fallen bodies.

I rolled away, a dull ache in the thick meat at the top of my arm, and Warboys raised the sap again as the AFOs came into the flat, only their eyes showing above their face masks and below their helmets, screaming their warnings – 'Drop the weapon now! Drop the weapon now!' – as they edged around the fallen officers, their assault rifles all aimed at the chest of Paul Warboys.

He charged at them, the leather sap raised above his head, still shouting about cow sons. The armed officers all carried a Sig Sauer MCX, the Black Mamba, a short, superlight firearm perfect for use in confined spaces. It is a weapon favoured by American Special Forces, although the ones the Met use are configured not to fire on semi-automatic, meaning that the ones levelled at Paul Warboys fired just one round for every trigger pull because the Met makes its officers justify every use of deadly force. That's why every AFO could be a highly trained armed officer at breakfast and the object of a murder investigation by lunch.

I braced for the explosion of gunfire, the sound that is always so much louder than you ever expect, steeling myself for all the noise and fear and mess of 5.56 rounds passing through fragile flesh and blood and bone.

But they did not fire.

Warboys threw himself into them, the sap rising and falling, but now striking the lightweight body armour that the AFOs wore under all that grey Kevlar.

One of them, a woman, stuck a reinforced elbow into Warboys' throat. He reeled backwards and she bounced the butt of her assault rifle off his chin. He stared at her with his watery blue eyes wide with shock, the sap now held loosely at his side.

She did it again and he went down.

Then they were stepping over his prone body, someone kicking the leather sap down the hall, and they were pouring into the small flat, clearing each room one by one, but the only sound was the noise our people made.

I looked for the great sloping head of Bullseye, his beloved English Bull Terrier, but Paul Warboys was a responsible dog owner, and his pet was already gone, and no doubt missing his master in some new loving home.

I picked up the black leather sap. It was a good one – eight inches long, flat, beaver-tailed black leather, weighted with lead at either end, with what felt like a semi-flexible steel spring running down the weapon's spine.

I walked into the living room, stunned again by that view of the Thames, a light flurry of rain coming down on the river as the sun glittered behind the glass towers of Docklands. The flat still didn't feel like a real home, despite the evidence of Warboys that was all around – the Otis Redding and Tamla Motown vinyl, the *World at War* boxed set on top of the home cinema, the framed photographs of his late wife.

No photographs of Tommy.

No photographs of Madam Theresa.

But then I guess you can love someone without putting their picture on your wall.

Someone shouted with joy in the tiny kitchen.

A uniformed officer held a box of Weetabix upside down and shook out red rolls of fifty-pound notes bound tight with elastic bands. There were more bundles of fifties in the tea, the sugar, in every corner we looked. A Specialist Search Team would do a search of the property that would take up floorboards, look in the ceiling and punch holes in the walls. But it felt like we hardly needed them.

Everywhere we looked, we found those neat rolls of fifties, and the smiling face of the Queen.

As they dragged Paul Warboys away I felt the weight of the sap in my hand, enjoying the slap of it on my palm, and I watched the sun rise above the river where his father had worked on the docks.

They called me when he was out of the hospital and tucked up in the holding cell.

Paul Warboys sat on the washable plastic bed in that cream-coloured room as if it was familiar territory. But he looked beyond tired, and it was more than waiting up all night for us to kick down his door, it was more than going a few rounds with coppers who were half a lifetime younger than him, and it was more than the concussion he got from the butt of the AFO's assault rifle.

The old gangster looked as though he was at the end of everything.

'I thought you were above living on immoral earnings, Paul. You know how much cash we found in your little flat?'

'It's not what you think. It's not from Theresa.'

I waited.

'It's from London property, Max. The reserve currency of the world. Better than gold. The money you found is rent money. Cash in hand, saves on the paperwork. That's where my dosh comes from – *my tenants*. Everyone wants to live here but there are only so many houses, only so many flats. I've been buying property all over town for donkey's years.'

Donkey's years. There was another one that would die with him and his generation.

'How did it work?' I said. 'Who recruits the women you brought in?'

He exhaled with frustration.

'I don't know what you're talking about.'

'Did you approach Imagine or did they come to you?'

'What's Imagine when it's at home?'

'Imagine are a bunch of British anarchists in the refugee camps of northern France. They don't believe in borders. They've been facilitating the people smuggling out of Dunkirk.'

He shook his head.

'Nothing to do with me. I could never stand hippies.'

I leaned across the desk. 'Your old flame was getting through twenty girls a week up at the Hopewell Centre. What happened to the women who went missing?'

He stared at me with his pale blue eyes.

'I don't know what they're doing up there in the penthouse,' he said.

I turned away. His voice stopped me at the door.

'You want the truth, Max?'

I stared at him. People will say anything. That's the first thing you learn. People will say anything to save their skin.

I waited.

'The truth is that I met a girl,' he said. 'And she stole my heart. Corny but true. Happens to the best of us and the worst of us. And she stole it even though I was a young married man with children. And she stole it even though I knew she had done bad things for money. We fitted together – I'm not good with words. Never had any education. So maybe that's the best I can do. We just *fitted*, Max. She was the best fit that I ever knew. And I thought about starting over. We talked about it. And she got pregnant and that just made it even better. But when the baby was born it all went wrong. And the baby – this beautiful little baby – there was something wrong with him that we couldn't understand and we couldn't deal with. So we locked him away and I think the shame of it killed us. We didn't *deserve* to be happy any more, see? Theresa and I haven't had any contact for years. For half a lifetime. We're *strangers*, Max. You can understand that, can't you? How you can

366

love someone and then they become a stranger? You had a wife once, didn't you? Now you tell me – do you feel like you still know her? Or does she feel like a total stranger, Max?'

I banged on the door of the holding cell.

'I'll see you in the interview room,' I said. 'But we will not be talking about the good old days, Paul. We'll be talking about lorries full of women left to freeze to death in Chinatown. And we'll be talking about the slave market you ran in that penthouse.'

He sighed and shook his head.

'All right, you cow son,' he said. 'Give me a pen and paper. I'll write it all down for you. Make it nice and easy. What you want to know about, Max? People trafficking? Prostitution? What are those hippies called – Imagine? I'll give you the lot if you give me pen and paper. Where the women came from. Who finds the drivers. Who gets paid at the border. Who gets paid all the way down the line. Is that what you want, Max?'

There was no pen and paper in the holding cell. I borrowed a yellow legal pad and green Ball Pentel from the duty sergeant on the desk outside and brought them back to Paul Warboys. Then I left him alone.

My phone began to vibrate as I was on my way up to MIR-1. I recognised the faint Australian accent of the Director of Nursing from Summerdale Psychiatric Hospital.

'DC Wolfe?' she said. 'I thought you would want to know.' I heard her take a breath. 'Tommy Defarge died at some point during the night.'

'What?'

'We will be conducting a full investigation, but the bottle we found in his room indicated that he had somehow obtained Fentanyl. He just slipped away. He wouldn't have felt a thing.'

She was still talking about how difficult it is for patients to get their hands on prescription drugs at Summerdale and how there would have to be a full investigation but I was already running down the basement corridor screaming for the duty sergeant to unlock the holding cell containing Paul Warboys.

As he struggled with the keys I looked through the small window in the door and I saw the arterial spurt that had sprayed the cream-coloured tiles.

Then as the door to the holding cell swung open there was the body of Paul Warboys, a heavy flow of blood pulsing from the hole he had punched in his jugular and, still in his lifeless fist, the pen he had used to gouge, tear and finally open up the veins of his neck.

35

Chinatown is underground.

The world flocks to the restaurants, medical centres and massage parlours of Gerrard Street, Lisle Street and Shaftesbury Avenue, but there is another Chinatown below the city streets, in basements and cellars down a narrow flight of stairs, and it has existed since the city's first Chinatown, Limehouse in the East End docks, was obliterated by the Luftwaffe.

It was down one of these unmarked flights of stairs, halfway down Gerrard Street, that I found Keith Li.

He was playing Mahjong in a low-ceilinged basement so huge that it must have stretched from Gerrard Street to Leicester Square. There were dozens of small square tables, each with four players, most of them elderly, every one of them Chinese, and the sound of their bone Mahjong tiles being banged together blurred into one unbroken cacophonous note.

Keith was playing with two old ladies and a man, none of them below eighty, yet they picked up and discarded tiles at breakneck speed, attempting to get three of a kind, four of a kind and running straight, but with a set of tiles that were three times the size of a pack of cards, depicting dragons, the four winds, bamboo, circles and a bewildering array of Chinese characters.

When the game ended and the tiles were face down and being shuffled – in Mahjong they call it *washing* – Keith stood up and looked at me for the first time.

'Do you understand this game?' he asked me.

'I tried to once,' I said. 'But I'm not meant to understand it, am I?'

He said something to his companions in Cantonese. Then I followed him to a small office in the corner of the basement, a tiny glass box where we could see all those grey, white and bald heads bent over their Mahjong tiles, although the noise was not quite so deafening.

There was a portable gas stove in the corner of his office, suitable for a camping trip, and Keith heated water in an aluminium pan and spooned some leaves into a cracked brown teapot. He offered me a small cup but I shook my head.

He settled behind his desk with a cup of boiling tea.

I remained standing.

'You have not come to arrest me,' he said. 'Because you would not have come alone. And yet you have not come to thank me because you will not sit and drink tea with me.'

'Who was she?' I said. 'The woman you came for in the Hopewell Centre?'

'Her name is Li Jin Jin,' he said.

'Li,' I said. 'The same family name as you.'

He shrugged.

'The same family name as ninety-three million Chinese. Li is the second most common surname in China. Many people are called Li. We are two a penny.'

I saw the glint of relish in his eye at his use of the phrase. *Two a penny*.

'So I'm meant to believe that it's a coincidence that you have the same family name as the woman you came for?'

The woman you killed for, I thought.

'No,' he said. 'Jin Jin is the daughter of my brother. She is nineteen years old. A student in Wanchai, an area on Hong Kong island. There are many bad people there,' said the head of the Wo Shing Wo. 'And she met a man who told her that he could help her find work in London. We say – *heiyu*. A snakehead. You are familiar with that expression?'

He still sounded like the man I had met on that first day, in thrall to a version of the English language that he had heard on the BBC World Service.

'A snakehead is a Chinese people smuggler,' I said.

He gazed out through the glass wall, as if anxious to return to his Mahjong. It seemed to be a game without

371

end. The washing of those bone tiles by all four players. The thundering clack as the tiles were matched and discarded to the cries of Chinatown's most senior citizens. And then again the washing of the tiles, face down, all of it done in a hurry.

'The Chinese invented many things,' he said. 'Do you know what we call the Four Great Inventions of Ancient China?'

'Gunpowder, paper, printing and the compass,' I said.

He was impressed. 'You know China, Detective.'

'Not really. But I worked Chinatown. When I was very young. When I was so young that I wore a police uniform. I don't know China. I only know Chinatown, Keith.'

'And yet you will not drink with me.'

I relented. He poured another cup of boiling water on to the leaves.

'We Chinese invented other things,' he said. 'We Chinese invented the snakehead. We invented the smuggling of people from a poor part of the world to a rich part of the world. The worst of our people have been doing this business for many years. So we are very familiar with the kind of people you are hunting. It is new to you. It is new to the West. But it is not new to us.'

'And is she all right?'

'My niece was fortunate. If nobody knows you're here, then nobody knows you're missing.'

'And how did you know she was up there?'

'One of my friends. She is out there now, in fact,' he said, indicating the great game that is played under the streets of Chinatown. 'She is one of the ladies you saw at my table playing Mahjong with me. She goes to that big glass tower – the Hopewell Centre – every day.'

'Why?'

'So she can clean it for them. All those rich, well-educated people – they can't clean it for themselves, can they?'

'She must be in her eighties. Bit old to be a cleaner, isn't she?'

'Chinese people don't retire,' he said proudly. 'Only Europeans retire. And then they immediately drop dead. So much for retirement!'

'Keith,' I said. 'There were other women up there who needed your help. There was a woman called Rabia Demir. She was in the cab of the lorry we found at the end of this street.'

'And you think my men and I could have saved her?'

After a moment, I shook my head. 'But I think we could have tried.'

There was a hard light in his eyes.

'We came for my niece. I told you, Detective. *We take care of our own.* I'm sorry for that woman. I am sorry for all the women in that place. And I am happy that coming for my niece also meant that we saved your hide.' He liked that one. *Saved your hide.* 'But I told you before – *this is why you tolerate us.* Where were your colleagues?'

'They got there in the end. Later than I would have liked.'

'And did you catch the snakeheads you were seeking?'

I thought of Paul Warboys bleeding out on the floor of a holding cell in West End Central. I knew that Madam Theresa would be in a cell for the rest of her life. And I saw Troy of the camp finished at the hands of the small man drinking his tea on the other side of the desk.

I nodded.

'They're all done,' I said.

It was time to go.

Keith Li stood up and held out his hand.

I shook it.

But there was one last thing.

'What was your niece studying in Hong Kong?' I said, although I felt that I already knew the answer.

'How to help people,' he said. 'She wants to be a nurse.'

36

When her grandmother had slipped into her afternoon sleep, Edie gently took the box of Milk Tray from the bed and settled herself in the small room's only chair. I made a drinking gesture and Edie gave me the thumbs up. We smiled at each other. I went off to the canteen to get coffee.

White-suited nurses were eating their lunch, their conversation like birdsong. They all wore the same identical white suit but they looked as if they were from every corner of the world. They did not look exhausted or depressed by their work. They seemed energised and happy.

As I paid for the coffee, I felt my spirits sink.

What's wrong with this picture?

I stared at their happy faces. One of them, Maria from the Philippines who always took such good care of Lil, saw me staring, and smiled back.

They came from Africa. South America. East Asia. They came from where one continent ended and another began. They were Nigerian or Ghanaian, Filipina and Chinese, Albanian and Turkish, Brazilian and Colombian. They spoke in English, even when addressing someone from their own country, but I knew their languages would have been the Ashanti Twi of West Africa, the Mandarin of mainland China, the Portuguese of South America and languages that I had never heard of and would never recognise.

But the white-suited nurses of Golden Years all spoke to each other in English that was getting better every day.

I returned to Lil's room as if in a dream.

'What's wrong, Max?' Edie said.

'The staff,' I said. 'These nurses.'

'They're great, aren't they?'

'Yes,' I said, suddenly aware of my breathing. 'But they're all illegal.'

I stared out of the window. In the car park a Bentley had pulled up next to my BMW X5. Doherty, the driver, leaned against the door, smoking a cigarette in his gloved hands.

'No,' Edie said. 'You can't know that. You can't be sure.'

She looked anxiously at her grandmother. The old lady moaned in her sleep.

'I hope I'm wrong,' I said. 'But I can feel it in my blood, Edie. Every one of them is illegal. That's why the women we found were all nurses. Hana Novak and the others in the lorry in Chinatown. Rabia Demir. Keith Li's niece. They were all nurses. They were coming here to do what they had been trained for. And do it well. And do it better than the locals. I'm sorry, Edie.'

'No,' she said. 'If you're right, then why did some of them end up working for Madam Theresa? It doesn't make sense.'

'It's the only thing that makes sense,' I said. 'Some of them never made it here alive and some of them were put to work in the Hopewell Centre. But they all came to do the same job.' Edie's grandmother had woken at the sound of our voices. 'I'm sorry, Lil,' I told her. 'I truly am.'

'That's all right, love,' Lil said, grinning happily, not a care in the world.

Edie was shaking her head.

'Max – please. Stop for a minute and think this through. You could be wrong.'

'But I'm not,' I said. 'Call it in, Edie.'

She made no attempt to reach for her phone. We stared at each other for a long hard moment and then I turned away. And as I left the room, I saw her reach for her grandmother's hand.

I walked out to the car park. Doherty saw me coming and dropped his cigarette. I held out my hand. The chauffeur stared at it as if uncertain what to do. I kept my hand there. He slowly took it. We shook.

And then I squeezed his hand as hard as I could.

I saw the look of disbelief on his face turn to shock and finally, as I increased the pressure, excruciating pain, the kind of pain that doubles you up.

Cursing, Doherty abruptly pulled his hand away, and bounced off the side of his master's car. His leather-soled shoes skidded and slipped on the icy ground as he broke into a run, his eyes streaming with tears.

It had been just shy of two months since the Champagne Room was torched.

And burns take a long time to heal.

Barry Warboys was smoking a cigar at his desk when I walked into his office.

'What's the life expectancy in this country these days?' I said.

His PA appeared in the doorway behind me.

'Mr Warboys? This gentleman just barged—'

'It's all right,' he said, dismissing her. He considered my question. 'Eighty years for men,' he said. 'Eighty-two for women. And rising all the time, of course.'

'Then this is the best business to be in,' I said. 'Reasonably priced residential care for the elderly. All these people who need looking after.'

'It's an expanding market.'

'But it must be hard to get nurses from affluent countries to look after old people. I imagine it's a hard, messy, thankless job for not much money. To wash them, to clean up after them, to care about them.'

He was watching me carefully.

'Frankly, it's hard to get their own children to care about them,' he said.

'But your nurses care.'

'Yes, they do care.'

'Is that why they're all illegals?'

He laughed like a man whose conscience was clear.

'Technically speaking, Detective, these nurses are not employed by me. These women are *not* my staff. They come from an employment agency. They are employed by that agency. So if there are issues with work permits, residency visas and so on, then you will need to take it up with the employment agency. It's the agency's job to vet them. Not mine.'

He looked at me like a man who knows his hands are clean.

'That ruse would work if it was just some migrant worker scam,' I said. 'It would work – and work well – if it were some cleaning jobs in London or a bit of potato picking in East Anglia. But the bodies are piling up. It's gone too far for anyone to just get a slap on the wrist for lacking the right stamp in their passport. Too many women have died, Warboys. And you're the man who shipped them in.'

We stared at each other.

And he still wasn't afraid. He exhaled a cloud of cigar smoke.

'I don't know what you're talking about.'

'Believe me, I can see the attraction. Your nurses work harder, cheaper and better than the locals. They do their job with good grace. It can't be easy, looking after people who are in their final years. And I can see that they are all highly qualified and motivated. But I bet that when we round up the staff here – and at all your other retirement communities – they will all have entered this country in the back of a lorry. Every single one of them.'

He looked out of his window. The Bentley was without its driver.

'Doherty's not coming,' I said. 'Your man did a runner. Why did you have him burn down the Champagne Room?'

His jaw tightened, the blood slowly draining from his face.

'I was nowhere near that fire.'

'Oh, I don't doubt your alibi is first class. My guess? It was all getting a bit too hardcore for your son, Steve. I met him a couple of times – but Steve wasn't quite as hard as he wanted to be, was he? Were you trying to shut him up? Was he going to go to the law about the lorries that were being unloaded out the back? Or did he just want you to stop using his car park for your filthy little business?'

He sucked on his cigar as if it was the cure for something.

He took his time exhaling and the smoke drifted from his half-open mouth as if he was releasing something that had been locked up deep inside for a long time. I believed that there would be no more empty denials. Barry Warboys was ready to talk.

And I realised that I had seen this kind of confession before in dozens of interview rooms and holding cells. They deny everything until it can no longer possibly be denied. But when the truth is finally so close that you can smell it, taste it, feel it in the back of your throat – then you can't shut them up.

'Stephen was – how can I put it? – a trifle squeamish,' he began. 'He liked to play the hard man out there in the Essex nightlife, but the lorry with those girls in Chinatown – well, it put the wind up him.'

Put the wind up him. Meaning to cause extreme fear. It was an expression that his own father might have used.

'My son wanted to see you and confess,' Warboys said. 'Which would have been good for his conscience but bad for my long-term plans.' He was suddenly exasperated. 'But I'm a businessman. You have to understand. I never wanted to hurt anyone.'

'Then why are so many young women dying?'

'Supply and demand,' he sighed. 'Market forces. We just had all these women coming in that we didn't need.

We didn't have any use for them. They were no good to us. They were surplus to requirements. I had all the staff I could possibly use. But once the pipeline was open and flowing, it was impossible to turn it off. You can't imagine the logistics, Detective – talent scouts at nursing colleges, reliable drivers for the journey across Europe, the odd anarchist to ease our way across borders. There were deliveries that were never even collected.'

'Is that what happened to Hana Novak? A delivery that nobody collected?'

The name was unknown to him.

'Who's Hana Novak?' he said.

I felt myself shaking with rage.

'Hana Novak died in that lorry we found in China-town. She wanted to be a nurse.'

He laughed shortly.

'Do you *know* how many qualified nurses there are in the world who want to come to this country? It's rather a lot. And even when I attempted to shut off the pipeline, and told that tattooed freak in Grande-Synthe that we didn't need any more, there were still all these women arriving. And then that old bag contacted me. My father's favourite whore.'

'Madam Theresa.'

'Madam Theresa! She was long retired. She contacted me about my *brother*.' His face twisted with disgust at the implied intimacy, and the last of the cigar smoke seeped from his mouth. 'Would I like to visit my *brother*? The old girl has done it quite a bit over the years – inviting me to hold hands with her retarded offspring. Make believe we are family. No, thank you! I told her that I didn't have a brother. But I *did* have a job for her. Oh, I knew what she was. And I knew what she sold. You see, we just were just bringing in too many nurses. It seemed a shame not to put them to work.'

'So it was never your father who was Theresa's sponsor up in the penthouse of the Hopewell Centre. It was you.'

He took a long drag on his cigar and the tip glowed red in the dying light of the late afternoon.

'Look, I was never interested in whoring. That's my father's area of expertise. Getting someone to have sex with you is absolutely *nothing*,' he said. 'But try finding someone to look after your old, dying parent! Try getting someone to clean the mess off dear old mum or dad when they've soiled their bed again! Now *that's* bloody difficult, Detective.'

A squad car pulled up in the car park.

And then another.

No lights, no sirens, no fuss.

Nobody wanted to scare the residents. So Edie must have called it in after all. I felt a huge wave of sorrow for her. And for the lovely old lady with the censored box of Milk Tray on her lap.

Warboys stepped out from behind his desk.

'I think you've earned this,' he said, and tried to stub out his cigar in my right eye.

I must have slipped because I felt the cigar burn and crumble against my shoulder and then his hands were in my face, the fingernails clawing at my forehead as he sunk his thumbs into my eyes, planning to push them into the back of my head as a howl of furious rage strangled in his throat.

Slip and rip, Fred had said. *Slip and rip*, Fred had drilled into me until it was second nature, no need for my brain to tell my body what to do, all of it done from muscle memory after repeating it a thousand times, and as I took half a step away from Warboys I dug a left hook into the bottom of his ribcage, and as he let me go with a squeal of pain I brought a right upper cut on to the tip of his chin, snapping his head back. There was a right cross ready to drive into his heart, but it was not needed. He was already going down. And as I caught him by his lapels and I held him up, I thought of the photograph that I had seen in the Black Museum of a small boy in a gym long ago, surrounded by all those leering, laughing hard men, the look of dread on his face, a son sick with fear in the presence of his father.

But I didn't feel sorry for him any more.

'You should have stuck with the boxing,' I said.

*   *   *

On Valentine's Day there was a party at the Finchley branch of Golden Years. Staff from all the other branches of the chain of retirement communities were invited. Mini-buses were provided to bring them from all over the country to North London.

The canteen was decked out in heart-shaped balloons in pink and red, and tables and chairs were pushed to the walls to create a dance floor.

A beat box was provided for music – pop favourites from the last twenty years – and a small selection of food and drink was on offer. It was not our show at West End Central, but I saw the budget drawn up by the UK Border Agency and they certainly made it stretch to a lot of cheese sandwiches, crisps and cheap wine.

Even as the dancing got started, large coaches were pulling up in the car park. Two vans of uniformed officers were already parked in the corner but they were relaxed and chatty, coppers who were not anticipating any trouble on this shift.

The nursing staff of Golden Years were all expected to go quietly.

But still, there was no harm at all in letting them work off a little steam on the dance floor before they were collared.

I saw Maria, the Filipina nurse who had changed Lil's bedding, dancing to ABC's 'The Look of Love' with a group of other Filipinas.

But I didn't see her stopped by one of the two uniformed officers who waited in the doorway of the canteen for when the nurses left, and I didn't see her being processed by the immigration officers who set up their desks in the lobby, and I didn't see her loaded on to one of the coaches that were waiting to transport them all directly to one of the UK's dozen Immigration Detention Centres, which are built to Class B – medium-security – prison standards and invariably close to an airport.

We don't call the facility a prison or even a detention centre. We call it pre-departure accommodation. They did not know it yet, but the staff of Golden Years were all going home.

As ABC made way for Abba, I went upstairs to Lil's small corner room on the first floor.

There was a half-eaten box of Milk Tray in the waste-paper bin.

But the bed was stripped down to its bare mattress, the room was dark and cold and Edie Wren's beloved grandmother was staying in some other care home tonight.

37

They came to the Old Bailey and they waited for justice.

It was not quite ten in the morning but many of the crowd gathered in Newgate Street had already done a full day's work.

They were the night cleaners who scrubbed the towers of glass and steel. They were the drivers of tube trains, buses and mini cabs who pulled the graveyard shift. They were hospital porters, security guards and nurses, and some wore the white-and-blue uniforms of professional carers. They came up from the underground and they came down from the skyscrapers where they scrubbed before the working day began.

The winter was over now but they still wore its clothes, wrapped up in thick fleeces and padded jackets, the clothes of those who wait for the night bus or the first tube trains.

Their faces suggested that they came from every corner of the earth and they stood in silence for Barry

Warboys to be brought to the Central Criminal Court, the proper name of the Old Bailey.

I flashed my warrant card to a uniformed officer and made my way to the main entrance where Dejan Jovanović of the Serbian embassy was waiting for me. As we were about to go inside, he tugged my arm.

'The boy,' he said. 'Nenad Novak.'

Nesha was standing at the back of the crowd on Newgate Street and I wondered how many other blood relatives of the victims were in this crowd. It was impossible to know where the curious ended and the bereaved began. I lifted my hand in salute to Nesha but he gave no indication that he had seen me.

'Here he comes,' said Dejan.

A prison transport van – a large white truck with eight blacked-out windows on each side – lumbered into view. A murmur ran through the crowd and they pressed closer to the road, held back by a line of uniformed police officers.

A single bottle exploded on the side of the van. A cry went up, filled with something like relief, and another bottle was thrown but the prison transport van was already disappearing inside the gates of the Old Bailey. Nothing in the city works quite as well as the Central Criminal Court. Gangsters, terrorists, and murderers – the Old Bailey sees them come and sees them go with little drama every day of the week.

'Go inside,' I told Dejan. 'I'll see you in there.'

I pushed my way through the crowd to Nesha.

'Go home,' I told him. 'Nothing's going to happen today. It's his first appearance. All they're going to do is hear his plea and remand him in custody for a later date. The trial will be six or eight weeks from now.'

Nesha shook his head, as if I had it all wrong.

'I want to see this man,' he said. 'And I want to see him punished.'

'I understand that, Nesha. You're here for Hana. You're here for your sister. But today is just the start. You're not going to see Warboys punished. And you're not even going to see him. They'll take him out the back way.' I gestured towards the far side of the Central Criminal Court. 'Warwick Square,' I said. 'They're not going to risk this crowd. Go back to the gym, Nesha.'

'I want to go inside.'

'The public gallery was full hours ago. There's nothing to see and there's nothing to do. Go back to Fred's and I'll meet you there, OK?'

But he was not listening to me.

He stared up at the bronze statue of a woman that adorns the roof of the Old Bailey, blindfolded Lady Justice with the scales of justice in one hand and her sword in the other, and he kept staring up at her long after I had turned away, as if expecting her to rise up and strike down the wicked.

The holding cells below the Old Bailey lead directly into the courtrooms and so there was something almost theatrical about the way Barry Warboys suddenly appeared out of the ground and into the glass-walled dock of Court One. He blinked and stared around, haggard and dazed, his thinning fair hair dishevelled, like some subterranean creature dragged up to the light.

A murmur ran through the public gallery. I looked up and saw Billy Greene's mother and his fiancée Siobhan sitting towards the back. And then it began.

'All rise,' the bailiff said.

The judge read out the charges against the defendant.

'Barry Warboys, you are accused of facilitating the entry of illegal immigrants into the United Kingdom. How do you plead?'

His voice was strong and clear, still the tone of a man who was accustomed to doing business, well used to every deal going his way.

'Not guilty, My Lord.'

It was all over in five minutes and the disappointment in Court One was tangible.

You come for justice, red in tooth and claw.

And what you get are well-paid men and women in

wigs and gowns and bewildering rituals that have not changed in over a hundred years.

Barry Warboys disappeared back into the ground like the punchline of a magic act. Up in the public gallery, those who had queued for seats since the middle of the night loitered as if something else might happen today.

But as I had told Nesha, nothing would. Even my colleague from the Serbian embassy seemed deflated.

'Not murder?' Dejan Jovanović said.

I shook my head. 'Not murder,' I said. 'Trafficking.'

'How long for this crime?' he asked.

'Fourteen years,' I said. 'Maximum.'

'I need a cigarette,' he sighed.

The courtroom slowly began to clear and we went out to Warwick Square. The enormous prison transport van was parked with its engine idling outside the back gates of the Old Bailey. Two uniformed prison officers stepped out with Barry Warboys handcuffed between them.

'Do you know this girl?' Nesha said, brushing past me, his voice shaking, as if the words were too much for his throat. 'Hey!' he said. 'Hey, mister – do you know this girl?'

He was holding a photograph in his hand. A hard copy of that last selfie from Belgrade. A brother and a sister smiling for the camera just before they said good-bye forever.

'Hey!'

I placed a restraining hand on his shoulder.

'Nesha—'

'This was my sister,' he said, as one of the uniformed officers noted his presence and took a pace towards him.

'Her name was Hana Novak and she was a nurse from Serbia,' Nesha said.

Barry Warboys looked at the boy without pity or interest.

The uniformed police officer placed a closed fist on Nesha's chest. The other officer helped Warboys on to the back step of the prison transport van.

And the boy was suddenly past him.

'She was *a nurse*,' Nesha said as he punched Warboys in the side of the neck.

'Oh,' said Warboys, falling sideways, trying to lift his arms to touch his neck but shackled by the handcuffs he wore, and off balance, so that when Nesha hit him in the neck again he went down hard, unable to hold his hands out to break his fall.

And I was screaming Nesha's name as the uniformed officers threw themselves on the boy, knocking him off his feet and pinning him to the deck with his face buried in the pavement of Warwick Square. And as the fight went out of him and he began to weep for his lost sister and for himself, I saw it all at once.

The knife still in Nesha's right hand.

The blood pouring from the wounds in Warboys' neck.

As uniformed officers bundled him inside the gates of the Old Bailey, I shouted Nesha's name.

But the boy was already behind locked doors.

I sat on the steps of the Old Bailey with Dejan Jovanović.

The crowds who had waited for a glimpse of the accused had gone home, sleeping on buses and trains to the faraway edges of the city, and they would not return until the night came and their shift began.

'What will happen to the boy?' Dejan said.

'They'll put him away,' I said. 'In the eyes of the law, Nesha's still a child so he'll go to a Young Offenders' Institution, probably Feltham in Middlesex.' I thought about Nesha in that place and it was not a good moment. 'And then, at the end of that, they'll throw him out of the country. Deport him.' I shook my head. 'What a bloody mess.'

'But this is a kind country.'

'You think so, Dejan?'

He nodded, staring thoughtfully at his cigarette.

'You don't send people back to their own country if it's too dangerous.'

'But there's no war where Nesha comes from, is there?'

'Not now,' he said, dragging deeply on his cigarette, and I remembered that Dejan Jovanović of the Serbian embassy was a man who had twice worn a soldier's uniform, and who had picked up broken bodies in two wars.

I watched him smile sadly.

'But who knows what terrible things will be happening in this world when Nesha Novak finally comes out?' he said.

'Yes,' I said. 'You never know your luck.'

38

The days were growing longer now and for the first time in months, natural light poured through the large windows of our loft as Scout and Stan were fed by Mrs Murphy.

We had put away our winter clothes. We had turned the radiators off. And Scout was suddenly an inch taller. The season had turned.

My daughter and my dog both glanced up from their dinner as I came out of the bedroom.

'Why are you dressed like that?' Scout asked with a mouth full of pasta.

I was wearing my new suit, white shirt and blue tie. I usually only dressed like this when I was getting married or going to a funeral.

'It's called style, Scout,' I said, touching her brown bell of hair.

Mrs Murphy smiled.

'It's called a date, Scout,' she said.

I was embarrassed. 'No,' I said. 'Not a date.'

'Go on with you,' Mrs Murphy said, flicking a tea towel in my general direction. 'Go and have a good time. You deserve it.'

I was not so sure. I knew I should have done more to protect Nesha and Billy. I felt bad that Edie's grandmother had been moved from the retirement community she loved. And I knew I would always feel bad about it. But Mrs Murphy kept smiling. More than anyone in the world, she truly wanted a happy ending for our little family.

She chuckled happily as I collected the flowers I had bought.

'What time is the young lady expecting you?' Mrs Murphy said.

'Nobody's really expecting me,' I said, and it was only then that her smile began to falter.

I am not one of those people who visit graves.

I never go to the small churchyard on the outskirts of London where my mother and father are buried. If you saw their grave, battered by time and the weather, untended and ignored, then you would think that this woman and man must surely be forgotten, unloved and unmourned.

Nothing could be less like the truth.

But I saw them both after they died, and the spark that had made them the man and the woman they were had gone to some other place or dissolved from the universe. I had no idea. But their souls had flown. So I can never convince myself that the double grave in the little churchyard contains my parents. They are not there. They are in my heart – that is where my parents rest.

And I don't need to see their grave to remember them.

Yet something drew me back to Chinatown and the place where we had found the lorry. Of the twelve women we discovered on that freezing morning, only Hana Novak was ever identified and claimed. I felt that we had failed them all, and everyone who loved them, and there needed to be some act of remembrance or gesture of apology. So I took flowers to the dim sum restaurant where we discovered Hana and the women whose real names we never learned.

I placed them as far away as I could from the diners passing through the busy doorway. The makeshift shrine that had briefly appeared outside the restaurant was gone now and my flowers were the only sign that lives had been lost on this spot. It was Saturday evening, the weather mild after our long hard winter, the crowds thronging Chinatown, and everything spoke of life apart from the solitary bouquet of flowers, alone in the shadows of the red-and-gold awning. I stood there for a moment, remembering Hana and the others.

But I had no prayers for them and I did not linger.

I let the city swallow me up in another Saturday night, walking down the length of Gerrard Street, the smell of roast duck making my mouth water, and then taking a random side street, where an older, dimly lit Chinatown still exists, and voices from doorways call out to a man walking alone.

I heard the heels behind me.

Click-click, they went. *Click-click*.

'*Ni hau*,' she said.

She was mainland Chinese, wrapped up for some sub-zero winter in Beijing or Shenyang, still new enough to this life to look nervous as we stood facing each other in the Chinatown twilight.

'*Ni hau*,' I said.

'Are you alone?' she said.

It was a good question. I shook my head, smiled, suddenly knowing that Chinatown had nothing for me tonight. I ran back to the car and drove north, parking outside the one-bedroom flat above a shop on the wrong side of Highbury Corner.

There was a light on in Edie Wren's apartment.

We had not spoken since the end of Golden Years. I did not know if the married man was still in her life. I did not know if she was angry with me for Lil having to leave the best place she ever lived. I did not know very much at all.

But I knew there was nowhere else I would rather be than standing on the street where Edie Wren lived.

It was Saturday night.

What else can I tell you?

I rang her bell.

Did you enjoy reading DIE LAST?

Do you want more of Max Wolfe?

Turn the page to read an extract of
Tony Parsons' new novel

GIRL ON
FIRE

1

I woke up and the world was gone.

All was silent, all was black, the darkness so complete that it was as if all light had been drained from the world.

The dust was everywhere. The air was thick with it – hot and filthy, the dust of a freshly dug grave. And a strange rain was falling – a rain made of rocks and stones, the fragments and remains of smashed and broken things that I could not name. The destruction was everywhere, in my eyes, my mouth, my nose and the back of my throat.

I was flat on my back and suddenly the devastation was choking me.

I pushed myself up, coughing up the strange dust, feeling it on my hands and my face.

I stared into the pitch-black silence and felt a stab of pure terror because for the first time I was aware of the heat. There was a great fire nearby. I looked around and suddenly I saw it, blazing and flaring, the only light in the darkness. The heat increased. The fire was getting closer.

Move or die. These are your choices now.

Then I was on my hands and knees, scrambling away from the fire, gagging up the filth that filled the air. A wave of sickness was sweeping over me, and I was aware of a pain that was everywhere but seemed to radiate out from the inside of my right knee.

I fell on my side with a quiet curse and touched the slice of glass that was embedded in my leg. It was a small but thick chunk of a plate-glass window that was never meant to shatter. I felt it gingerly, my knee raging with pain, trying to make sense of it all.

Where had the old world gone?

What had happened?

I remembered that I had been in the Lake Meadows shopping centre in West London, buying a new backpack for my daughter, Scout. She wanted a plain and unadorned Kipling backpack now that, aged seven, she considered herself far too mature for the backpack she currently carried to school. It was only a year old but featured the female lead of last summer's big blockbuster movie, *The Angry Princess*, a beautiful cartoon princess who looked fierce and threw thunderbolts from her elegant fingernails. And Scout was done with all that little kids' stuff. She wanted me to buy her a big girl's backpack. And that's what I had been doing when it happened.

I remembered paying for the new grown-up rucksack and stepping out into the concourse wondering where I could get a decent triple espresso.

There had been people and lights and smiles, the smell of coffee and cinnamon rolls, the soft sounds of shopping centre music, some song from the last century. It was something other than a memory. It felt like a dream that I was forgetting upon waking.

And now the light ebbed and flowed because the darkness was broken up by the great fire but also by some weak grey light from the outside world creeping into the ruins through a shattered roof or wall.

Now I could see the bodies in what had been the shopping mall.

Some of them were unmoving. Some of them tried to sit up.

But this new world was silent.

Then I realised that the world was not silent. Not really. My hearing had gone the moment that everything went away.

There was a young security guard sitting on the ground nearby. His uniform was covered in the grey dust. He turned his face towards me and tried to speak.

No – he was speaking but I couldn't hear him.

I pulled the broken glass from my knee, cried out with pain and crawled to his side.

His mouth moved again but his words were indistinct.

I stared at him, my eyes streaming in the dust, shaking my head.

He repeated his words and this time, above the ringing in my ears, I heard him.

'A bomb,' he said.

'No,' I said. 'Too big for a bomb.'

'My arm,' he said.

He was holding his arm, staring at it with confusion.

His right arm was missing below the right elbow.

I put the bag containing Scout's new rucksack beneath his head.

Then I took off my leather jacket, pulled off my T-shirt and tore it into three pieces.

The security guard was trying to hold his injured arm in the air, using gravity to stem the flow. I nodded encouragement.

'That's good,' I said.

People were slowly walking past us. They were not running. They were too dumbfounded to run. They staggered out of the swirling clouds of dust, some of them still carrying their shopping, too numb to drop it, too shocked to let go of their bags, as if none of this was possible. I placed a strip of T-shirt in the security guard's wound and held it there.

The blood seeped through almost immediately.

I left the scrap of bloody T-shirt plugged into the wound and placed a second piece of the T-shirt on top. This bled through more slowly.

As gently as I could, I removed the guard's tie, measured approximately four inches above the wound and tied a tourniquet on what remained of his right arm. Then I placed the final piece of T-shirt on the wound.

And this time no blood came through.

My hearing was back now and I could hear the screams and the sirens. I could see bodies scattered in the ruins. I could feel the great fire. The horror flooded over me and made it difficult to breathe.

I thought of my daughter and I didn't want to die.

Objects began to rain harder from the sky. And now some of them were as small as pebbles while some of them were chunks of matter big enough to break your neck. The security guard and I flinched and cowered and tried to protect our eyes.

The sky was falling down on the living and the dead — great clumps of concrete bringing with it more clouds of dust, as if the sky itself had been made from these things, and now it was smashed for ever.

A piece of something struck me on the shoulder. I felt nothing, but the pain in my right knee made me clench my teeth until my jawbone ached.

I took the security guard's left hand and guided it to the scraps of T-shirt stuffed into his wound. He was still attempting to hold his arm in the air. He was doing good.

'You're going to make it,' I told him. 'I'll get help.'

Then I was on my feet, and I began to walk towards the sound of the sirens. But my right knee no longer worked the way it should.

I felt it buckle beneath me and suddenly I was down on my hands and knees again.

I slowly got up and walked on, favouring my left leg now, trying not to put too much weight on the right side.

I could feel the heat of the fire and I could smell the stink of the fire.

Kerosene?

But an ocean of the stuff, all of it ablaze, and that made no sense. Where would that much kerosene come from?

A man in a business suit walked by carrying a bag from the Apple store, every inch of him coated in the grey dust that filled the hot, fetid atmosphere. I spat out some filth and took a deep breath, inhaling the burning air. It seared my lungs.

The fire was getting closer.

Move or die.

A life-size puppet was hanging from what had once been the basement roof of the shopping mall. There were long thick straps of webbing attached to the puppet's chair and they held him from the ceiling, as if

6

waiting for some giant hand to move him. The puppet was close enough for me to see the expression on his unmarked face.

And I saw that this had been a man. The man had been a pilot. And some freak accident had prevented him from being smashed to a billion pieces after falling from the sky.

I had heard of this happening but I had never believed it.

But now I believed.

And now, finally, I began to understand.

That reeking, sickening smell was Jet A-1.

Aviation fuel.

Move or die!

'Excuse me,' an elderly woman said, her politeness heartbreaking in this new world. 'Please stay with us.'

She was sitting on the floor, cradling the head of a man her own age who looked close to death. I knelt beside them, gasping as the pain in my knee surged through the rest of my body, and as I took her hand I saw what had brought this new world into being.

'A bomb,' the lady said.

'No,' I said. 'It's too big for a bomb. A helicopter came down.'

And through the smoke and the dust and the twilight ruins I saw a smashed and crumpled Air Ambulance, its cockpit a ruined pulp of red aluminium and steel and glass, the four rotor blades twisted and bent yet somehow not broken.

It looked like a giant insect that had been swatted by some enraged god.

Behind it was a wake of wreckage that seemed to stretch on forever, twisted and burning and broken, a tangled mess of steel and glass and concrete, flesh and blood and bone, human beings and buildings. Everything smashed.

But there were new lights now, the red and blue lights of the first responders.

'I'll bring help,' I promised.

And I left the old man and woman and started off towards the red and blue lights, but my knee went again and I fell flat on my face in what remained of that shopping centre.

So I got up and tried one more time, treading very carefully so as not to step on the bodies that were scattered all around, moving very slowly to protect my busted knee, as if everything that I thought I knew would have to be learned again.

And as the tears cleared the dust from my eyes, I saw this new world clearly.

I saw the men and women who came with the red and blue lights of the emergency services.

I saw the trail of total ruin that had been left in the wake of the fallen helicopter.

And the rage choked my throat when I saw the injured – that gentle little euphemism for those who now carried terrible wounds that would never heal, not in this lifetime.

Then I wiped my eyes with the back of my hands, sucked in some air and began to stumble towards the reds and blues of our lights.

2

I stood by the side of the low stage, sweating inside the stab-proof Kevlar jacket despite the chill of the hour before dawn, my right knee still pulsing with pain seven days after the Air Ambulance helicopter came down on Lake Meadows shopping centre, killing dozens of innocent people.

The current fatality list stood at forty-four, but the number crept higher every day as the emergency services continued the painstaking work of sifting through the crash site. Nobody knew for sure exactly how many had died and I suspected that we would never know with total certainty.

I was in the briefing room of Leman Street Police Station, Whitechapel, feeling the weight of history. Murder detectives hunted Jack the Ripper from this station. Today it is the base of SC&O19, the specialist firearms unit of the Metropolitan Police.

The briefing room was packed.

Rows of Specialist Firearms Officers in grey body armour worn over short-sleeve blue shirts were listening intently to the young female sergeant on stage. There was a lectern up there but she stood to one side, tall and athletic and affable, and I thought that she was young to be a sergeant in any part of the Met, let alone the firearms unit.

Specialist Firearms Officer DS Alice Stone.

She sounded far more relaxed than she had any right to be.

Behind her a large screen showed a photograph of a three-storey house.

It was a small, neat Victorian terrace on Borodino Street, London E1, its bay windows covered with net curtains. Only a postcode away. We believed it contained the men who had brought down the Air Ambulance helicopter.

The young sergeant touched the iPad she was holding and architectural plans appeared on screen. She began talking about the morning's MOE – method of entry – and I felt the sweat trickle down my back.

It had nothing to do with the weight of the Kevlar jacket.

Someone always has to go in, I thought. *After all the hours of surveillance and analysis of intelligence and briefings, somebody still has to go through a locked door and into the unknown.*

'The entry team for Operation Tolstoy will be breaching the front door of the target with Hatton rounds fired from a shotgun,' DS Stone said, her voice calm and classless, just the hint of some affluent corner of the Home Counties in her accent. 'Distraction stun grenades will be deployed immediately prior to entering the premises.' She paused. 'We have every reason to believe that the men inside are armed fanatics who would actively welcome a martyr's death. So it's CQC when we are inside.'

CQC is Close Quarter Combat, moving through a series of rooms and corridors until the inhabitants are subdued and dominated. Many SFOs either have military training or they have grown up around guns – shooting game with their family in some muddy field.

I wondered which one it was with young DS Stone.

Then she smiled. She had a good smile. It was wide, white and genuine. The trouble with most smiles is that they are not the real thing. This was the real thing.

'And then we're all going for breakfast,' she said. 'On me.'

The room full of SFOs in grey body armour all grinned with her.

Still smiling, she turned to the side of the stage.

'DC Wolfe?' she said. 'We're ready for you now.'

*

Coming March 2018

TONY PARSONS

GIRL ON FIRE

Order your copy now

TONY PARSONS

I always knew that I would write. I knew that nothing would stop me. I always loved stories, I always found books engaged me like nothing else, and helped me to make sense of the world.

I left school at sixteen, did a number of low-paid unskilled jobs, and I was working on the night shift in Gordon's Gin Distillery in Islington when I was offered my first job in journalism on *New Musical Express*. Since then I have become an award-winning journalist and bestselling novelist, and my books have been published in over forty languages, most recently Vietnamese. My semi-autobiographical novel, *Man and Boy*, won the Book of the Year prize.

The last few years have been all about Detective Max Wolfe for me. *The Murder Bag* was the first in a series of crime novels featuring Detective Max Wolfe and his world – from the Murder Investigation Room at West End Central, 27 Savile Row, to the Black Museum in New Scotland Yard to the home he shares with his daughter and dog in a loft high above Smithfield meat market. Then there was *The Slaughter Man*, *The Hanging Club*, *Die Last*, and *Girl on Fire* is next.

I live in London with my wife, our daughter and our dog, Stan.

Don't be a lost contact. Keep in touch with me at:

www.dcmaxwolfe.com

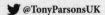 **f** / TonyParsonsBooks   **y** @TonyParsonsUK

ENTER THE LONDON OF DC MAX WOLFE

Starting at West End Central,
explore London locations
as DC Max Wolfe gets
on the trail of a serial killer.

Find the clue in each scene that
takes you to the next location.
Complete the journey and sign up
to be the first to hear more
about DC Max Wolfe.

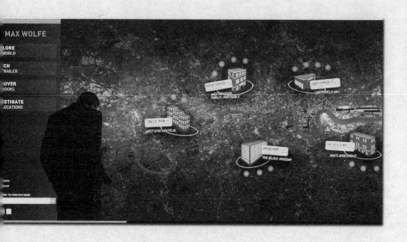

www.dcmaxwolfe.com